Pauli   **HA** nn grew up in Galway and started acting while
study   This   ory of Art in Dublin. She has played many stage
roles   the   ot to fame as the inimitable Mrs Doyle in *Father
Ted*.   late   ther television work includes *Aristocrats* and
Bren   not   *rd and Fortune* and, most recently, the hugely
popu   Pe   nedy series *Jam and Jerusalem*. Pauline has read
sever   bl   *ks at Bedtime* and her appearances on cinema
scree   ──   lude *Angela's Ashes, Quills, Gypo, Heidi* and *An
Ever*   *Piece*. Pauline has contributed to *Girls' Night
In*, i   War Child, *Magic*, in aid of One Parent Families,
Mom   aid of Tsunami Relief and the serial Irish novel
Yeats   *ad*, in aid of Amnesty International. She has
writt   ee extremely successful comic novels featuring
Dub   vate detective Leo Street, *Something for the
Wee* | | *etter than a Rest* and *Right on Time*, and the
high   17   med novels, *The Woman on the Bus, Summer
in th*   nd *Bright Lights and Promises*.

Prais   5   ssing You Already:

'McI   ks from the heart when she lays bare the truth
of A   s: her descriptions of the ruthless and irrev-
eren   d the consequences for Kitty and May are so
beau   vn, rallying as they do between hope, despair,
acce   back again that they had me gulping back
tears   and horror. In *Missing You Already*, McLynn
brav   ome serious subjects with sensitivity, honesty
and   It is an insightful and ultimately uplifting
nove   nted writer'   *Irish Times*

'Be prepared for a rollercoaster of emotions that will
have you reaching for the Kl   A fantastic read'
                                                            de

PAULINE MCLYNN

Missing You Already

headline
review

First published in 2009 by HEADLINE REVIEW
An imprint of HEADLINE PUBLISHING GROUP

First published in paperback in 2009 by HEADLINE REVIEW
An imprint of HEADLINE PUBLISHING GROUP

1

Cataloguing in Publication Data is
available from the British Library

ISBN 978 0 7553 4340 9

Typeset in New Caledonia by Palimpsest Book Production Limited,
Grangemouth, Stirlingshire

Printed and bound in Great Britain by
Clays Ltd, St Ives plc

Headline's policy is to use papers that are natural, renewable and
recyclable products and made from wood grown in sustainable
forests. The logging and manufacturing processes are expected
to conform to the environmental regulations of the country of origin.

HEADLINE PUBLISHING GROUP
An Hachette UK company
338 Euston Road
London NW1 3BH

www.headline.co.uk
www.hachettelivre.co.uk

For my mother
Sheila
and in memory of my father
Padraig

ACKNOWLEDGEMENTS

I have a great fear of acknowledgements, and usually avoid them, as I am always certain I will forget someone whose input was vital. Therefore, first, I say a far too general and inadequate thank you to all who helped in the making of this book. I have rarely encountered such generosity of detail and emotion. I am particularly indebted to Darragh Kelly, Owen Roe, Rosie Cavaliero, Salima Saxton and Carl Saxton Pizzie, Sue Johnston, Kate Hoban and Andrea Henry. I hope I have done some justice to you and yours. And, as always, Clare Foss, Richard Cook and Faith O'Grady have been of inestimable help. No words can adequately express my gratitude to you all.

ONE

Pennick is on the way to somewhere else. People pass through and think it's as cute as it seems. They see the main street, which has a clutch of Olde buildings, and a few garish window boxes in summer. The purists say it's in Norfolk, and it probably is as it's flat enough, for one thing, but its position near the county lines of both Cambridgeshire and Lincolnshire makes it susceptible to getting lost in the geography of the area. You know those romantic scenes in films where characters stand on a mountain and say, 'Look, you can see three counties from here,' and everything is wonderful? That's how it is somewhere else, not here. Occasionally, a rock star thinks he's discovered the last unspoiled bit of England and buys a crumbling pile down a meandering gravel lane, but then gets driven to more drink and drugs by sheer isolation of the place and the fact that he's trapped in it when it floods.

Pennick doesn't seem part of anything but its own ordinariness. Perhaps the geographical ambiguity is contagious and we natives are unsure who or what we are, or should be. We're pretty good at misery and feeling hard done by, if we have any sense at all. Mostly we're stoics, accepting what can't be altered. After all, this place was fashioned long before any of us got our hands on it and change comes slowly in these parts. I've lived here all my life and hate it as much as anyone has a right to. Which is also to say that I love it. Love has such a crooked logic that nothing about it should ever surprise us. And so Pennick is home to me and I'll defend it to the death, which action is unlikely to be required.

I work at the railway station, running the office. Most trains keep on keepin' on down the line and don't bother themselves with us or we with them, I guess you could say. To be honest, we're little more than a junction with lines going to far more interesting places. A few services have to stop, for passengers to make other connections or some locals to return after unsuccessful attempts to escape.

I'm being harsh, I know, but I'm allowed. Pennick's my hometown. This is like having a go at family: it's expected, par for the course. And if I truly hated it, I'd've left it long ago. Or at least I assume I would. That sort of thinking – conjecture, Mum would have called it – is useless anyway. The what-ifs. I'm going nowhere. I deal in reality these days and it's not very pretty most of the time.

I'm waiting for my holiday cover to arrive so that I can show her the ropes of the station office. I take the fallow time to review the items on my special shelves. Aside from a whole section at the back of the office devoted to forgotten umbrellas, I've got a walking stick, three pairs of spectacles (one with prescription sun lenses), a lunchbox (which I have relieved of its banana sandwich and juice carton), a jolly-looking turquoise windcheater, and a Busy Lizzie plant up front. It's not bad, only seven items. Sometimes the shelves groan under the forgotten and misplaced pieces of other people's lives. There isn't a peak season for being lost or found, except in the case of umbrellas, or at least if there is, I haven't spotted one. It's a constant, but sometimes there's a little more lost in the world. I like to help things be found.

People forget things every day. They miss their stop. They leave an extra bag on the train seat or resting by them on the station platform bench. Travelling is stressful, although this doesn't fully explain the way some of the townspeople's bits and bobs keep turning up here. Pennick is big enough for a police station but not a Marks and Spencer. People here dislike the criminal taint of handing in an article to the cops, as if they might be suspected of coming into it illegally or through some other unsavoury activity. So impromptu Lost Property departments are springing up everywhere. I know Longley's the newsagent's has one, for instance, ditto Springfield Medical Centre and the Frog and Firkin, though the latter usually re-homes items promptly when its customers sober up. I think they once put a hen up for a weekend because the farmer thought it had flown away. He recognised it when he came back the following Monday, complaining about how you couldn't get faithful stock any more.

The Springfield gets a surprising number of medical aids left behind, things that are designed to help people cope and perhaps were even what they came in for in the first place. You have to wonder if we aren't a hell of a lot more adaptable than we think, us humans, and just prone to cosseting ourselves needlessly a lot of the time. That said, they found a false leg in the car park once which was very quickly reclaimed, I hear. Happy reunions are what we aim for, at best. At worst, it's a shelf-ful of knick-knacks, trapping dust and taunting me with unfulfilled promise.

The station did once have a formal Lost Property office, in the far-off glory days of rail travel, when rail workers had recognisable uniforms and there were porters on the platforms wearing peaked hats. With time, and the erosion of old travelling decencies, the staff was streamlined as were the posts. Lost Property and Left Luggage merged then disappeared, to be replaced only by a general remit to look after those who pass through our hands here each day.

Dan is the Station Master and I have known him since I was a kid. He was at the root of me coming to work here. I was drifting at the time. He didn't need a nine-to-fiver just then but somehow he wangled the budget for it and here I am. He deals with the upkeep of the station, with ushering on the local departures, and keeps things in order for the many trains that simply whizz past without a by-your-leave.

I look after the administrative side: ticket sales, paperwork, phone enquiries and lost property.

We're not the only staff here. Nights are looked after by Benny, who likes the dark and dislikes people so the shift is perfect for him: his dream job. He charts the ghostly goods trains travelling in the down time, some carrying succour to supermarkets, some full of other poisons, the waste shunted from place to place as if to keep it moving will somehow make it invisible or matter less. There's a small band of contract cleaners who come in daily to keep the place as spruce as it can ever look. Sometimes they find used hypodermics in the loos, proof that we're as poisoned a backwater as anywhere else. And then there's Roly, the biggest cat I have ever encountered. He strolled in some years ago, decided he liked the set-up and stayed. He's the ratter and mouser and keeps to his own schedule. In more inclement weather, he'll choose a spot in my office and snooze; mostly he prefers the sheds out by the sidings. He delivers gifts for the pantry as thanks for the shop-bought and homemade cat food he gets in the office. I have become used to encountering dead rats on the doorstep, though not quite inured to it, and must praise him if he's still around when I see them. He's big on manners like that.

The railway has played a major part in my life. As kids we took the train to school in Fetchley, twelve minutes up the line. 'We' was Daniel, Donna and I: the Three Amigos, Three Musketeers. There were other neighbourhood children, friends even, but they were peripheral to us. We three might as well have been siblings. As it is, I am the lone only-child of our posse but, even though the others had some each, we meant more to one another than any brother or sister. We took one another for granted, and we took the railway for granted too. We needed it, it was there, we used it, attaching no great importance to it at the time. But it ran in our blood all the same.

Donna and I went to the Benedictine Girls' School and Daniel attended Farnworth College. They were within spitting distance of one another, a fact that the boys were keen on proving regularly during term-time. Richard Crabtree once got Sister Hilda's habit by accident as she floated through the playground. She was away with her many saints and never noticed the creamy gob on her long, black skirt. It was disgusting but it set a new standard and thereafter to hit a nun without being caught was all any Farnworth boy longed for. It was only a shame that Punk was long dead by then. We could have put Norfolk on the map.

The schoolkids still travel by train. It's the part of the day I like most: the jostling, the energy, the hope. I miss that during the holidays, though lots of the kids are still around and get out of town to the sea as much as possible, to escape the drear flatline of Pennick. That goes for winter as well as summer. Some aim for glory and get as far as Norwich before being recalled. It gives them a taste, though, and if they're lucky they'll get out altogether and go to college.

I didn't. For some reason, I wasn't cut out for it. It's strange to some because I am the product of two academically bright people but have none of that sort of mental alacrity. It's not something I've ever lost sleep over. I didn't care enough about it then, and I still don't. Anyhow, I see similar things in other lives. There are kids out there born to plain-looking parents who inherit some rogue beauty gene and are blessed with movie-star looks. Equally I have seen the ultra-plain kids of beautiful parents, children who display the worst of both parents' features. Those are the genetic breaks and not scoring brains was mine.

My name is Kitty Fulton.

Margo slumped on the uncomfortable chair listening to Kitty explain the workings of the office. She was not particularly interested but this job was only temporary and she needed the money. She might have shifted to a more viable pose, probably should have, but couldn't get the will together for that. She studied her nails instead, wondering what colour to choose next. There was a silence and she realised that she was required to answer something, or perhaps comment on what had gone before. Kitty was smiling which looked vaguely condescending to Margo but she didn't want to get kicked out in spite of the fact that her uncle was the one in charge and had said she could fill in while Kitty was on her holiday, so that was a done deal as far as Margo was concerned. She rearranged her eyebrows to acknowledge that she was still paying attention.

'So, do they break off when you type?' Kitty asked, referring to her bright pink false nails.

'Nah.'

If Kitty expected more she didn't get it. Margo had no wish to be drawn out by an old person. I'm only in my thirties, Kitty wanted to shout, knowing that any such explanation would appear irredeemably uncool. 'Any questions?'

'Will this be cash?'

'That's for your uncle to say.'

Margo grunted.

'Is that all?'

Did Margo detect an edge there? Was she supposed to have some hugely intelligent question to ask about the drudgery that went on here? She felt she'd better ask something, to keep the older woman happy.

'What's with the Muster Point signs?'

Kitty frowned. 'I think they're self-explanatory, surely?'

The girl's mouth took a down-turn as if she had smelled a bad odour. 'Yeah?'

'Dan saw one somewhere and decided he liked the sound of it.'

Margo shook her head in sadness and pity.

'The lost art of mustering,' Kitty said. 'It amuses him.'

A vision of her Uncle Dan grinning at something so lame had Margo shivering. 'State-of-the-art weird,' she declared.

Margo's gaze shifted to the station concourse, which she had been half keeping watch over through the main window of the small office. Fred Rowland and his mates were kicking an empty can around and waiting for the 16.08 to Fetchley-on-Sea. Kitty followed the direction of the girl's eyes. She saw a greasy gang of yobs who couldn't help making twits of themselves.

'He's quite attractive,' she conceded, in the face of Margo's pained and adoring expression.

'Yeah, well,' came the reply, which marked an end to their conversation, apparently.

Kitty walked the familiar route home along a stretch of railway line and in through the allotments. Her own plot was here, close to Dan's. She always stopped to check on it, however cursory this might be. Today, tiny spiders floated from the trees on gossamer threads. They were supposed to represent money or a windfall and, whereas that was always handy, there were a lot of things money simply could not buy for Kitty any more. The sky still showed some daytime blue. Soon, an extra hour would be given for a longer night's sleep and they would be plunged into months of darkness that the stolen hour could never make up for. The air was crisp with the promise of the first frost and all around allotment owners were harvesting. Shivering, Kitty pulled her cardigan close about her. Her mother had knitted it a decade before and it was always a comfort to wear. She regarded it as a shield, sometimes, its elaborate Fair Isle pattern dated but resonant and, above all, safe. It stood for something.

It meant the past, and there were times now when Kitty felt that was all she had.

Her allotment neighbour, Jed, was attending to a patch of his beloved onions. He was of another century in outlook as well as language, his Broad Norfolk scattered with words and phrases little used in the modern parlance. Kitty asked how he was and he gave her his usual 'fair ter middlin'. Jed could tell the weather from a sniff of the wind. And sometimes he'd declare it, with no less accuracy, according to how his cats faced the window or fire or a bowl of milk.

'Nip in thet air,' he told her. 'Frost's com'n, dew yew arst me.' He was wearing his fingerless gloves in preparation for the cold. Even through the wool Kitty saw the carbuncular swellings of his arthritis. His long-dead wife had knitted those mitts, as he often reminded her. They were both held together, Jed and Kitty, through the medium of craft, she thought. Jed wore a shop-bought, woollen hat but it stopped short on his head and his ears were livid with the chill. She wondered if he would wear a pair of ear-muffs if she got him some. She'd need an occasion, like his birthday or Christmas.

His bushy grey eyebrows met. 'Yer rum friend was 'ere, gorpin at yer shud.' He nodded a few times. 'There's suffin savage 'bout that 'un.'

She didn't need to think hard to know whom he was talking about. 'You mean Donna?'

'Crockin' then she were.'

Crying? This was not good.

'Ollust be cairf'l thair,' he advised, nodding as if he had seen it all before. He probably had. She wouldn't have been surprised to discover that Jed was three hundred years old. Kitty thought, He's warning me.

'Thank you,' she said. 'I appreciate that.'

He shrugged. 'Jest wantet ter tell yew.' He turned away. 'I shall hatter keep a' dewin here. No time for mardlin.'

My journey home takes me past the graveyards, old and new. A fresh plot is gaping, ready to take the latest inhabitant allocated it from the town. It's probably someone I know. Pennick is small enough for everyone at least to have heard mention of the names of the other people who live here.

I think back to my conversation with Jed and remember how Dan adopted the old man's pronunciation of Pennick when we were young. He'd declare that we lived in a town called Panic. It always seemed ludicrously funny that such a sleepy place would ever sound so racy.

I hear Mum's voice as I come through the door. It's good to know she's home and safe. She threw a cup of hot tea at me this morning. She missed, but that's hardly the point. Perhaps I annoyed her into flinging the cup but I doubt it. Even so, it's the thin end of some wedge and will have to be discouraged. She is practising her words. Mr Bishop wants her to do Bs on her next visit and she'll have a head start if she thinks of beginning with his name. He assigns the letter at random so that we can never second guess what he'll choose next. My theory is that she practises a lot in the hope that more than she'd be expected to remember might become lodged in her head and have to come out if she wills it. She is still an incredibly determined woman. Happily, she won't have to make sentences using only these words. That would be a call too far.

'Bound. Bale. Bland.'

These are all good. She is having a good day. She is beaming when I enter the kitchen. I must tell her that: Beaming.

'Beauty,' she says, looking me in the eye and I choose to believe it is deliberate, a gift to me. (Believe, another B – it's an expressive letter, this.)

'Billy.' She pauses. It's a name but at least follows the B rule. She runs Backer and Bike together and it makes her smile. I think there's a story attached but, if there is, she doesn't share it. 'Bite. Bored. Bla . . . bla . . . bla . . .' she's getting stuck '. . . black.' It's a B and fully formed, so well done. I add 'sheep' quickly to make a joke and ease over her hesitation, and we laugh although it's not that funny. We have to keep things light and happy. There is no room here for Bleak or its cousins. They will join us in time. But not yet.

But. That's a handy one. It keeps a situation current, ongoing. There is still some wriggle room with a But. It's an invitation for more of whatever you need to get by. By and Getting are what we are about now.

I see the shopping basket in the kitchen and I know she has done her chore for the day. The list is still inside and each item is ticked off. I begin to check them myself, casually so she won't notice, looking in the cupboards to see that they are put away properly. Although the list said cucumber she has bought a courgette, but never mind: it's an easy mistake to make. I flick the switch on the kettle and ask Mum if she'd like some tea. She looks puzzled. 'I think I've had some,' she says, and consults her notebook. 'Yes,' she confirms. 'Says here I enjoyed it too.'

'Good. Would you like some more?'

'Maybe not, dear. In case I didn't go to the loo last time.'

She is careful not to give her body any further chance to betray her.

I check the main diary and see that Hannah, a neighbour, has been in and has written that all was well today. Mum had a sandwich for lunch, then went on an outing with her support group to paint landscapes. I don't see any evidence of that but I'll ask in a while. I open the fridge door to get the milk and notice the hairdryer on the bottom shelf. When I look back I see Mum about to pour tea into an upside-down mug, knowing there is something wrong in this picture but wondering what it is. I rush to take the pot from her before she scalds herself. She will be sixty years old next January.

Our house, number 15, The Cottages, is small, unremarkable, red brick, in a terrace of many others. Evidence of the way we live is everywhere. The Post-its on the wall by the front door remind us about our keys. In this regard I am as bad as Mum for forgetting so I'll share responsibility for those. The Post-its are also all over the back of the door should any distraction occur between picking the keys up and heading out. Again, those could be meant for me. The hall table has little areas marked out for keys, umbrellas, gloves; if there's a gap, it means the system isn't being adhered to. Important numbers are clearly displayed by the telephone. We used to have a portable handset but it kept getting misplaced so we're back to the traditional one attached to the cradle now.

A visitor might take in the sheer volume of thrillers and detective books on our many sets of shelves. Pieces of, largely abandoned, knitting spill from some bags on the floor, none terribly coherent in pattern but the colours are vivid and welcoming. I am forever threatening to feng shui the lot, more because I realise that clutter presents hazards for Mum than from any inclination to find money corners to leave free or to keep invisible energies flowing throughout the space. I suppose it's all a lot of old cobblers, especially to people like ourselves with huger issues to deal with. It's not a streamlined or neat house, then, but neither is it in total chaos, which is a minor wonder given that we're not always up to keeping it in order. There is a constant soundtrack, of radio or television or stereo, especially during daytime hours. I try to keep it to a gentle level so that if Mum found herself at some sort of disadvantage, she wouldn't be further confused by the noise.

My mother May is a sprightly Irishwoman with naturally dark hair and blue eyes. A Celt, she would say, if she remembered to claim it. I am dark also but hazel eyed. We're both of medium height and have no remarkable distinguishing features that I am aware of. You would pass us on the street and not take a second glance, I think.

The garden out back is testament to Mum's green fingers. She began it many years ago. It's a riot of colour in summer and a symphony of structure in winter. 'Plant well,' she told me, 'and the garden does the work for you.' In the late-September light, thistle tops stand ready to catch snow and frost, shrubs have been clipped to add pleasing shapes and a small rowan tree holds red berries to cheer the birds along.

Whenever we are at home the door is kept on the latch and neighbours come and go regularly. They always have, but make sure to now. Spare sets of keys reside in about ten houses around 15, The Cottages so there is never a problem with anyone gaining entry should they need to.

At face value the picture is one of rumpled domestic harmony, and often that's true of the little house. It might even look regular or humdrum but for the Post-its. Some are rectangular yellow, some square and blue, and some recent pink additions are heart-shaped. On the day Mum took a marker to the plasterwork to write herself a reminder,

I was forced to admit that the writing was now well and truly on the wall.

It was Dad who first noticed that something was wrong. My father, Stephen Duke, is the publisher of a small imprint that specialises in academic tomes and collections of poetry. That's how he and Mum met and became involved. She worked as a copy editor for him. Words have always been her thing, which makes this new situation doubly tragic for her. He sought me out one day about eight years ago to ask if she was having her menopause. I asked why, wondering if this was going to be one of his occasional mini-rants about how they should never have hooked up and that I was the only good thing to come of the union, to be followed swiftly by a denial that there was only one good thing, though I was assuredly the best thing, and that they simply exasperated one another and not to mind him letting off steam. But this time it was a lot less and, in fact, a lot more.

'It's just that it looks as though she's edited that last book I gave her with a knife and fork,' he explained.

I didn't think much of the remark for a time. They often had artistic differences. I was pretty sure it was not the menopause, that was past. Unless it could make a return, like a hormonal grace note? I asked around and that didn't seem likely. But Dad was right that she did seem more distracted than usual. A tad forgetful. She would have to search for the appropriate word, sure, though actually I didn't find that bit at all odd. She liked to be precise. As I've said, words were her thing.

'I can't find the whatchoocallit,' she said one day, her accent more Irish-sounding than usual. When you've lived away from the country of your birth for a long time it gets less pronounced, I think. Now her lilt was emphasised. So I noticed that. And then she began to cry. 'I can't seem to find it.' She was desperately upset, a lot more than she should have been. After all, what could be so important that it would drive her to tears? Later, I realised that it was the *word*, not the *thing*, she couldn't locate and that, for her, was an awful admission. She was frightened by it. We've been frightened by bigger things since, but on that day it was the worst thing that had happened to her in a long time and not, as I finally began to suspect, an isolated incident.

Mum was never the kind to panic easily so she was obdurately against supposing this was, actually, anything but a hormonal surge or a symptom of creeping stress. She had always been a bit scatty about domestic details – bills to be paid (until she set up direct debits), keys, her purse, the usual stuff. We muddled along.

Then Mum began to bulk up. She had always been a trim woman who took care of her appearance. Now she was inclined to leave a skirt zip undone for comfort. I thought nothing of it at first, putting it down to the hormonal imbalance she insisted was at the heart of her problems. There did seem to be a lot more food in the house, and a lot more

17

going to waste for that matter. I found abandoned halves of sandwiches and baguettes by the many paperbacks she liked to read. I would tip them into the bin without comment. Then Mum would ask where her lunch had disappeared to. It could be ten in the evening by then. I found receipts for the supermarket; my mother was clearly going once or twice a day. These featured chocolate that never entered the house, along with crisps, sweets, popcorn. No wonder she was packing on the pounds.

'Are you putting on a bit of weight?' I ventured one evening, but there was no tone that could take the sting off that remark for a lady who was conscious of how she looked and I almost held my breath, waiting for the answer.

Mum's eyes narrowed. 'What if I am?'

'Well, I guess, no reason, except that it's hard to shift it once it goes on and it's bad for your health anyhow.'

'I can't help it if I'm hungry a lot.'

'No.' I didn't know where to go from here. 'Are you hungry now?' I asked.

I saw my mother check the clock. It read 9.15. We had eaten our evening meal over an hour before. I noticed her do some calculations and answer, 'Of course not,' adding, after a pause, 'it's eight o'clock,' for good measure. It was then that I knew two things: one, that Mum didn't remember eating and, two, that she was hiding a lot more from me. The idea that my mother was lying to me on a regular basis made my heart shift in my chest. She'd never lied to me, aside from about Santa Claus (which was no big deal when the truth emerged as the gifts kept coming) and saying that Granny had gone to heaven. I had been taken 'home' to Ireland to meet Granny on a few occasions and, young as I was, even I knew that the malevolent old crone would be welcome in no god's hereafter. Now my mum was applying subterfuge to exclude me. My guts wrenched.

'We didn't have pudding,' she said. Her voice was high with a mixture of longing and providing an excuse for wanting more, or anything at all. It was also wily, a new nuance to her speech.

We rarely ate dessert at home. It was time to act.

I think life gives us time to digest news, particularly when it's bad. And the medical profession is no different. It has to be like that, otherwise hospitals and surgeries would sink under the weight of tears and anguish and no one would be cured, least of all the curable. We have to be given a chance to digest the facts, as far as they can be known. Even death at close quarters slows down our perception so we can get past the first awful fact and prepare ourselves for the grief that we can see approaching, in slow motion but on its way nonetheless.

So it was when it came to my mother's diagnosis. We were drip-fed facts, such as they were and are. Even so, there is no absolutely certain way that her condition can be called what we all feel it is. A slew of tests relegated other dementias. When she's dead they may take a slice of her brain and examine it and say, 'Yes, May Fulton had Alzheimer's Disease,' though we all know that to be probable right now. However, only her poor addled mind can give the definitive proof and it's too invasive to do that while she's still alive. She is young to be affected, as mostly it's an increasingly elderly population who present with it. I've heard it called Old Timers a lot. But it's not a discriminating disease and will take whomever it pleases, just to show it can, I sometimes believe.

Trying to convince her to see a doctor in the first place was arguably the hardest part. She did seem perfectly hale, other than being mithered. In fact, with the weight she'd gained, she looked to be blooming. She argued and prevaricated but eventually gave in. We had to know, to act, and I'm so glad we did as I think it has bought us extra time. There is nothing so satisfying as snatching back years that the disease might have denied us.

Mum's mind is tangled. Bit by bit, proteins made by her own system are strangling her brain and killing it. All of her physical abilities in general are being impaired to some degree, hijacked by this sneaking disease. We've had the best of the early medication and that returned her to near normality for a long time. We almost felt we were beating the thing for a while, which was cocky and inaccurate. What the drugs did was work on the symptoms not the disease itself, boosting the brain's supply of neurotransmitters while unable to rid her of the underlying damage. I hear of kids stealing the stuff to take before exams so that they'll enhance their brain capacity. It's a mad but strangely practical thing to do, I guess, and no real surprise.

After all, people are injecting botox, a bona-fide poison, into themselves to erase their frown lines. That came from someone noticing there was a lucrative side-effect in the medical response to a debilitating condition. I'll bet there's some boffin in the laboratory of a large cosmetics firm right now trying to find the right ratio of flesh-eating disease to cream so that we can smear ourselves with something that will deal with cellulite. It's all a matter of degree.

As for Alzheimer's sufferers, there's always the hope of a general cure in the long term. Though not for us, as it happens. Mum is too far gone for that. But we make the most of what we have. And it's a good most.

Mostly.

TWO

The box of ashes was a first for the station.

'No one has ever left a dead relative before,' Dan said.

'It could be a cat or a dog, even a horse,' Kitty argued.

'That's hardly likely if it's from Jensen's the undertakers,' Dan pointed out. 'They only deal in human beings, unless they've branched out in the last day or two.'

'How could anyone forget one of their own, even if they aren't exactly flesh and blood any more?'

The box was dark and lacquered and bore no name aside from Jensen's – and chances were it wasn't one of that family or else all faith put in their abilities to run their business had been misplaced. Kitty opened her ledger and entered the find, with the date and time it was taken in and a short description.

'Should we look inside?' Dan asked.

'Doesn't seem right to.'

'Don't think the occupant will mind.'

'It might be disrespectful.'

'Fair enough. Have you ever seen human ashes?'

'No. I heard they're stranger than you'd think, though. Denser. Greyer. Gritty.'

'What will you do now, Miss Marple?'

Kitty loved the detection angle of this sideshoot of her job. 'Obviously I'll ring Jensen's and see if anyone's missing their box or urn or whatever they call it.'

'Box, I'd say.'

'Doesn't seem enough, does it? Box? Urn is better, surely?'

'Not an urn, though.'

'No. It's definitely a box, all right. A handsome one.'

They gazed at it some more before Dan said he should go and check on the 10.12 to Shrifley. Then there would be a run through to Norwich that he would probably stand on platform two to wave to. He usually did. That was the boy in him still, she thought. Kitty watched his broad back as he walked towards the door. He was wearing his uniform jacket with its fluorescent yellow stripes. He was proud of the words 'Station Manager' displayed on it. He needed a haircut but she liked the way his wavy hair touched the collar.

'Donna was up at my allotment last evening. Jed saw her. She was gone by the time I got there.'

He stopped, didn't really turn around but inclined his head three quarters back to her. 'Fuck,' he whispered.

❋   ❋   ❋

Dan moved into the next street from us the summer I turned five. I saw the removals truck pull up, followed by a car packed with him and his family and the things that couldn't be squeezed into the more substantial vehicle. I had never seen such a head of red curls before and I ran over to touch them without any thought that he was a stranger. He laughed into my face and I fell headlong for him. 'I love you,' I said, before running to tell Mum that the new neighbours we had been expecting were here and marvellous beyond words. I really didn't have anything else to shout but, 'They're here, they're here. He has wed hair. WED!' I had a problem with my r's then. I've had a problem with him since.

I finish the petty cash reconciliation, a chore that always leaves me feeling dissatisfied. I hate the way it eats up so much time for so little result. Now I feel like a reward. There's no chocolate in the office tin, which means either Dan or Benny has been raiding it again, so it looks like a quick run through the crossword will have to do. I'm tempted to try to fill it with random words, to see if I can make them all match up. This is a lot harder than it sounds. Words are tricky customers.

Mum and I have always been partial to a game of Scrabble. We are vicious at play. I learned early on that it was all very well to want to make interesting words on the board but you had to rack up the scores too or face ruin. Mum kept a dictionary of obscure terms handy in case of disputes, of which there were many. The game might have been an indicator of her vocabulary loss if we hadn't already had decades of weird spellings. 'Ba' appeared after her diagnosis but I didn't bat an eyelid, having seen it many times before and knowing it to be the Egyptian word for soul. 'Xu' is a Vietnamese unit of money, and her use of it might be co-incidence or not. She knows to reach for the dictionary no matter what. At least she has always enjoyed the games even if I am allowing some entire rubbish through now. It's all about her happiness.

I tried puzzles to keep my own noggin ticking over but they weren't for me. I quite liked the logic of Sudoku, but bored of it quickly. I caught a programme on the television recently about very old people and they all said that the brain was the main thing you had to keep stimulated. It was a sad piece. Nearly all of them were at a loss to know why they were still here, and most didn't particularly want to be. All of their friends and a lot of their families were dead and they were trapped within an ancient casing. One woman kept referring to the damn' chair she was stuck in.

As much as I quite like puzzles, I hate magic or what passes for magic on television and variety shows. I always want to roar, 'It's nothing but trickery.' That sort of magic is an illusion, a deliberate obfuscating of facts and techniques to fool us. I also get very agitated when I don't know how these so-called magicians are doing their trick. I need to understand, not presume. I cannot give blind faith and I have lost any sense of wonder that might permit me the indulgence of magic. I would like to think there is real magic still out there, of a kind that can never be explained away. But I have no time for sly trickery now.

Kitty phoned Jensen's the undertaker's in Norwich to ask about the shiny box full of ashes. As helpful as the receptionist tried to be, she could shed no light on who might now be in Kitty's care. 'Cremation is a very popular choice nowadays,' she intoned. 'It's what I want for myself.' There was an attempt at a knowing chuckle here that came out rather smugly on Kitty's end of the line. 'And people don't always call to collect immediately the ashes are back with us. This package could belong to a number of people and I'm sure you'll understand that I cannot give you clients' names over the phone.'

'Would you email them to me, then, or post them?'

'Er . . . no, that would not be acceptable either, I'm afraid.'

'How am I to trace the owner then?' Kitty asked.

The answer was delivered with such emphasis, such precision, that Kitty was left in no doubt it had been unreasonable of her to ask in the first place. 'All I can do for you, Miss . . . ?'

'Fulton.'

'Quite. All I can do is wait until the unfortunate who has misplaced their dear departed gets in contact with me, and then I can forward your details to them.'

The superior tone got to Kitty. 'This is not exactly

doctor–patient confidentiality we're talking about here,' she pointed out.

'In all my years in this heartbreaking business,' the face-less, and increasingly annoying, woman began again, 'I hope I have never – and I repeat, *never* – been insensitive to a client's needs. I cannot have you, a stranger, upsetting them at this delicate time by calling up out of the blue while their grief may have returned in all its raw manifestation.'

Oh, shut up, you pompous old bag, Kitty wanted to shout. Instead she took a breath and said, 'Surely it would be more sensitive to let me help track down whoever is responsible for this box, to reunite them with their relation?'

'Perhaps you might simply return the item to us?'

That cloying suggestion was never going to fly, not on Kitty's watch. 'The *item* is now the property of the railway and here it will stay until it is claimed. Thank you so much for your valuable time and good day.'

'Good day?' Kitty whispered to herself afterwards. Where in hell had that come from? All the same, she had handled the call badly and now had no lead to follow up. This *item* was well beyond a lost umbrella in importance and she felt honour bound to reunite it with its owner. If anyone could ever be said to own another person, that is, ashes or not. Come to that, how could anyone lose so unusual a package? Ashes in a box weren't exactly an everyday package to be toting, were they?

She'd had brushes with beautiful finds before, in this line

of her work, and been obliged to stop herself from getting overly protective of them or inventing stories about them that could never be matched by reality. A charming mother-of-pearl music box had turned up in a basket of sundries once and she couldn't resist opening it to see the inside and hear the tune. The tinkling song was both eerie and uplifting. She'd read and seen enough ghost stories to imagine a darker scenario, but when she found the hidden drawer with some photographs and a love letter inside she immediately assumed she was holding in her hands the relics of a great romance. An octogenarian lady arrived to reclaim the bag the following day and Kitty couldn't help but confess that she'd found the secret cache.

'Splendid,' said the woman. 'Saves me the trouble of working that out.'

Kitty was dismayed. 'So it's not yours?'

'Oh, no. I bought it all as a lot at a car boot sale, hoping it's of some value when I flog it on. This discovery of yours might just swing it for me.'

Never assume, Kitty learned. Life is often a lot more basic than we would like to think.

She popped the lacquered box in pride of place at the front of her main shelf, patting it twice for comfort as she settled it in. This one was different, she felt.

I sip herbal tea and wish I had someone to talk to. The station is in a lull. I could phone Dad but both he and I are at work and, besides, I don't have anything new to tell him. Best not waste his time, even if my own is going a-begging now. Also, I feel odd about making personal calls on company time. Roly appears and nudges around my legs before fading away into the shelves. I hear him scratch about a bit then settle somewhere in the gloom. I am tempted to buy him a proper bed.

These days I miss conversation the most. I have Dan to talk to here at the station, sure, and Dad on tap at the end of the telephone line, but talking to men, however close they are to you, is not like a good girlie chat. Mum has her limitations now and although we still communicate a fair deal, it all depends on how her day is going. Often it's just fractured reportage of her doings as opposed to a decent account of this or that. It's also usually in rather basic terms as her mental grasp on complex issues fades. We used to discuss a whole range of topics. We'd take one, maybe prompted by the newspaper, toss it about, chew it over and park it in the corner for future mauling. In those days we told one another most things but there are always matters that can only be discussed with your own generation and, in my case, without a sister to confide in, Donna was the one who filled that role. Don't get me wrong, I talk to people every day. I spend most of my time dealing with the public and colleagues and friends and neighbours. I'm lost for choice with people to pass the time of day with. But it's all small talk. I don't have a real confidante any more.

The last time I spoke to Donna she was uninterested in any of my news. I suppose I can hardly blame her when it's all the same now. Mum and how she's getting on is the main subject of my life, and I wouldn't have it any other way. In the old days, my lack of ambition drove Donna round the bend. I haven't changed much. I love the allotment, our garden, reading books, tending to Mum, worrying about what will become of her, re-homing the items in my Lost and Found. These precious elements in my life mean so much to me. If that's lacking in ambition, so be it. The tag of my herbal tea bears a message from some yogi reading 'Love what is ahead by loving what has come before'. I'll try, Mr Yogi, I'll try.

The Bartletts' house was no bigger than ours but it was packed with people, all the time. At our house there was only Mum and me, and sometimes Dad stayed over, but not regularly on account of him and Mum not being married or together any more. The Bartlett sisters had one chaotically full bedroom, the boys another, and the tiniest was filled with their mother and father's double bed from which issued forth new offspring, each more adored than the last, it seemed. I loved blending in with the family. I wasn't the only other kid from the area subsumed into the workings of the place, and extra mouths to feed at mealtimes went unnoticed. Donna hated having to share so little and so much with so many.

'You just love this place 'cos you can go home to yours afterwards,' she'd often say to me. It was a taunt as well as a fact. I did love to go home to my mother and our quieter abode full of books, and to have those things all to myself. I rarely had friends home, though Donna and Dan were regular enough visitors. I just about allowed them. I wonder now if I was bad at sharing or just selfish, but back then that was too hard to think about so I ignored it and got on with my life. I was good at ignoring awkward things.

On the day of her tenth birthday Donna was given a comb and brush set the like of which had never been seen in Pennick before. It was mock tortoiseshell and no less beautiful for its fakery. What marked it out above all others was that a mutual and clever hinge in the handles attached brush to comb. It was a treasure beyond compare. I sat with Donna and a gaggle of her sisters and friends on one of the two sets of bunks in the small bedroom and wondered at its beauty. Donna alone was allowed to handle the thing, which was only right. Again and again she went through the routine of how you pulled away one instrument and combed your hair then flipped it and brushed. Then, with a snap, it was closed and neat again. It glowed with genius and desirability. Donna had the hair to go with it: long, glossy locks of a dull blond, envied by every girl in the parish.

When they'd finally tired of yet another demonstration of the brilliance of the contraption, Donna's mother called that it was time for cake and everyone bundled down the stairs.

All but me.

I couldn't leave the birthday gift, now abandoned on the coverlet. I knew I was forbidden from touching it but I was mesmerised. It dared me with its magnificence. I couldn't help myself. I reached out and took it reverently in my trembling hands. I relished the fabulous object, turning it this way and that to admire the light on its surface. It was covered in Donna's greasy fingerprints, but undiminished in my eyes. Finally I summoned up the courage to open the wonder. And it snapped in two in my hands.

I let it fall with a small yelp and felt bile rise in my throat. I shook with terror and uncontrollable fear. I had destroyed the most precious thing I had ever been close to. And it didn't belong to me. It was the property of my Best Friend. I would die for this. Actually die. No punishment could exact the retribution Donna would need to atone for this crime. Death would be too good for me. The rosy wallpaper and grubby bedclothes began to close in on me. Sweat stuck my t-shirt to my back and I was genuinely afraid I would shit myself with fright. Tears began to roll down my cheeks. I took one long jagged breath before wiping my face quickly and sneaking down into the crowd of shrieking youngsters, none of whom had noticed my tardiness in joining them. They were all singing 'Happy Birthday' with gusto, I myself as loudly as any of them. Later, at home, I threw the cake back up and my mother spent an hour sponging my clammy back with cold water and blaming the sickness on too many sweets and fizzy drinks.

The first time Dan and I made love was in his father's potting shed, and for the most part that's where we meet now. I was fifteen on that occasion. It was glorious and sweaty and he didn't really know what he was doing. But I did, or well enough. You see, as much as I loved Dan, it was Donna who had me first, in a way. She was always ahead of the game.

It started on a day when Dan couldn't get out to doss about with us. His mother had a room that needed painting. Donna and I mooched around the copse of trees near the allotments, that we grandly called The Forest, then settled on going to Dan's hut there. We could listen to the radio and gossip. Donna might smoke because that was her latest fad. But not today. I should have known she was up to something. She was especially attentive to the way I looked, and I was flattered. I made us both an instant coffee. Then she began to tease me about liking Dan. I told her to shut up because that was embarrassing, an area I couldn't put words to and didn't want to because I knew it would skew things between the three of us. Anyhow, it made me go all red and I was sure that wasn't an attractive look. She reached over to tickle me and soon I was helpless with giggles. Then she kissed me. It was all quite natural, actually. I got a bit fired up when she put her tongue in my mouth. It was lovely. It was Donna. I would have done anything for her.

'Take your top off,' she whispered and it seemed the most natural thing in the world, so I did. She looked at my bra and held it and my breasts in her hands. I liked it. She stuck a thumb inside and brushed a nipple, which immediately sent a tingle through me. Then she cupped both breasts, brought them forward and kissed them. I was swooning with the closeness of her and the thrill in my body. 'You like that,' she said. A statement, dispassionate in hindsight.

After that she played with me for about a month, going a little further each time. I knew she was probably just experimenting but I didn't mind. I was discovering things about myself I might never have had the courage to try without her encouragement. We spent afternoons on my bed, as mine was the more private house. Sometimes she just sat and watched as I did what I was told. I was only allowed to touch her once but it did nothing for her, or me for that matter. The whole thing petered out through this mutual lack of interest and we never talked of it again.

Dan was duly amazed by my knowledge of my own body and what I needed from the experience when we made love. Donna had destroyed my inhibitions. With Dan the experience was so much more than I would ever have dreamed. I knew from the first time he touched me that I was properly lost in someone else. I guided him as he undressed and kissed me. I was light headed as his fingers found me. 'You are very, very wet,' he said as he explored. I moved against him as he probed me, unable to resist him. We lay back on the battered sofa and, at my suggestion, he lowered his face and began to tease me with his tongue. I could hear and feel his words on me as he said, 'I love this, I love this.' As difficult as it was, I held off until he thrust into me and we were both ready to climax. It was the most logical and exhilarating thing we had ever done. Dan pulled away, gasping, and said, 'Christ, you're electric.'

I was.

I had been primed, groomed almost, for this moment, just as Donna had prepared herself for her turn when it came. And she made sure that it did.

Donna awoke a physical hunger in me that has needed sating ever since. I may not be a great beauty, as she is, but I am entirely at ease with my body and my sexuality. I'm not sure if Donna is aware of what she did and I can't imagine she's pleased if she is, but I am.

She always said it was a rites-of-passage thing that we both slept with Dan. Perhaps that was true. Maybe she even believed that, or still does. It broke me at the time, of course, and that may have been intended too. But I learned to deal with it and get on with my complicated and compromised life. After all, no one died, right?

Once Donna got her claws into Dan she hung on in there. It was as though she saw him as her ticket out of here. I was eviscerated by the double betrayal: I lost them both in one go. I was cut adrift. Weirdly, we did not stop seeing one another, in twos and our threesome, but it was never comfortable again and it was always made clear to me when I was to leg it and leave them alone. Dan was blinded, besotted. I hated Donna then. I even hated him. They held hands and giggled, usually without telling me why. Well, I knew why they were holding hands. And more than once I saw them go further. Lord help me, I watched too, alone in my misery, turned on by how beautiful they were together, appalled by their lovemaking yet horribly fascinated by it too.

I didn't know how to deal with this altered, unwelcome status quo. I didn't have any alternative friends in case of emergencies so I took to staying in the house a lot more than usual. Mum knew there was something major up but left me to it, which was entirely the correct thing to do. A teenager with a broken heart is best left to stew in her own agony. Interference, or any hint that her predicament is known, would only result in screaming rows.

I couldn't concentrate on my schoolwork. I had been tipped for third level but that altered almost overnight as my mind circled through its own hellish rings and scenarios. I pitched up to my exams and stared out of the window, unable to put much on paper that would persuade anyone to invest in my further education. I was letting myself get stuck in Pennick and I didn't care how trapped I would be. The world had ceased to matter and the future was a burden. In the meantime Donna grew more beautiful and was signed up by a model agency in Norwich. She was on her way and didn't hesitate to point that out to everyone, whether they wanted to hear it or not. The local rag announced that Pennick would be put on the map by this teenage beauty. Dan puffed his chest out and looked a bit of a twat, I thought. I detected a new, idiotic swagger in his step. Neither of them noticed my anguish, and even if they had I am not convinced they would have cared.

Then things began to go awry for Donna. She had trials with bigger agencies, each surrounded by more hype than the last, but nothing seemed to come of them. Over the months, there were stories of the flu, untrustworthy managers, a change of direction. The *Pennick Post* grew tired of reporting on nothing. She retreated and went to ground. Occasionally, the paper leaked rumours of great news to come, that a waiting game was being played by our Donna as she chose the right path. But gradually the nascent career faded, was dropped as a topic of interest by the local hacks, and never mentioned again.

I don't know how she managed it but Donna blamed Dan for all her woes. I was delighted to see them fight. They raged and screamed, taking turns to wound each other. I was used by both for sounding off against, whether I wanted to be or not. They sought me out. We didn't travel as a trio any more. We did not function as one. It was a tragi-comedy and we were our own three stooges.

Then Donna got pregnant, and I did not, and they cleaved together again and made plans to get married.

✳   ✳   ✳

'May, if you don't get a move on right now you'll be late.'

'I'm coming, Mammy.'

The little girl had been looking forward to starting school so much she couldn't sleep the night before. Her brother and sister scoffed at her, told her she was mad, a fool, but she was impatient for this new experience. Her school bag had been propped against the wall by the door for a week, full of empty copybooks and sharpened pencils. When the longed-for morning came she was ready and waiting a good hour before the off. But she'd dozed again and now she was behind. She wore a grey pinafore hand-me-down from Ellen over a new blouse. Her white tights were greying and bobbled with age and a bit short, so inclined to creep down her thighs, but her shoes shone with vigorous polishing.

She skipped all the way to the school, hanging off her mother and asking questions by the dozen. Her mother stared straight ahead and rarely answered, but that didn't matter. At the main door other small people were ready to go about their education. She knew some of them and waved and chattered. They were led into a huge light-filled room with miniature desks and an enormous blackboard. It was overheated and smelled of wax and chalk. Paint peeled gently from the walls but May saw only glory. She couldn't wait to get learning. She needed to know everything. Her hands itched to lay out her copybooks and pencils on her new patch. A nun stood tall and dark by the door. She wore a long black dress and full veil with a white starched wimple. May was so happy she forgot to breathe and became faint till she realised what the problem was. The mothers retreated and the crying began. May couldn't figure out why this was happening. Then, thinking it was the etiquette for the occasion, she joined in, wailing with the best. A smell of pee soured the air. Some of the mothers were summoned back to soothe their distraught children. May watched hers disappear straight-backed out of the yard, never looking back.

Suddenly the woman came to, as if from a sleep. She jerked, looking around for her bearings, alert to a change in them. This room seemed familiar but she couldn't place it. She looked at the hands resting in her lap, amazed to find that they belonged to an old lady. Oddly, though, they were her own, which startled her. This is home, she thought, but couldn't be entirely sure. How odd. The past was perfect in her mind, each detail remembered with precision, down to the visceral smells and sensations. The present was a mystery, and the near-past shrouded in a haze of uncertainty. She felt afraid, then, but knew it would get her nowhere.

THREE

This morning Mum can't find the cat and she's worried about him. He's been dead two years: a lovely black-and-white called Pegasus. The name suited him: he seemed to fly through the air when he needed to. Times like these were the ones I had greatest difficulty with at first. I would try to correct her. The point is, though, that when she believes a thing, like the cat being alive, her brain is away somewhere I cannot go. It's a place that has its own logic. It's somewhere I cannot even be invited. Correcting her would only lead to confusion and unhappiness. Also, she wouldn't believe me, so that could give rise to an argument and then paranoid behaviour from her for hours. Why was I trying to deliberately thwart her? Why was I trying to confuse her, to lead her astray in the head? And so on. So I learned to let things slide. 'He'll turn up,' I tell her. Now, at least, she'll stop worrying about the cat and may never actually think of Pegasus again, for all anyone knows.

She loved that animal. He had no expectations of her except for bed and board, accompanied by adoration, and he got all of that. He didn't notice when she began to change, or if he did it didn't bother him overtly. She never once raised her voice to him, although I got plenty of that as she slid into darker areas of faded understanding. She was content to sit for hours stroking him and he was happy to accept that. It was a lesson for me, too. Acceptance. After the railing 'against the dying of the light', as she liked to put it, loftily. That was when her verbal powers were still with her. They have not truly deserted her yet, but are more difficult to call, to predict. We never know when they will return, and whether that will be with some vigour or just enough to make her self-aware and unhappy. Increments of dissatisfaction, that's what we deal in.

I make sure Mum joins me for breakfast every morning. We're usually early to rise. We eat and chat, listen to the radio and try to keep abreast of the outside world. Mum still appreciates this but can't always hold all the details of a story together. Still, it's a routine and a fairly enjoyable one. It gives me the opportunity to measure her mood and to judge what might lie ahead for the day. I supervise her shower, gently and unobtrusively. The dial on the apparatus to deal with temperature is now as foreign to her as telling the time on the round kitchen clock. She deals better with digital figures; her sense of space and form is fading. More often than not I say, 'I think I got the water just right,' in the hope that it will stop her from jiggling with the thermostat and burning herself if she gets it going in the wrong direction. If Mum notices the subterfuge, she allows it, generally.

If she's had a restless night and plans to go back to bed for a while, I write on the bathroom door and the door of the shower that she has washed so there'll be no second attempt at it. We have long ago agreed all of these systems and now don't even comment on their existence. Planning, as with the planting of the garden, is everything. When the building blocks are firmly in place the house is less likely to fall down.

Kitty stepped out into the flint-sharp nip of cold that Jed had promised. She passed along row by row of red-brick houses, identical as meticulously capped teeth. Early-morning Pennick was furtive, a tissue of secrets hinted at or revealed. She observed the creeping about of those who wished not to be seen or couldn't afford to be. There was Bert Silver returning home before his children woke so that they might think he still lived with their mother. Andrew Faber and the nurse who looked after his bedridden wife walking their dogs and nuzzling close to one another, a love story born of Multiple Sclerosis and necessity. Ali Barton staggered back to base after another epic binge of drink and who knew what else.

Kitty made her way in the wan morning light to her

allotment, to dig over a bed. Glenda Parfitt rode by on her horse Jack The Lad, along the bridle path, also taking in the sights but never commenting. She waved to Kitty and moved on. Dan would already be at work, having taken over from Benny after night duty. Everything had to be in place for the new day. And the less time he spent at home, the less grief he got from his wife. They were all escaping something in their own way.

Even now, years after taking ownership of her allotment, Kitty was still unearthing shards of crockery and small stones. The earth was forever moving under its surface, shifting cradled treasures, throwing to the surface those that could be dispensed with, at seemingly random intervals. She had a bucket for collecting interesting bits of china and hoped to make a mosaic one day. She wondered about the people who had shared her little site. Had there been a dwelling here once? She must look that up sometime. Jed might know. Perhaps the ancients had only passed by on occasion and left behind the bits no longer needed on their journey, the lame and the halt of the cup and saucer world.

By the door of her hut lay a small bunch of late roses wrapped in newspaper. She didn't need a note to know who had left them. It made her smile. She had her secrets too. She trawled through her brain for a phrase she'd heard in a play once about flowers given as a love gift, though an un-requited love. It had been poignant, she remembered. It fitted these, although hers were not a symbol of unreciprocated feelings. She crooked them in her arm and made for work. She crunched through the dying leaves, kicking up swathes of brown and yellow through to scarlet. Nature hurt most when it was most beautiful, she thought.

'Lovely blooms,' Dan said, smiling, as she brought the chill with her into the office.

She stopped to catch her breath, to savour a moment with him. Early-morning commuters milled and shoved on the concourse. Edie Wallace shouted through that the Marshton-on-Fore connector was late.

'Again,' Dan conceded with a shrug.

'"Beautiful, mournful, autumn roses",' Kitty said, bringing him back to her. She had remembered the line. At least, she thought she had. It would do. Memory was now whatever was useful to get through the day. Anything extra was a bonus.

Dan watched as she put the flowers in water and placed them by the box of ashes, to honour the occupant. She thought she caught a strange look from him then. 'What?' she asked.

'Oh, nothing,' he said, before moving off, half smiling, wholly assured.

I spend a lot of time looking at the back of that man's head, Kitty thought, noticing again how his hair had darkened. No longer the 'wed' of their childhood but a more muted shade: 'burnished', she might have chanced, but expected he would give 'rusted' as an alternative.

Donna turned up at noon. Kitty had been expecting her. She couldn't have explained why, exactly, she just knew it would happen. Kitty knew Donna and that ran the other way too, she imagined. Donna looked dreadful, for her: complexion mottled, hair unkempt. Although she was moody and drawn, she still looked a million dollars to Kitty's eyes, and probably always would.

'I hear you're taking a trip,' she said. 'Egypt?'

'Yes.'

'Good for you.' Not delivered in a totally positive way.

'Mum's always wanted to go, and now seemed the right time.' Although she wasn't, Kitty felt she was gabbling. Donna often had that effect on people. The atmosphere in the office was suddenly bleak, the air thin. Donna seemed unaffected by it.

'Would you like a coffee?' Kitty asked.

'No. Just thought I'd come in to see how you're getting on. See what you're up to.' Then Donna's eyes lit on the roses and a curtain came down behind them. 'I'll see you around, no doubt,' she told Kitty. Sounded like a dark promise she intended to keep. She stopped at the door as if hijacked by a sudden thought. 'We've known each other a long time,' she said.

'Yes.'

Donna looked almost amused by that. 'Have a good time in Egypt,' she said, and was gone.

❖　　❖　　❖

Donna and Dan thought I was exotic, an only child with parents living apart. They professed envy of my situation, which I never understood. I loved my life, no doubt about that, but I couldn't grasp why anyone with a rumbustious home of their own would want to swap with me. We didn't have a quiet house, exactly, but the quality of the noise there was different. Mum would listen to Radio 4 or play her whirligig Irish music, sometimes dancing about to it, which made me curdle inside, particularly when I was a teenager. Other times she might argue with the television – again shockingly cringe-inducing for me. I often told people she was mad and they seemed to accept that. She was different, that much was sure.

I did want to know why I had no brothers or sisters. It seemed an outrage when I was a very young child, not that I wanted for company. I didn't understand, though, why I couldn't have more family if I wanted. The big question was always, 'Why not?'

Mum: 'You can't have another slice of pie.'

Me: 'Why not?'

Mum: 'You are not to go traipsing around the fields without your coat on.'

Me: 'Why not?'

The answers I got to all the other questions were logical enough but I couldn't grasp the one about siblings. I did get that she might have liked more children, but the idea that she wasn't lucky enough was impossible to grasp. She had no answer to the 'Why not?' that made any sense to me but told me she'd explain properly when I was bigger. The answer, later, was that she'd been getting on when she had me and didn't want to tempt fate by trying for any more children, especially as I had turned out so well, she said. This made me both self-congratulatory, in secret, and embarrassed, in public, and I prayed she'd never say it to any of my friends. It also meant that luck hadn't come into it. I took it for granted that Dad would be the father for these mythical brothers and or sisters. It never occurred to me to ask about that. It would have been a very interesting 'Why not?' if the answer hadn't suited my youthful tunnel vision.

Sometimes, when I was a kid and he stayed over, Dad slept in the tiny spare bedroom, sometimes he was in Mum's. There was no pattern to this and I never questioned it. Just as it wasn't odd to me that Mum had a different accent from everyone else. We all had a lilt; hers was simply from another country. It didn't mean I spoke any differently from the other children in my class or on my street, and that was all I cared about. There was an awful moment around my twelfth birthday when Mum wondered if I would like to use Dad's surname attached to the end of hers as my full name. I would then have been Katherine Fulton Duke and the mortification a disaster for me. I let it be known that the idea was not appreciated, especially as they hadn't bothered to get married. I made liberal use of the Big Statement to drown out anyone else's reasoning in those days. It was never discussed again. Oh, and there was the time Mum suggested I call her May and my dad Stephen, which also went nowhere as a notion. Nowadays I call her May a lot as the mixture of it and 'Mum' is needed to attract her attention.

Dad has been brilliant all along. I must tell him that. It always seems that the people you most value are the ones you take most for granted. Such is love. My father is also a master of understatement and of those tiny gestures that make up a lifetime of devotion and care, so he and his actions tend to get overlooked. He's been supplementing our income so that we can buy any of the drugs we can't get on the NHS. He let Mum work on for as long as he possibly could. And she was capable for a while, after the diagnosis and with the assistance of some good medication. Then she lost interest. The lack of concentration and disappointment in her own waning abilities got to her. She had other things to pursue that had become altogether more important. She planned what would happen to within an inch, wanting to bear most of the burden she would become for as long as possible and setting systems into place so that it would be smoother and easier to handle for everyone when things began to run downhill. But while we're organised, life is untidy and plays by slippery rules that change without warning.

Mum instated the large house diary and the system of notes. We are on our seventh now, one for each official year of her affliction. She rigged up the cooker to shut down after a certain time, in case she forgot to do it. In fact, she put in all sorts of switches and levers to safeguard that sort of thing around the house. She wanted the transition to be virtually unnoticeable when these things became vital.

She tried changing her diet. We got a bit faddish, I'll admit, following advice in articles about turmeric being useful or Vitamin E after some report on that. She upped her caffeine intake when it was said to aid those susceptible to Alzheimer's because their higher cholesterol compromised their blood/brain barriers. That resulted in headaches and the jitters so we got her back to normal doses of tea and coffee.

She found a support group and joined. She actually helped out at the beginning, although she is now one of those who need the help. She has moved on, if that's the right way to put it. The local group, which serves a few towns in the region, changes all the time, as people die and their families fade away. The relatives feel incredible guilt about that, I know, but their fight is over and they are entitled to a break from the beast. I met one chap in the chilled food section of the supermarket after he'd buried his dad, and he looked so ashamed. We stood there, perished by the fridges and wiping our noses.

'I feel such relief,' he said, looking around to be sure no one heard the heresy but me, as if it was obscene. 'I'll be back when I get over it all,' he promised, before scuttling off to fruit 'n' veg. I knew I wouldn't see him again.

Dad has been there for us on the journey. We never lived together as a family and as a result I never knew any other way for us to be. I had two homes, if I wanted, though Pennick has always been my base – I suppose you could call it the mother-ship without stretching credulity too far. Even when there was a threat that I might do well enough in my A-levels to go to university, I never really considered Dad's offer that I could stay with him in Norwich. I managed to do badly anyhow and stayed where I was. If either of my parents was disappointed they kept it largely to themselves, though Mum would sometimes ask if I might like to travel and see the world, in that casual way older people have when they're slyly trying to gauge a life.

Kitty was not home long before Val gave his tootling knock and entered the house. Her face lit up to see him. Val had that effect on most people. He was infectiously positive. May smiled and waved from her chair. She was watching tele-vision, flicking from channel to channel without lingering for long on any.

'Brought these back,' he said, producing May's missing painting accoutrements. Kitty knew he'd probably visited a few homes returning forgotten items. He always did after leading a support group jaunt. That's where she'd found him and persuaded him to moonlight, looking after May when he had the spare time.

'I wondered where they'd got to,' Kitty said. 'Kept expecting to find them in the coal scuttle or the airing cupboard.'

Val took out May's latest effort and looked at it from different angles. It was an abstract in vivid colours that could have been of anything but was probably a local church. 'I base that on the fact that it was St Michan's we visited on the day,' he said.

'How was she?'

'Animated. She and two of the others, Phil and Roger, spent their time laughing at themselves and anyone else they met. I had the distinct impression they were teasing passersby with their supposed madness.'

'Naughty.'

'Yes, but great to see a bit of spirit, still ready and willing to mock others and mess with their mojo. Mind you, if I'd heard them sing another nursery rhyme, I might not have been answerable for my actions. You all set for the hospital check-up?'

'I think so. She's been preparing a lot, so I hope that stands to her. I can't think she'll fool Mr Bishop but so long as she's pleased, I'll be happy.'

'Well, good luck with it all. I can't stay, which I know will break your icy heart, but try to be strong.' He kissed both of her cheeks in farewell, then quietly asked, 'Are you still wasting yourself on that married bloke?'

Kitty spun her head to check that May could not hear them but her mother was still gazing at the television.

'Val, don't.'

'You are.' He sighed. 'I don't have time to give you my sermon on the subject today but you can be sure that I'll treat you to that again.'

She was.

'You know where to find me when the inevitable disaster strikes. You will so get dumped, my dear. But I'll be here, ready to pick up the pieces.' Then he sang, '"Why? Because I love you"' from an old ditty that neither of them knew the rest of.

When he had first come into their lives he'd told her Val was short for Valentine, 'As in "My Funny".'

'Elvis Costello does a fine version,' she'd said.

'I think I love you,' he'd told her, the first of many times. He had been hers ever since, according to his version of events. Dear, sweet, hopeless Valentine, she thought. And then, I am a condescending bitch. She did feel for him, just not in the way he would have liked. She watched his strangely agile seventeen stone of kindness through the window as he waved to a neighbour across the road then turned back to blow Kitty a kiss. He knew she'd be looking. She couldn't remember how it was that he knew her biggest secret but she was certain he wouldn't have told anyone else.

May thought going to Mass was very boring but everyone had to, that's what Mammy and Daddy said. The neighbours would ruffle her hair outside the church and say, 'She's the image of her father, so she is.' That was nice. It made her preen. Inside, though, in the echoing cavern, there was nothing to do and May hated sitting still. Her mam and dad would wedge her between them because she was a giddy goat. Lots of other people thought it was boring too because there'd be a lot of coughing and that was a sign, May thought. Father Justinian's voice made her teeth itch and he talked forever. She never understood what he was going on about. Sometimes he made Mam shift about in her seat too. He'd say things like husbands were in charge, the same as Christ was the Head of the Church. Mam would snort quietly then and Daddy would have a smirk on his face. Mam would be in really bad humour after one of those Masses.

Sometimes they could hear Daddy doing things to her that sounded bad. She'd be moaning and crying a bit, but trying to be quiet about it too. Michael Junior ran in once and told him to stop hurting her and Mam brought him back to his bed and told him it was fine and May thought Mam was actually laughing but she couldn't have been if Daddy had hurt her, though May knew he wouldn't have meant it if he had, it'd have been an accident.

And sometimes they heard them shouting at one another if they were by themselves in the house.

Kitty marshalled May into the back garden. The frost had killed off a lot of the summer annuals and they lay black and forlorn in the ground. Best to gather them up for the compost bin and tidy everything for the dormant winter period. The garden didn't look dead at all, of course. May had seen to that with her planting. Red berries shone on the small rowan tree, the mahonia sported yellow plumes and a fuchsia still held its bell-shaped flowers like a tease over the ground. They worked in tandem with Kitty staving off mistakes by her mum. May hummed and was happy with the physical labour. The temperature had improved enough for a misty rain to sift gently from the sky. May lifted her face and said, 'Doesn't that feel great?' Kitty had to agree. It was soft on her face, soothing to the skin.

'Donna was very interested in that little tree,' May said, indicating a young oak still growing in a pot on the postage stamp of decking by the back door.

Kitty stopped work with a jolt. 'Donna was here? When?'

May frowned. 'Couldn't tell you, dear.'

Kitty took some breaths to give May an opportunity to gather any thoughts she had and to give herself a chance not to fall in a heap on the ground.

'What did she want to know about the tree?'

'Whether it was dead. I told her no, it's just . . .' She was lost for the word. 'Asleep,' she chose at last.

That wasn't so bad, then.

'Will you be taking it to plant at the . . . patch place?'

'The allotment? Yes, I must take it in the spring.' Kitty only kept it here to hide it. Dan had given it to her after a trip away during one of his marital crises. He had stayed in

Devon in a guesthouse called Twin Oaks where the land-lady bred Labradors and oak trees grown from acorns. She'd gifted him a couple of saplings and he'd kept one and given Kitty the other.

She remembered him commenting once that he'd been asked why he kept a dead twig in the garden. He had laughed at the ignorance of it. 'Donna didn't know it was deciduous.' He shook his head. Was it any wonder they were in trouble? he asked. Kitty had stopped him then, feeling guilty at how much better she felt to hear the details of his wife's folly. At that moment, for the briefest whisper, she was not the Other Woman. That mean-spiritedness had come back to take its toll now. That, and so much more. Suddenly the rain no longer felt pleasant and kind. It was cold and wet and soaking her through. She shuddered. She felt the beginning of the end, here in this sodden, English garden in a town no one wanted to know about. She began to shake then, great heaving rumbles of unhappiness.

'Let's get you in,' her mother said. 'You'll catch your death out here.'

Donna wanted to get married quickly before her bump began to show. She wasn't all that pleased to be pregnant but it did take the heat off her going-nowhere career. She reckoned a bridal splash in the local rag would help, too, and form a useful section for her portfolio. She actually went on a diet. I was chosen to be a bridesmaid although she already had three sisters doing the honours there. She kept me on a short leash, as in friends close and best friends even closer. It is such a fine line, after all, between friends and enemies. She chose frilled, apricot-coloured monstrosities for us to wear while her own dress was an ivory, sleeveless, bias-cut satin with beading at the neck and hem. Outside the wedding preparations I took to wearing shapeless black clothes and tried to disappear into the background. Bit by bit, I was succeeding.

Donna took time out to be with me. She was glowing. It pleased her to ask my opinion on her approaching nuptials and what her life with Dan might be like thereafter. I pleaded ignorance of any knowledge or idea that might help her and tried to smile a lot. I knew she couldn't decide whether I was genuinely happy for her or simply refusing to bow. I wonder now why I ever put up with a lot of what Donna doled out. I think it was an attempt to stay as close as could be to Dan. And a part of me still adored her. I was under her spell and had been since I was a child. Between them, Dan and Donna held me tight and refused to let me go. Then again, did I really want to be let go?

Regular conversations went something like:

Donna: 'You amaze me, you know?'

Me: 'Really?'

Donna: 'Yeah.' She would wait and wait until I crumbled and spoke again.

Me: 'Why?'

Donna: 'You're kind of a freak.'

Me: 'Oh, yeah?'

Donna: 'Well, you should have got out when you had the chance. There's nothing for you here. Now.'

That 'now' was calculated to wound, and it did. She was right. I was losing my old life. I didn't have anything to look forward to. I couldn't help but think it was deliberate on her part. By now we were toxic for one another but I couldn't see it. I thought it was par for the course in a friendship like ours, close enough to be family yet far enough apart to be rivals.

Through it all, Mum was at my side. She may have known what I was going through. Even if she could only guess, she was solid, an anchor. Her tiny kindnesses every day made all the difference. She ensured I was always made up and smelling fragrant. She treated me to more flattering widow's weeds, while gently hinting that the Goth look drained me and she hoped it was just a phase. She made me get my hair done. She was wonderful.

Donna was relentless but, looking back, I think she was giving everyone a hard time. She had an effect on the whole of her extended entourage. We all fell into line when the Diva barked instructions. I was miserable in the extreme and then, one ordinary day, I began to get angry. I knew better than to let Donna see it as I thought she would be both gratified and spurred on to torture me even further than she had already. Besides, I had one up on her. I still had Dan. We met more often than ever at the allotment.

He began to shrink with the worry of the wedding and a family on the way. He was also terrified of being married to Donna till death did them part. In lighter moments, which we rarely allowed ourselves, he joked that she'd expect him to be hers till his death but reckoned there'd be a different set of rules for her. Looking back, it was horribly disloyal of him to say it and of me to encourage him to. I asked repeatedly if he couldn't see it was wrong to marry under these circumstances. He would shrug and say he had to stand by her. Dan has always suffered from a bad case of loyalty, however misplaced. His brother Graham was set upon for stealing a bicycle once and Dan got five stitches in his head for sticking up for him, though he knew Graham was guilty.

I myself was losing weight with each day nearer to the catastrophe awaiting us all. On the night before it, Dan and I made frantic love and I begged him not to go ahead with this fiasco. It may have been reprehensible but I felt I was fighting for my life. I had no shame any more. I pressed my words against his chest, willing them to infiltrate and infect him with my longing. My voice rose as my panic mounted and the inevitable approached. The sky was lightening outside and my heart was tearing itself to shreds. Again I implored him not to go ahead with the ceremony.

'I have to,' he said.

'You don't. You so don't.'

'I do.'

'Please, Dan, I'm begging you, don't do this.'

'I have to.'

'Why? Tell me why?' And then I took the biggest gamble of my life. 'If you can say to me that you love Donna, I will stop asking you not to marry her.'

He took his time then gently said, 'I love her.'

After he'd left I cried until I felt physically injured and it was time to go home to get changed. I didn't wash because I wanted to smell him on my skin and I suppose I half hoped that Donna would too and call the whole charade off. Mostly I didn't want to believe that he loved her, but in a side compartment of my heart I think I probably did.

I stood behind them at the altar that afternoon as they took their vows, and we all stepped through the portal to a new life. The animals went two by two into the Ark, I remembered, not in threes. Must have been a good reason why. Whichever way I looked at it, I was surplus to requirements.

FOUR

We both hate the trips to the hospital. The news is rarely good these days. An improvement is unlikely and so we are constantly measuring degrees of disappointment. The place itself is worn out with caring and I know how it feels. I just hope that I don't smell as much of disinfectant and disease, though both are large elements of my life too. The linoleum bears the tracks of legions of the ill and their families. We get funny looks when we turn towards the psychiatric end of the building. We are the nutters, the loopy ones, to be observed from a safe distance, as in olden days when the public visited Bedlam and laughed at the lunatics from the other side of the bars. No one meets our eyes. They are there to deal with cancers, cankers, the flu: stuff that's easy to under-stand. And beatable. You can taste the relief as they quietly realise, There but for the grace of God go I. Looking at Mum and me, it's hard to decide who's in for the check-up, I'd say. That often gives us a smile but it never gets far past a grimace.

Mr Bishop has a firm handshake and a frank gaze. He's appraising me as well as Mum. 'She's in trouble if you are,' he'd said at the start. What did he see now? A tired spinster of a certain age. I look him directly in the eye and say, 'We're doing well,' and that's close enough to the truth for both of us. Then I ask whether they'd mind if I went outside to make some phone calls, and they say that's fine. It's all part of our hospital routine, a courtesy we pay one another. Mr Bishop and Mum like to leave the door ajar so I can be a part of it yet apart. I sit outside, listening to her consultation.

I hear her go through her words. I know she is nervous and likely to be the worse for that. But then again so does Mr Bishop. He's seen so many like Mum. I often wonder why he doesn't go quite stark raving daft because he can't cure anyone. What a strange area of medicine to be in. It's practically palliative care: he can help but he cannot make my mother better or whole again. He waits, as his patients do, in hope of a cure.

'Band, bar, ball, but, born, bee, beer, basket . . .' This is the only two-syllable word she manages. My heart is hurting for her. She so wants to do well. She is trying her trick of starting a word and letting it finish itself. She gets a few more out this way then ends with 'bad'. And it is.

I hear Mr Bishop ask her to do the clock test. I know this will also be bad, worse even than the words. She cannot manage the numbers and how they relate to one another on the round dial. Time is beyond her. It's too abstract. So is space. Mr Bishop still smiles, I can hear it in his voice, and he tells her she's doing well – and she is, for what she's capable of now. We are both a little in love with him. He understands our situation and doesn't judge us for it. He is kind without pitying us. That counts for a lot.

A man approaches to take his place beside me in the small queue in the corridor. He is next up. He starts to cry without meaning to. His wife sits next to him and taps his leg as if to say, There, there. I don't know why but I take his hand in mine and squeeze it. I have never met these people before but they are comrades in trouble. I don't know which of them is to be assessed. Of course it's both, whoever has the screw loose.

Rain clouds glower in the sky above us, waiting for their moment. If it doesn't pour down we'll have a new set of umbrellas handed in at the station. When the rain comes people don't need reminding to put them up. When it is dull but doesn't deliver, the brollies are left behind. We sit on the station bench, our silence heavy after the hospital and the journey ahead not interesting enough to get excited about.

'We're off soon,' Mum says.

She might be referring to our return to Pennick or our upcoming holiday. It's best to keep the conversation open.

'We are,' I agree.

'I'm looking forward to it.'

I know this to be a handy phrase, just as I know Mum is not really capable of imagining the future properly now. I have been reminding her of our foreign trip each day and night, hoping that it's embedded somewhere in her conscious-ness that hasn't been devoured by her perfidious brain yet.

'There's not a whole lot to be happy about now but the holiday.' So, it was Egypt she was referring to.

'Mum, you heard what Mr Bishop said: you're doing well. In fact, you're a bit of a marvel. You did better than he expected.'

'It's never going to be good, though, is it? I cannot beat this thing. I can keep it . . . off.' Whatever phrase she wanted to use here wouldn't come.

We've been over this ground many times. In earlier days, Mum had similes about thrashing waves and expecting the tide to retreat. She very rarely manages these any more. Now it is more a case of tilting at windmills without fully understanding why, only because they are there and in the way.

I've always thought that windmills look as though they are constantly warding off attack, whirling their sails to confuse and strike, if necessary. They seem to be under perpetual siege. Even at rest they look poised to deliver some sort of leisurely karate chop to an assailant. Ever-vigilant, the wind-mill. As we must be now.

'I get so tired, Kitty.' I know this continual compromise

is wearing my mother out and, although she doesn't say it, she's scared too. We have an unspoken vow not to go into that territory as it makes us both extremely uneasy and that feels only a breath away from panic.

'Mum, just think. Two weeks from now you'll be swimming in the Red Sea. How about that?'

'Will I, dear?' She is suddenly bewildered by the notion. My stricken face sends her to deflect mode. 'I've always wanted to, haven't I?' She begins to search in her bag, as if busily following a plan, unwilling to let me see her confusion. 'I must pack my pink dress.'

'You do that,' I tell her.

My mother doesn't have a pink dress.

Mum responded to her diagnosis by devouring information about the disease. She read as much as she could about it as if that would give her the leverage she needed to deal with it from the upper hand. She became obsessed with new developments in treatment and was every doctor's nightmare, namely a patient who took an interest. The first battery of tests were notable for the way I fared only slightly better than her on some of the questions. I failed to name the correct date or time; I have clocks and calendars for all that. I was rubbish at counting backwards in sevens from one hundred. Mr Bishop laughed gently and said he had problems with those himself and that stress often produced similar symptoms to what they were looking for. He also invoked 'benign senescent forgetfulness', which I found out was a beautiful way of saying we're all getting old.

The MRI scan revealed the extent of the damage to Mum's brain and afterwards I knew all too exactly where her temporal lobes were and how diminished her hippocampus was. These were new and unwelcome pieces of information and we left the clinic feeling low and wondering how to proceed.

'I have no choice but to face this full on,' Mum said, which was when she began her researches.

'Are you not the one constantly declaring how dangerous a little learning is?' I teased her.

'That's me being ironic. Knowledge is the only way we'll get through this with any dignity.' She sighed. '"Second child-ishness and mere oblivion".' I must have looked puzzled. 'Shakespeare,' she explained.

'Surely you're quite like that now,' I pointed out.

Mum gave me a watery smile. 'You'll be living with a lunatic eventually,' she warned.

'That's a long way off yet.'

'But when I get there I intend to be a regular size twelve again. Time to lose some weight.'

She was so determined to continue as if everything was normal. But of course it wasn't and never would be again. Drugs modified her symptoms, took the edge off them. She set about her self-imposed tasks, learning as much as she could, and then trying to learn it again, as assimilating information was now getting beyond her. It was like those absent memories of things that had recently happened to her; the memory of the event was not lost so much as never formed properly in the first place. What bits she could grasp and hold on to she worried like beads, trying her utmost to fathom the new information and what it meant to us.

And then she began to get angry. She raged, which was a side of her seldom seen before. My mother is a gentle creature who loves poetry and her garden. Where was she within this angry woman? How could she be in there? Would she come back out again or was this my new mother? Again, it was just a phase and she eventually calmed down. We reached an acceptance. In a way, I felt it was the hardest stage to absorb.

We've all had this conversation. It's the one where you see someone in extremis, in the street, a hospital or on TV, and say to your closest, 'If I ever get like that, shoot me.' Seems simple. You point out you'd do it for a dog, so why not your nearest and dearest? Mum and I had The Conversation early on. We both knew, and still know, that a time will come when she'll be lost to herself and unable to cope with even the most basic things. She wants to retain some dignity. Who doesn't? I've told her I'll help. But it's an abstract notion as yet. She brings it up occasionally, to check that I am still onside.

She took the optimum moment to discuss it oh-so-casually, but I knew she had been thinking about it a lot. She was reading a report in a paper about a man and his wife who had travelled to the continent for her assisted suicide. Mum read the article aloud and with some relish. She liked to give her own emphases to a passage, make it more interesting and usually more dramatic than it was. There was no need here. It was a detailed account, though the facts that delighted her most might have passed other people by. That was what I loved about Mum, that urgent and sometimes wicked sense of humour, on the very edge of propriety. It tickled her that the man described what a lovely day out they'd had before they sat down to the deadly cocktail of drugs that would end his beloved's life. His wife had been suffering from a virulent cancer and had decided that she'd like to leave on her own terms, which she did.

'Isn't that great?' Mum said. 'She did what she needed to and he gave his support.' Then she returned to the newspaper and paraphrased; 'We had a tremendous day out and then my wife killed herself, as scheduled.' Mum stifled a chuckle. 'And just think how economical it was,' she pointed out. 'As far as flights go, they only needed one single and one return, so good value on top of everything else! The wife's carbon footprint won't have taken too much of a battering either.' A wicked analysis, off beam but full of admiration for the people involved.

We toasted the couple, their thoughtfulness and courage,

then got sidetracked into a chat about leaving nothing behind but your footprints and how, logically, that didn't really apply to air travel but if we had wings we could measure feathers. See? An abstract madness, but fun. Then she brought things skilfully around to her own predicament and I agreed to help, though we didn't go into detail. Her hope is that she'll swim out to sea one day and I won't call her back in. I'm hoping it'll be that easy.

It's not that I disagree with her wishes. I want her to enjoy her life as fully as possible. And I want her to leave it her way. It's the ultimate act of love, surely, and an honour to be asked to help. But I cannot actually imagine doing it. Perhaps it'll be the most natural thing in the world when it presents itself. I hope so. I don't think I am a brave person and I do not want to fail her in any way. It will be the biggest moment of both our lives and I don't want to fuck it up.

Stephen Duke was not convinced that his daughter's trip to Egypt was a good thing but he kept his own counsel. Kitty seemed sure that it would please May but Stephen felt it would be beyond her straitened capabilities. Another new world to fathom was a tall order for her already addled brain. She was aware of the holiday, in general terms, but had no informed opinion about it that he could see.

'Egypt will be nice,' he'd said one day.

'Egypt will be nice,' she'd parroted.

She had taken to repeating phrases, buying herself time

while she figured out what on earth people were talking about or asking her. He was increasingly conscious of her failing vocabulary. Her speech was plain now, simple. She had moments of descriptive ability but they were occurring further and further apart. She was a pared-down version of the May he'd known. It was strange to watch a woman fade with each week that passed, her new transparency a sad reminder of the forthright spirit who had lived to talk, discuss, dissect language and beauty. This disease was a cruel bastard.

'Would you like me to come along?' Stephen asked his daughter.

In fairness to Kitty she did not dismiss the idea out of hand or immediately.

'No, Dad,' she said after due consideration. 'Thanks for the offer but I think we'll be fine. There'll be less pressure on Mum if it's just me and her. I think she feels like a lab animal sometimes, with us both watching her so closely. The scrutiny amazes her when she's having a good day and annoys her when she's not.'

'Have you thought some more about extra home help?'

'Yes. It's expensive, you know? I'm hoping we'll manage a while longer without it. The neighbours are wonderful, so is Val, and really between us all it's like proper care in the community stuff. We've created a kind of sheltered accommodation for her here.'

'The time will come,' he said, letting the statement hang between them.

'I know it will, Dad. In fact, I don't think it's that far away.'
This admission of the inevitable scored hard lines into Kitty's
already tired face. 'We'll do what we can till then. And make
the tough decisions when we have to. Mum's prepared us
well for this.'

I worry about taking Mum to Egypt, of course I do. It's
a high-risk trip. It will take us beyond her comfort zone,
such as that is now. We should have done it years ago but
it never seemed to be the right time. As you go on you
realise there is never a right time for anything, there's
only doing something and getting on with what follows,
or not doing something and taking that path instead. I
make sure to talk to her regularly about it so that it won't
be too much of a shock when we set off. At this stage
she's confused enough to be totally excited about going
one moment, and fed up with hearing about the holiday,
the next – like a child that's been told about a new brother
or sister too soon and loses interest long before the baby
is born.

The whole town knows about the trip and has an opinion
about what we should do there and see, whether or not they've
been themselves. The library is fresh out of Egyptology as
friends and colleagues go out of their way to help. They mean
well but sometimes, when I'm low, it feels ever so slightly
patronising. People want to be involved, and our neighbours
have been sterling, but they like going back into their own

homes and shutting the door against the big bad wolf that has May Fulton in his grasp. Her fate, unfolding before their startled eyes, reminds them too much of their own fragility. Every time they walk from one room to another now, wondering what they came in for, I am sure they think they have what May has. Just a touch, a little start up. Most of the time it's simply that they have too much on their minds. Not something Mum has to worry about too often these days. She's slowly drifting back to the safety of yesterday, which is a place she remembers surprisingly well. Of course, when I walk about forgetting what I intended to do, I am reminded that this may well be a prelude to the same disease for myself. Maybe not. We can hope. Or in some cases we can.

That's what makes us such adaptable creatures, I think, hope. It's the chance of a change, of catching a decent break in the cosmic order, the opportunity to improve our lot. We look forward. Or maybe hope makes idiots of us, toying with our dreams, delivering just enough to keep us hooked and never fulfilling its end of this bargain we made with ourselves in the first place. Humans are fools to themselves, then? You don't catch domestic pets getting hung up on the future and they care little about the past either, yet they have trained us nicely to do their bidding.

We base our futures on a set of results from the past. Looking at Mum now, I wonder about the wisdom of the system. Her past is eroding and with it her future. I feel her absence all around me. Her energy is dissipating, that fantastic aura of possibility and wonder she brought with her, the relish for life. I miss it. I mourn for it. Strange to grieve ahead of time but that is what this disease has forced into our home. I cannot avoid it as less of her appears each morning at the top of the stairs.

May's daddy was the most handsome man in the world. He was funny too. Mammy said he could make a cat laugh. Then she'd say he couldn't get around her that easy. He sold things. That was his job. He'd go down the country and sell people things they needed like thread and soap. Daddy said he was a Knight of the Road. Mammy said it was a poor thing he had to leave town to peddle his blather when there was plenty would believe his nonsense here. Then he'd make her laugh and might pull her on to his knee. But she'd give him a kind of smack and say there'd be no more of that, three children was enough.

There was another baby for a while but he didn't last and they must have given him back at the hospital because that's where they brought him one day and came home without him later on. Ellen said he was dead but that didn't seem likely to May.

Daddy never minded answering all May's questions. Sometimes Mammy said he should tell her the truth and not fairytales but May trusted him to say what she needed to know. He had a rumbling laugh, like the train coming from a long way off.

He made lots of sounds that May loved. Her bedroom was over the kitchen and in the morning she heard the tap-tap-tap of his razor off the side of the big white sink as he shaved. She'd snuggle deeper into the mattress, feeling safe. If she was downstairs watching him, she'd hear the graze of the blade as it scraped his face. He would ask her nonsense questions and then shake his head and say, 'Oh, not by the hair on my chinny-chin-chin.' And Mam would warn him that there better not be one single trace of him in her sink and she about to get food ready for the whole family and that it was unhygienic and she didn't know why he couldn't take a basin into the backyard like any other man in the parish. And Daddy would say that he was not like any other man in the parish and Mam would say, 'Don't I know it?' and sometimes that was a good thing and sometimes it wasn't.

Dan Gibbs was not a fanciful man; that had been knocked out of him long ago. But he did feel he was a soul in torment and that a lot of it was of his own making. This did not make him feel in any way sorry for himself. He didn't much like self-pity in anyone. He wasn't cut much slack for that kind of behaviour at home, and was usually too busy at work to indulge in it. What he did like then was to beat the living daylights out of a piece of engine or track. That normally did the trick.

He was worried about Kitty. She looked tired. In fact, she was worn out but beyond feeling exhausted by the constant grind of her daily life. She tried to wear her burden lightly but was not always successful. He had taken to calling in at her home, to check if she and her mother needed anything doing. Often May recognised him and that was gratifying. If she did not, he gently prompted her to acceptance that she knew him and could trust him to be there. It was a delicate operation as she grew tearful if she felt she wasn't grasping the nub of a situation. He couldn't bear to see her cry. He felt even worse when her daughter did, which was not often as Kitty was rarely self-indulgent either. They had been through too much together for that.

Today was a good start as May greeted him by name and led him into the kitchen. She made tea and said Kitty had gone out but would be back. Dan was fairly sure he could hear her upstairs.

'Did you get married yet?' May asked.

'Indeed I did.' He chanced a wry grin as if to say, I must have been mad.

May was surprised by the news. 'Oh. Was I there?'

'Yes, you were. Thank you for coming along.'

'Well, of course I did, silly.' She came over all conspiratorial then. 'Now tell me again, why did Kitty not wear white? She hates it if I ask her anything about it.'

He should have just lied but Dan had denied Kitty enough and he couldn't bring himself to it. 'I didn't marry Kitty, May.'

'Oh. Why not?'

There was no answer he could give, not even the truth, so he sat feeling dejected and ashamed of himself. I have not been fair to Kitty, he thought, ever.

'Is this a pot or a bowl?' May asked, holding up a yellow basin. 'I can only put the bowls in that zap thing.' She looked at the microwave and back at the basin. 'It'll never fit,' she said, puzzled all over again by life's intricacies.

The house is a mess but I'm thinking of leaving any major changes till after we get back from Egypt. Dad or Dan might come in to clear out some things for me while we're gone and I'm presuming Mum won't notice. I want her to know she's home when we return but not to miss anything that's been chucked while we're away. We have accumulated a lot of rubbish. There are the Post-its, for starters, which could do with sifting through and sorting out. Some of the messages are quadrupled reminders. It makes Mum feel good to put them up. She'll have forgotten about the first by the time the second goes up, let alone the umpteenth one. The knitting is becoming a jumble too. She can't follow a pattern any more so she makes it up as she goes along. I call it Jazz Knitting with its eclectic colours and textures, and it gives Mum great satisfaction, but it doesn't half clog up our living area.

She hasn't bothered with the photo albums in a while. At first she sought them out and immersed herself in them. She began with the oldest, touching a sepia print of a boy who was fading before her eyes, repeating his name. At her sister's portrait, she read her name aloud. In turn, she said her mother's and her grandmother's. All the while she fretted at the images with her fingers, willing them to commit to a memory she could no longer trust. Names, incantations, pleadings. She was trying to fix the facts of her life by repetition, like cramming for an exam. When she seemed convinced she had won some of this battle, she moved on to the albums full of photos of us. But they are past phantoms too, capturing a moment, no more. Still, it is our history and she wanted to acknowledge it, consume it.

She had read about the notion of creating a Memory Palace, where a house is created in the mind and memories and events deliberately distributed throughout its 'rooms'. So, in the hallway might be images of a birthday, treasured holiday reminders in the main fireplace, mementoes of the birth of a child on a table, and so on. She tried to do this but found it a very difficult exercise and frustrating in the choosing of what was important and what not. The mind is capricious and constantly throws up random memories that may have no lasting significance to anyone, even the person recalling them.

'I am hijacked by trivia,' she'd complain.

So, we decided to try to use our own little house to embody, physically, a type of Memory Palace. We selected photographs that held special significance, framed them, and put them in a sequence that pleased Mum and resonated with her in some way. All of the frames have labels on, identifying the people pictured. Similarly, we put the paintings and books she cherishes most at prominent points in the main room. Music she likes was categorised and made easily accessible. We are both quite scattergun so it was an interesting exercise to put some order into these things. Since then I make sure everything is where we decided at that time so that it is constant in her world and can be relied on. I wish we had a bigger space to deal with, as it's hard to stay neat in our cramped house, but the totemic items of our mini-Memory Palace are never disturbed unless it is by Mum as she tries to puzzle out their significance for her, after which I return them to their assigned places.

The books could do with culling, loath as I am to get into that. I try reading poetry to Mum as it brought her such pleasure when she was fully aware of such things. I think she still likes it but, more and more, she enjoys the simpler pieces, especially anything that rhymes. She's getting very into the advertisements on television too. They seem to hold just the right attention span for her. It also means she comes back from the supermarket with every-thing she's been told about by the box in the corner. I like to think it proves there is a viable subconscious still striving away inside that poor scrambled head of hers, even if we don't need nappies for new-borns or the no-tears shampoo for kids, but it could just be coincidence and the attractive, shiny packaging.

I've been enjoying the poetry myself. I think I resisted it down all the years because it was Mum's thing and I didn't want to conform to that. There was an element of rebelling against the school curriculum too, I suppose, though it was a rubbish revolt as I quite liked my teachers and my time there. I'm beginning to realise that I was the one missing out. Mum likes to repeat the words that especially resonate with her. I cannot tell whether it is their sound or meaning that pleases her. She struggles with the more abstract works. I find I am drawn to pieces that explore grief and how we deal with being human, but I keep those for myself alone so as not to upset Mum. A gentle trot through a poet's despair can be a cathartic experience when the day has been a shambles. It's comforting to participate yet remain detached from someone else's problems: looking on and experiencing an aspect of this other life, and deriving wisdom from the poet's burden. It's also a vindication of one's own feelings. People get as much from observing Mum and me, I suppose.

The house smells of shoe protector, which I am hoping will fade while we are away. Mum used it instead of furniture polish a few days ago, in a rare moment of domesticity. Well, now we're shored up against the elements should they decide to storm the place; another barbarian at our gate, but this one a bit gentler than the disease Alois Alzheimer lent his name to. When I say this to Dad his love of wordplay kicks in and he insists we go the full Mrs Malaprop on it and say another Bavarian is at our gate. It makes me smile to picture a man in feathered hat and lederhosen yodelling out our doom, and the gaiety is a welcome thing. The niff, however, is nasty. I suspect she may have used the shoe spray as an air freshener too, while she was at it.

Dan's niece Margo took over the afternoon before Kitty left town, to practise giving holiday cover. The thinking was that if there was a problem, she would have back-up and would also get used to running the office without too much pressure. It made Margo tut that anyone would assume she'd lose sleep over working in this two-bit place, and anyway Uncle Dan was going to be around so what was the big deal? It would be a doddle. She was a lot more bothered with how she'd dress for the fortnight she was on duty, and how she'd get out on to the platforms looking busy and fabulous when the local stud Fred Rowland was passing through with his entourage.

Kitty had left a list of things that might be handy for her to know. She ignored it after getting to the bit that explained again about her stupid Lost and Found system. As far as Margo was concerned that was extra work and she was not being paid to do it, so she wouldn't. No one would be any the wiser. It was a typically finicky thing for a spinster like Kitty to set up. She couldn't believe the woman had tried to tell her about increased security risks associated with abandoned packages too. As if any self-respecting terrorist would waste time blowing up this shit-hole.

Margo shifted the shiny box of cremated ashes to the back of the shelves because it gave her the creeps. She chased out the smelly, ginger cat, Rory or whatever his name was. 'Scram!' and a rolled-up newspaper did the trick there. After an hour of strangers arriving and riffling through the umbrellas she got royally fed up and hid most of them. Mad Marty Faber asked after a lunchbox he was missing, like she could be arsed looking for that, so she ran him out of the place.

Then a tall saddo came in saying some undertakers had sent him. Too weirdoid by half for Margo and she was so not going to get involved. She told him that Kitty Fulton would be back in two weeks' time and she was who he needed to see. Then Margo forgot all about him and began to paint her nails and dream of when the tracks on her teeth would come off, revealing a set of to-die-for pearlies that Fred Rowland would want to run his tongue along forever. She worried she might catch being a spinster just from sitting on Kitty's chair.

Outside, as the rain began to drive from the heavens in sheets, Simon Hill knew he should have been more forceful about the package he had misplaced, but he was so ashamed to have lost his father in such a way that he dared not draw any more attention to it than he had. Sullen teenagers were utterly beyond him, and the girl at the desk had made him even more awkward than usual. He was positive he'd stuttered and had just missed going arse over tit on the wet tiles on his retreat. His old man would have to forgive him and remain in the station at Pennick another fourteen days. It's not like the old guy had plans to go anywhere else in the meantime, Simon reasoned.

The earth had shifted again. Kitty used her last afternoon before the holiday to finish digging over her plot. When the frost came again it would kill all the exposed weeds for her. This time the ground yielded a small bundle wrapped in sturdy linen. She almost missed it, so dirty was the cloth, but it stuck out at an angle from the rest of the soil, calling her attention. She carefully prised it open to reveal a grubby toy of some sort. She tucked it in her pocket and continued with her work then forgot all about it as she prepared lists in her head of things to do before their departure.

The rain had upped its tempo and the earth smelled ripe and strong. There was a mildness in the air that made her smile. Jed stood under the eaves of his shed, bundled deep into his coat, and called, 'Reckon that'll be with us best part of some time.'

'Good for the veg,' she said.

'Yer away on hol'day termarra?'

Kitty smiled and nodded.

'I'll hatta keep an eye so agearnst yur patch git harm'd.'

'I'd appreciate that, Jed. Thank you.'

'An yer maam?'

'She's doing fine. I'll let her know you were asking after her. We'll bring you back a camel.'

'Egypt,' he said in awe. 'Sich a thing,' he added, shaking his head.

Kitty and May had a calendar showing how many days to the off. It was like the advent countdown. Each night they put a line through another day and prepared themselves further for their trip. Kitty knew that her mother needed structure now, a routine that could be relied on. Confusion was an enemy and if it could be avoided it was. Even though May's memory was not good, the reiteration of the little ceremony each night allowed her to be reminded of the shared plan. Now, it was time. That night Kitty handed her mother the thick red marker and breathed in the chemicals as May ceremoniously drew her mark across the date, the pen squeaking on the paper. They stood back to look at it together and May said, 'We're going, aren't we?'

'After a good sleep. Now come on, the sooner we go to bed, the sooner morning will come. Then we can get our train and our plane and go to see the Pyramids.'

Kitty remembered Christmases from her childhood when excitement was peaking and her mother had used a similar line on her. Is it inevitable that we become our parents? she wondered. Does history always repeat itself, even in such small ways?

✿   ✿   ✿

May's dad taught his family to swim on a day out by the sea. Mammy packed a picnic and they got the bus to Burnstown. He showed them a dog paddling in the water off the narrow pier that led out into the sea then threw them in one by one, in spite of her Mam's objections. 'They'll either sink or swim,' he said, and he was right. Ellen sank and Michael Junior and May swam. For months afterwards Ellen had to be coaxed to wash, much less go into the ocean again, whereas May and her brother wanted to go every day. Sometimes they shared a stick of rock and once they had a candyfloss. May loved the sweetness in her mouth after the salt of the sea. By then she could do more than the doggy paddle, having copied other children doing the crawl. Daddy called her Esther Williams but she didn't know who that was.

That summer was the happiest of her young life, the whole family together going on trips and arguing. A year later Michael Junior was dead, hit by a car whose driver never stopped to help or admit to the crime. May saw her brother laid out in his coffin on the kitchen table, and cried. He had a small cut on his cheek and a bruise on his forehead but otherwise looked as though he was asleep. Why would he not wake up? It wasn't funny any more, she told him, but it did no good: he had always been a stubborn boy. May's mother stopped speaking much and would sit for hours holding his favourite jumper in her hands, sometimes bringing it to her nose and inhaling really deeply as if she could breathe him back in if she did, and then maybe breathe him back out alive too while she was at it. She would take out a pair of baby's booties and that made her even sadder. She kept muttering about her two boys gone and Daddy would try to jolly her along saying, 'You still have me,' but she told him he was nothing but a fool. After a long time spent sitting in her kitchen she said she wanted to get a job and out of this place, but Daddy wasn't happy about that at all.

One day May's dad went on his rounds and never came back. May heard the women whispering downstairs after the children had been packed off to bed. Her mam said, 'He couldn't give me an inch of freedom without it nearly killing me as well as him. How will I manage now?' Then she wailed a bit which was an awful sound, not like a person at all. Granny Larkin said, 'Good riddance to bad rubbish,' but May knew she didn't mean it. Daddy made her laugh too. He used to read out bits from the papers in funny voices and she would have to cover her mouth so no one could see the space where her top teeth should be when she hadn't her dentures in.

May didn't think he was dead, just gone off. But she did think their baby was dead by then because of Mammy and the bootees. May wasn't sad about the baby, even though she knew that she should be, but she'd only seen him the once and he looked like lots of others babies except maybe smaller. She missed Michael Junior like mad and would have given up all the swims in the world to have him back.

She could smell the smoke from the women's cigarettes and hear them going 'Shush, now, shush' to her mam when she said, 'I drove him away'.

Ellen turned in the bed to May's right and moaned. She felt the mattress grow warm as a stream of her sister's wee reached her legs. Soon it would go cold. She tried to get to sleep before that happened.

Kitty and May took a cab to Pennick station where Dan fussed over them like a porter looking for a tip.

'Is it royalty that lad thinks we are?' May asked, preening at the attention.

'Well, I think we're special,' Kitty said, 'so we deserve special treatment.'

He offered tea and coffee while they were waiting, a service other travellers looked most interested in.

'Are you all right for money?' he asked.

'For the umpteenth time, yes.'

'Will your mobile phone work over there?'

'Yes.' Kitty didn't know the truth of that and it didn't worry her. There was little that couldn't wait till their return, she guessed, and precious few people to call from over there who wouldn't be satisfied with a postcard.

Dan saw them to their seats when the train arrived, stowed their luggage, promised yet again to feed Roly. The cat hadn't turned up to see them off. Dan had rarely been without Kitty for this long a stretch. She thought that was why he looked so gaunt. It made her happy that he would clearly miss her so much. For his part, Dan knew his expression was not solely due to this but that news could wait the length of the holiday. Their lives were about to change again, utterly. He wore the expression of a man condemned.

As the women waved goodbye to him through a mud-streaked window, May asked, 'Are we going to find Daddy?'

FIVE

We're in Cairo before our introduction to the others who will be with us for the duration of our tour. There are seven of them, all Brits, mostly getting on in years in as much as I am the youngest. I spotted one called Liz at Heathrow, yelling instructions at her husband Bernard. It made me wonder if he was deaf or whether her voice was always this strident. I find out it's the latter as she must be the one who is hard of hearing if she can make that sort of noise without wincing. Mum is fascinated to recognise 'the loud one' and, as much as it pleases me that she does, the fact that she points and bellows this just as loudly as Liz takes some of the shine off the achievement. Liz has seen and heard her and I expect retribution at some point in the future from the look she shoots us. Bernard seems pleased, though. They have a stray woman in tow called Rita who looks as if she might bolt at any moment but for Liz's steely grip on her arm. There are two couples making up the group, a pair called Sue and Mags who announce themselves as 'The Merry Widows', and Jim and Edna who are just merry, having spent the entire journey drinking gin and laughing together. We met as we gathered under the 'Faraway Holidays' sign held aloft by a man in a suit in the baggage reclaim hall. He sees us to the door of the terminal and hands us over to another smartly dressed man who sees us to the minibus in which a third suited man sits beside a driver, ready to escort us to our hotel. The second suit waves us off but stays put.

Cairo is all lit up as we whizz through it to our hotel. The others chat happily about what we can expect and loudly ignore the fact that our guide and driver might speak better English than most of us. 'They' expect tips all the time, is Jim's pronouncement.

'Baksheesh,' I supply, quietly, having done my homework.

'Pardon?' he roars into the back of the minibus.

I shake my head to indicate that it was nothing.

Mum points at the palm trees silhouetted against the orange of the streetlights and the minarets reaching into the night sky. She is chattering animatedly and making no sense that I can discern, but then neither are the others and no one notices. We finally pull into a sprawling hotel in the suburbs, isolated from the city hubbub, all marble columns, clipped greenery and busy staff. We are given our keys, an itinerary, and then abandoned to more staff and our touristy fate for the evening.

There is a large swimming pool on the way to our room and I make a note to lock the door in case Mum takes to wandering in the night. The room is decorated in lots of browns and has a slightly jaded air. I know how it feels. I give the porter too big a tip because I have not been able to change any of the large denomination notes I got at the bank. He is delighted and I realise with a sinking heart that he'll spread word we are a couple of flush women and we'll be mobbed. As I let him out I check the door. The lock seems serviceable enough. That pool out there is trouble with a capital T and I cannot risk its allure. Mum is staring at screen disturbance on the television.

'Just like the moon landing in '69,' she tells me. 'Your father had a small black-and-white set and we watched it on that.'

'Before I was even thought of,' I say, and she looks at me as if I am the hired help forgetting my position. I let it go. I know she doesn't mean any harm but there are times when I crave an unforced hug or words of unexpected praise, like in the old days.

There is no point in unpacking much as we'll only be here two nights before leaving for a cruise on the Nile. We head back to the main body of the hotel for something to eat. The rest of the group lie in wait for us, drinks in hand. The pack has spotted an anomaly and wants an explanation. I feel so weary but I refuse to give in. This slender life is too important for that.

* * *

Kitty kept a smile pinned in place to deflect the worst of the intrusive enquiries. It was too early to be intimate with these strangers. They could stew in their curiosity. This was only the initial phase of getting to know one another and distractions were easy to find on that first night. Amateurs, she would tell her dad when she reported back to him. When Kitty and May's turn for scrutiny came it was simple enough to keep the talk on Norfolk, which most had visited if not Pennick. Or if they had passed through they couldn't remember it, which was no surprise as it would have been little more than a station platform glimpsed from a train or an obscure mention on a road sign pointing in the wrong direction. The Merry Widows had travelled on the Poppy Line, the heritage railway in the north of the county. And wasn't there another pretty line through the Broads National Park? the women wondered, almost to themselves. Bure Valley Railway, Kitty could tell them. Jim and Edna had sailed on the Norfolk Broads. Bernard's eyes shone as he lovingly described a visit to Houghton Hall near Kings Lynn which has the largest collection of toy soldiers in the world. His wife Liz shut him up sharpish, having obviously loathed it, though she did decree the estate to be a fine one. Their mate Rita looked lost and barely uttered a word. Perhaps Kitty and May were not the only ones concealing something.

What could Kitty have said to redeem her home town's reputation? What was there to tell that would hold their interest or whet their appetites? It was functional, not hugely attractive, like a fixture used every day, without mystery or particular menace. It was probably no worse than anywhere else. It hosted people from birth to death and most of them were content enough with that. It didn't make big promises it couldn't keep: people went to Norwich or Manchester or London for that. It was comfortable. She realised this was the damning with faint praise that a town could do without, so she kept schtum.

Kitty monitored her mother's wine intake. Two glasses was more than enough. The last thing they needed was a hungover May, who would be cranky yet not remember why she should feel bad. Paracetamol and an explanation only went so far any more. They ate some lamb and couscous as soakage and May enjoyed it.

'Always tastes better away,' she said, and everyone agreed.

They were nearly getting by. Her mother began to yawn on cue and Kitty made their excuses and got them out of there.

'We'll see you bright and early,' Liz called. It sounded partly like a promise and awfully like a threat.

The following morning was the first of many early starts. A clear, blue sky heralded the expected good weather but the shade was chilly and Kitty and May hugged their linen jackets close. There was no escaping the gang. Kitty steered her mother through the less-used door of the dining hall and shielded the two of them behind a few pillars but they were caught at juices and rolls and had to join the Brits' table.

The breakfast buffet offered meats and cheeses, a chef stood by a griddle to make omelettes, yet still there was the longing mention of a good old British fry up. Kitty felt the heat of embarrassment.

'Are they mad?' May asked, a little too loudly again.

'A bit,' Kitty said in a low voice and distracted her with some yogurt.

The men had the alert look of naughty boys who'd stayed out late, drunk too much but refused to admit to the damage they must feel. Liz had donned a kaftan and probably assumed she'd gone native as a result. Rita was downcast and the Merries pale. It looked as though they'd all over-indulged the previous night. There was a nightclub housed within the hotel complex, the men reported in the martyred tones of pioneers who had explored on behalf of the group and the good of all. Kitty suspected several bottles of duty free had taken a battering in the quiet of the bedrooms after the official festivities had ended.

Liz read aloud from the brochure, bossily telling them they would visit the Egyptian Museum first. 'Museums,' she tutted, as if this was a waste of time.

'Eejit,' May muttered.

'What did she say?' Liz asked, hard voiced and slit eyed.

'Egypt,' Kitty said. 'She loves it. We both do.' She smiled broadly and her mother tittered. She understood that, Kitty thought, and glowed a little.

❀   ❀   ❀

We have not been here more than ten hours and already the pecking order within the group is clear, with Liz putting herself forward as leader. I pity the guides. She is so busy talking about being 'out foreign' that she's missing the delights of our first proper drive. Mum points to the horizon and says, 'Pyramids,' and sure enough there they are. The pyramids of Giza are visible in the distance just beyond the outskirts of the modern city. I am dumbstruck by the sight. These are the last Wonder of the Ancient World still in existence. It's like meeting an impossibly famous film star and dribbling like an imbecile instead of saying something lucid, or anything at all. All I can do is repeat the word and point. And dribble. The guide smiles. Her name is Mary, nothing more exotic than that. 'We will see those up close later,' she promises. The Pyramids spin by like a three-dimensional postcard and I still cannot believe we have seen them. I feel like Mum has discovered them all over again and hug her.

I ask about the large expanse of low buildings between the roads.

'That is the Dead City,' Mary explains. 'It is the cemetery.'

Liz starts to fan herself as if she's never heard the like of a graveyard in a town.

'It's not so dead,' Mary goes on. 'Lots of the poor live in there, perhaps half a million Cairenes between here and our other big City of the Dead.'

Now Liz is beginning to voice her outrage at such savagery.

'They want to be close to their loved ones,' Mum says.

'Yes,' Mary agrees, and smiles happily. 'It is important to be close to family, though many are poor and have no choice but to live there. But, yes, it is a comfort to be near our ancestors and we have a long tradition in my country of living close to family graves.'

'There's a lot of building work going on,' I say, pointing to unfinished roofs with steel bars sticking up into the bluest sky I have ever seen. It's as much to change the subject and stop Liz short as anything else.

Mary laughs and says something to the driver in Arabic. He laughs too, but not in a mean way. Mary turns around in her seat again. 'That is to avoid paying taxes. If a building is finished it is more expensive.'

'"Nothing is certain but death and taxes",' Mum says, half-quoting Benjamin Franklin's famous phrase.

I am thrilled that she has dug this up and bursting with happiness that we have come here, and nothing Liz can do will spoil that. Then Mum says 'taxis' to reinforce her point and I want to phone my father immediately and tell him the funniest thing: that the only two things we can be sure of in this life are death and taxis. Everyone looks at me as tears run down my cheeks. The expression in their eyes is unmistakable. They think I'm a loony.

The shaving mug was cracked and generally knackered. It should be binned, Simon Hill knew, but he was finding it difficult to cull the most personal of his father's things. How was it possible to choose some beloved objects above others? Why was this particular item giving him such trouble? Perhaps it was that this was something his dad had used every day of his life since he was given it. As far as Simon could remember it had been a Christmas present from Mum. He'd had no such trouble with the brush as it had long ago gone bald and been ditched by the old man himself. The current one was no better and could easily be jettisoned. He forced himself to take a rational approach. He loved this mug, would use it himself and be cheered every day by seeing the Blue Delft figures. He set it aside along with the ivory comb, the sort that was now illegal and available only in the most secretive and expensive of stores. He could still picture his father running that through his hair every hour, maintaining his quiff with the aid of a little brilliantine at first and then on to gel, no less, in his latter years. In poorer days it had been water and his hair's natural oils. 'Costs nothing to make an effort,' he'd say. And there had been hard times, and hunger, and cold. Proudest day of the old man's life? Simon's graduation from Oxford. First of the family to go to university. He looked at the few possessions which represented the life he was tidying away. There was no one to remember Dad but him now. Saddest day of the old man's life? There were many, but probably realising he had no grandchild to leave his all to – the 'all' being his cherished opinions and the tiny insurance policy that had been severely depleted by the last stay in the old folks home.

And what would Simon do with the few items he had chosen to hang on to? Put them in a box alongside his mother's things, in yet another attic? At least when they had chosen those mementoes, Simon and his dad had been together, grieving but busy. This was the second time he had stuffed the remnants of a life into black sacks for charity. He wondered how many of his dad's things would find new homes and how many end up in landfill as if they had never mattered.

He was getting maudlin. There was too much to be done for that: moving house, the new job . . . and getting the old guy back from that ruddy station. He would give a piece of his mind to this Fulton woman when she came swanning back from wherever the hell she'd flown off to. Cufflinks went into the staying pile. Ditto the navy tie with the paisley design. His dad had been quite the dandy, really. And it was Simon's own stupid fault he'd left the box of ashes on the platform.

The guide gave them a pep talk before they entered the museum building. This would be the largest collection of Egyptian artefacts they would ever visit and it was impera- tive they stick together, she warned. Liz took it upon herself to repeat everything Mary said, in spite of the fact that they were both speaking English. Everyone looked a little as if they hated her then, especially her husband Bernard. He also looked like a man whose hangover had started to hit home. The Merries, Sue and Mags, just giggled, the naughty girls of the class. Jim and Edna bore the hallmarks of a couple in the aftermath of a tight-lipped, hissy row. The first days of a holiday were always the most tense, Kitty thought, everyone over-determined to have a good time and finding it impossible to relax. She herself never relaxed any more so she didn't miss it like the rest of the holidaymakers. She rarely ever made an instant decision either as it could have so many consequences undreamed of in any other person's normal day. But she had practice of that, sneaking around with Dan for so long. This pulled her up, the fact that she might think about them in this way. She felt a faint uneasy sense of betraying them both then but buried it and moved on: now was not the time, this was not the place.

Museum-goers thronged past and Kitty linked one arm firmly through her mother's. She was surprised to feel sad Rita clinging on to her free arm. After that they entered the place to be amazed. And of all the things that impressed Kitty there, May's recall of facts about Ancient Egypt was the most astounding. She identified Pharoahs and gods. She chatted happily with Mary about Osiris and Isis, Tutankhamen and Rameses, mummification and theories about potential treasures still to be unearthed. But any time Kitty asked her a question, her mother looked as if she'd just encountered a crazy woman and pointedly clocked their arm-lock as if a stranger had latched on to her but she was too polite to brush her off. I am not part of that section of her brain, Kitty thought. I do not feature in this area that seems untouched by the disease. If we could isolate that and flood it with her lifetime's experiences, perhaps we could beat the thing.

They hit the Khan al-Khalili Bazaar, fresh meat to the traders, and Kitty spent her time forcing things back into different displays, promising May she had bought them all and annoying the shopkeepers as they went by. She had learned the words for 'No, thank you' from Mary earlier and chanted 'La, shukran' over and over. The urge to point at her mother and then at her head was tempting, but she did not. My mother is not mad, she reminded herself, she has simply lost her mind.

Simon Hill was tired of goodbyes. He stood on the threshold of another. His whole life was made up of them. His father's job had moved the family from town to town, so no childhood friendship could ever last long. He didn't have siblings but spent a lot of time alone and with his own thoughts. After a while he found it easier not to get too involved with anyone else and kept acquaintances at a safe distance. He rarely expected to see anyone again once they'd moved on, and he rarely did. University was the longest consecutive time he'd spent in one place. Four years was just asking for trouble. It was inevitable, he thought, looking back, that he would finally fall hard. And he did. Her name was Louisa Walcott and he hadn't a hope of emerging unscathed from that experience. He didn't.

The first time he saw her, he thought she was the living embodiment of the description 'fragrant'. She spoke to him, which was a shock. Later she told him it was for a dare but she kept it up because she found him 'quirky', which latterly morphed into 'creepy' and was then accompanied by a range of singularly unfragrant sounds and gestures. She was a petite blonde who played on her diminutive size, wore a velvet hairband, belted coats to emphasise her tiny waist, and tottered across the college cobblestones in impossible heels, refusing to give in to fogeyish tradition. 'Next they'll be fining me for not wearing my sword,' she'd declare. This Simon took to be evidence of rare wit, falling further under the spell that would almost do for him. Any glance she threw exclusively at him knocked another nail in his coffin. He was hopelessly in love and easy pickings. It was still chastening to realise that one year's love could be another's hopeless infatuation, with the twenty-twenty vision of hindsight. He wondered if all experiences were transmuted in this way or if some resisted the prism of time. Even his speciality, history, sometimes failed to stand solid. Everything was subject to interpretation, when you thought about it.

Back in the day, Louisa told him what to wear, where to go, what to eat, how to behave. Simon had to hand one thing to her, though: she awakened in him a passion that he would never otherwise have suspected he'd harboured. It took them both by surprise. He was awkward in company, or 'socially autistic' as Louisa liked to declare, but a wonder in bed. He discovered there was nothing he didn't like to do for a woman and, although he'd never sustained any lengthy dalliance thereafter, he had no shortage of transient admirers, especially as reviews of his skill were disseminated throughout the sisterhood in whatever town he fetched up in. His complete lack of moral hang-ups helped as well. Marriage was someone else's problem, not his. If a woman was hitched, he really couldn't care less. It wasn't mentioned. There was only the here and now of an affair which always remained discreet and usually brief. The instant commitment was suggested or scandal was threatened, it ended. Sure, there were vague regrets but only in a sentimental way. He had never fallen in love, or if he had it had passed unnoticed and was consequently a great deal less earth-shattering than he had been led to believe.

Now he was headed for Pennick to take up his new post. He bade farewell to the bungalow he had detested in Kings Lynn, with its noisy plumbing and woodchip wallpaper, and turned his back on that chapter of his life. He wondered what had happened to Louisa. He'd been surprised to see her once on a London street, carrying a little extra weight and looking a little drunk. He'd walked on, as he always had, without looking back.

❖ ❖ ❖

It was the Great Sphinx that Kitty loved most on that first day. It was noble, chipped, forlorn and steadfast. She looked at the photo in her guidebook that showed it buried up to its chin in sand, over a century ago, and then back at the excavated monument. The sea of sand still lay all around, waiting for the next chance to reclaim its treasure. It would ebb and approach, taking a sliver here, a detail there, ineffably powerful. It had all the time in the world, having seen off generations of men. She wondered how much more lay hidden beneath the dusty, innocent surface of the land. The myth of the Sphinx was that Napoleon's men had used it for target practice during the eighteenth century but, according to Mary, this was not the case. They all chuckled at the way the truth should never be allowed to get in the way of a good story. Beyond, the Pyramids were swarming with visitors: buses rushed their cargoes back and forth through the desert; cars and camels buzzed about the pale triangles set in relief against a turquoise sky. Everyone seemed to be in a tearing hurry to devour history and pick over its bones, covering as many millennia as possible before purchasing plastic reminders to display to neighbours at home as proof of a good time.

Kitty had to be herded forcibly from her perch to join the expedition to a nearby perfumery where Liz bought knock-offs of famous brands and got a lot of free ornate perfume bottles to go with them. The guide discreetly stayed behind to collect her commission and Kitty was glad that

Mary had really had the last laugh there. At the minibus, May pointed to a fast food joint across from the car park, within sight of the ancient Sphinx, and said, 'The Colonel is everywhere.' They took in the two wonders, each instantly recognisable, each relevant in its different way. Kitty knew which one she preferred. As she ushered May on to the bus her mother asked, 'Are we not getting a chicken bucket?' as if the world had gone totally mad.

They were in the foyer bar when Rita shyly enquired about May's condition. She kept her voice low so as not to alert the rest of the group, who were debating which of the hotel's restaurants to hit. Rita was demolishing her third large glass of wine. Kitty checked that May was otherwise occupied, and apparently she was, reading a brochure and looking like it made sense to her. 'It's Alzheimer's,' she confirmed. 'She's just about tipping into late onset.' The admission exhausted her and she took a hefty swig of Egyptian beer.

'So strange,' Rita said. 'And sad,' she added, after a beat. 'Here I am, drinking to forget, and there she is, unable to remember.'

Kitty took in the lines of disappointment across Rita's forehead, dragging at her eyes and the corners of her mouth. Her makeup was carefully applied and maintained but it couldn't hide the evidence of her disintegration, etched deeper by each night's drinking and each new day's sadness and thirst.

Rita seemed to think she should confide a secret too. 'I used to be Liz's sister-in-law. Still am, actually, though he's gone now.' She grimaced and tried to look wryly accepting. 'Younger model, clichéd as that might be. Liz keeps me around to torture me with kindness, and to assuage the general family guilt and feel better by comparison.' She shrugged at these notions as if she hadn't decided their worth and thought it redundant to do so anyway.

'Cheers,' said May, joining their conversation.

'Cheers,' Rita agreed, holding her glass aloft.

Kitty looked from one to the other and then down at her own hands. They were all separate and lonely in their own way. Her mother was trapped in a body whose mind was on the mitch and about to depart permanently, Rita was now surplus to requirements in a life she'd thought secure and safe, and Kitty was a spinster of a parish located in the midst of nowhere, a nobody to all but a handful of people. She wondered how many doors were shut in the faces of stranded women just like her all over the world each day. Kitty thought of Donna then, and how she was a lonely person too. She rose to buy another round of drinks, having no other answer to their separate problems.

'Is it someone's birthday?' May wanted to know. 'Shouldn't we have a cake?'

The brown paper parcel was tied with string and her name was written on the front. It crackled like a fire as May's mam turned it from side to side, checking the postmark again and again, but all it gave away was that it came from Dublin. There was a card, too, and Daddy's writing said 'Happy Birthday to the prettiest girl in town'. Her mam left the package on the kitchen table and went out into the yard, and banged about there while May opened her present. It was a pink dress and the most beautiful thing she had ever seen and she squealed as she held it up to her. It had puff sleeves and a big frill all around the hem and there was a sash tied in a bow at the back. She ran out to ask if she could put it on and her mother snarled back that it was her dress and she could do what she liked with it. It didn't sound like she thought the dress was lovely, but May didn't care because it was from her daddy and maybe it meant he was coming back and that would make everyone happy, not just her.

She went upstairs and laid it on the bed and stared at it a long time. And then she realised that she couldn't wear it that day or any other and suddenly tears spilled down her face. She thought she'd never be happy again, and neither would anyone in that house. They'd be like princesses in a fairytale who were enchanted so that they could never smile or laugh. And suddenly she hated her dad because he was the one who had put this spell on them.

She marched downstairs and out to her mother and said, 'I don't like it. It's too frilly and stupid. Only a kid would wear it.'

Her mother had smiled then, breaking the curse a little.

Later on May rolled the dress into a ball and hid it in the wardrobe. She couldn't send it back. There was no return address on the parcel because Daddy didn't want to be found.

Mum is having trouble with her dinner. She's sitting looking at it, holding her cutlery poised above the plate in a puzzled sort of way. As odd as it may sound, I think she's forgotten how to cut and scoop up food. I don't want this to come to anyone else's attention so I lean across and ask, 'Can I taste that?' poking a vegetable, stabbing it with my fork in a slow, clear movement and bringing it to my mouth. Mum follows suit. We move on to the meat and in time she gets the hang of chopping it up and I leave her to finish at her own pace. I'm glad we aren't eating anything complicated with bones in it. I feel unpleasantly hot and sweaty, yet shivering at the realisation that Mum has lost a skill so vital to her. I hope it's only temporary. She has no problem with dessert and, once she's done with it, I get us out of there pronto on pretext of needing our sleep before the early start tomorrow.

In the brown room she watches television, some music videos, then asks, 'Why are the little men dancing in the box?' I am starting to get seriously worried that she won't be up to the rest of this holiday when she suddenly turns to face me and says, 'We're all right, Kitty, aren't we? We're doing okay?'

I could wail with joy. My mother is back. I fight for my voice. 'We are, Mum, we're doing fine.'

'I'm so confused,' she admits. 'And I get so frightened, Kitty. I never know when I'll be back, and when I am it's for less and less time. It scares me.'

I can feel tears threaten but I mustn't let them out. This is a moment to be savoured and dealt with properly so it's not ruined by sentiment. There'll be plenty of opportunity for that. I put my arms around her. 'I'm here, Mum, and so long as I am, you will be fine. Better than fine. And I will always be with you, so we're sorted.'

'I love you,' she whispers.

'I love you,' I say.

'And when I swim out into the Red Sea you are to let me go, do you hear?'

I stiffen. I wasn't expecting this, not now.

Her voice hardens. 'Do you hear me, Kitty? You are to let me go.' She pulls back and stares at me, hard. Then she puts the knife in. 'If you love me, you will let me go.'

A song comes on the television that distracts her and she wriggles away again. She gets off the bed and begins to dance. I am torn apart and she is dancing. It strikes me that this sums up our situation as well as anything else.

The station at Pennick was beginning to assume an unusual significance for Simon Hill. He supposed he could have travelled with the removal van but the driver had smelled of cigarette smoke and he rather suspected the cab would stink to high heaven. So he went by rail with a few cases cluttered about him. Now, as he stood on the platform in the wake of the train, he counted his bags, determined not to abandon any more of his life in this place than he had already.

A man of his own age, with a pleasant face and faded red hair, asked if he needed a hand and Simon said he'd kill for a cab. They agreed that probably wouldn't be necessary and walked through to the station forecourt and a telephone with a direct line to the taxi office. With a car on its way, the man shook his hand and turned to go. Simon fumbled in his pockets for a tip.

'Ah, no, no,' the man said, shaking his head almost sadly at the mistake. 'I'm Dan Gibbs, the Station Manager. I'm not a porter.'

Simon burned with embarrassment to have made such a gaffe but thought that to apologise would only make things worse so instead he introduced himself. 'Simon Hill, idiot and new Town Librarian.'

'Happens all the time,' Dan said easily, though Simon suspected it did not. 'Have the powers-that-be finally managed to retire Mona Fletcher?' he asked, clearly intrigued that such a thing could be accomplished.

'Yes. I hear she is a hundred and forty-five years old now and was finally made to see sense.'

'As long as she can still walk, you'll never be rid of her. She'll camp on your doorstep. Rumour is she made a deal with the devil centuries ago that she'll never lose the power of speech. Be prepared to be told many times where you're going wrong and how she likes to do things which is, of course, the right way.'

Simon wondered, briefly, if he and this man might be friends. 'Advice gratefully accepted, sir. While I have your ear, might I ask about the lady who runs your Lost and Found?'

'Kitty?' Dan's eyes took on a kind of shine.

'I believe she's currently on leave.'

'Yes. Egypt. Why?'

Simon indicated the station office. 'She seems to have my father in there, in a box.' He'd rarely felt more self-conscious. First, he'd made a fool of himself offering this man a tip, and now he was topping it off by admitting he'd lost his own dad's final remains.

'I've seen him.' Dan nodded, as if all was perfectly in order.

'So, should I collect him now or what?'

'If I were you, I'd wait till Kitty returns. That way, things will be done properly. Besides, she'd like to meet you, I'm sure. She takes a great interest in reuniting people with their possessions.'

'Fine,' Simon said, unsure that it was really and wondering if he would ever see his father again.

SIX

We love the boat and feel all Agatha Christie as we pose on deck. I try to relax but I'm anxious about the low railings and the fact that we are now afloat on a deep river. I encourage Mum to stand back from the edge whenever possible and hope she'll get the message. I am going to have to be extra-vigilant on this leg of our trip.

The Nile is shockingly serene as we glide along. The banks sprout postcard-pretty reeds and rushes, of the sort Moses would have known. He sailed in a little cradle made of them at the start, didn't he? And was rescued by a Pharaoh's daughter. We still have my Moses basket in our attic, ready for my child should I ever be blessed. That's not looking so likely as the years tick on. Beyond the water is the narrow delta of lush greenery this river has nourished for centuries. Behind that we see desert and sky. The sand is never far away, waiting. The sky watches as it always has done, and will forever. We hear donkeys braying somewhere in the distance. The only sign of modern life is the occasional concrete bridge with a few cars and trucks passing over it. Mum settles in a deckchair and dozes. She is like a cat basking in a sunbeam, a lazy half-smile on her sleeping face. There is timelessness in the air, the ghosts of millions of other people who have sailed this watery superhighway. Other cruise ships pass by and we wave to the passengers without feeling foolish.

If Liz doesn't shut up wondering about dinner, and whether it's 'safe' to have a massage from the young man on the middle deck designated to provide the service, I may kill her and then we'll have our very own Death on the Nile. Rita is hitting the cocktails, the men the beer, and the Merries are checking out Egyptian wine. Edna is caught in Liz's line of fire and unable to escape. She looks as if she could murder too so Rita puts a green-coloured concoction into her hand and she downs it without hesitation.

Our first stop is Luxor. In spite of having been to the museum in Cairo and around the Pyramids, I am unprepared for these temples. They have a whole different kind of grandeur. I love the huge columns, set stolidly in the earth while soaring towards the open sky; the avenues of mini-sphinxes with rams' heads; the wealth of minor detail like the ducks and seeds depicted in the hieroglyphs. I love this flat art, its calm regularity. There seems to be such order in the illustrations by the different dynasties represented here when in fact they amount to a fantastical mishmash of beliefs and events, all cobbled together. The walls are teeming with messages. At Karnak we see the name of Alexander the Great hewn into the wall, part of his prize for being the first Greek to conquer Egypt. I don't wonder that he wanted this fabulous jewel of a land.

Mum touches the carved stones, delighting in the sun's warmth on them and the beauty of the artwork. It reminds me of when she touches the photographs in her albums at home, hoping to make a connection, retrieve a memory. Those are her hieroglyphics. I point the camera at her amidst it all and suddenly wonder who will want this record after we are gone. There is only her, and me, and Dad, I guess, but if the natural order is followed they will go first and then it's all down to me. I have no children of my own. I have no siblings and therefore no nieces or nephews, no cousins. No one will keep pictures of us framed on a sideboard for remembrance. We'll end up in boxes of old knick-knacks at car boot sales, sold off to a smart boy in advertising or comedy who'll make the pictures into funny cards with a witty slogan that people will laugh at and buy to send to their friends, with no notion who the subjects really are and even less interest.

These thoughts make me long for Dan but I know that he isn't mine either. He can never hang my portrait on his wall. When I tell him of my adventures, I must hope that he locks my stories safely away within him and doesn't forget the details that make them important to me. He needs all of his powers of recall, and cannot rely on visual prompts like photographs, because he is someone else's husband. If I take him home a gift, it must be something he can keep at the station which will seem nothing out of the ordinary between friends. Because he is someone else's husband, not mine.

Atop one wall, far above our heads, is the clear outline of another, part of a much later church. This holy place was built when the temple was buried beneath the sand. Now, the exposed architecture is like a barometer of the ages. It looks like history's version of those marks parents make in kitchens or bedrooms to chart their kids' growth as they shoot up, becoming more ready by the year for the final leavetaking. Protected under eaves here and there we spot flashes of colour, undimmed by the centuries of weather that have scorched and lashed this place. Such endurance is astonishing.

We see graffiti from past centuries chiselled into the ancient stone. There are the names of eighteenth-century travellers declaring emphatically that they were here. Beautifully done, and in Latin, but vandalism nonetheless. And who were these people? They are long gone, and their signatures now tell us no more than some instantly forgettable names, but *how* they wanted to be remembered. Their daubings may now vindicate their quest for perpetual remembrance but are as confusing to many as the more ancient illustrations were before the Rosetta Stone was discovered.

I will soon need a deciphering system of my own: the time is coming when I will have to interpret my mother's needs, her pain, her life. I try to notice every detail about her to help me when that happens, but there is so much to learn and I am unsure what I should be concentrating on the hardest. For now, she is happy to pose among these relics of the ancient world, the woman I recognise who is slowly being taken over from within, hollowed out, a shell left behind after the invasion of the body snatchers.

They had to move to a smaller place, Mam said. They were broke and her job didn't bring in enough and 'your father isn't providing for us any more'. She made it sound like it was the girls' fault that their dad existed at all, let alone had gone and left them and wasn't sending enough money – or any money. And while she was at it Mam didn't want to hear any whingeing about the move or where they would live or their rooms or anything at all . . . and that *especially* went for May. Ellen's lip began to quiver and Mam told her to button it tight or else. They trudged behind a car filled with their stuff, each carrying bags that were too heavy and big. It was like following a hearse. The local children ran alongside, laughing and pointing. A huge, grey cloud followed, just waiting to piss down on them. It looked as angry as Mam.

The new place was smelly, like too many rashers and cabbage had been cooked in it and other stuff that was nasty but hard to name. May's shoes stuck to the floor in the hallway and made a sucking noise as she walked. It was freezing cold. Her nose began to drip. Ellen looked as if the world had ended. Mam's face was set in hard lines. Granny Larkin was waiting for them in the tiny kitchen. She had lit the range and a kettle was boiling for a 'nice cup of tea'.

'It'll take more than that to fix things,' Mam warned.

'I have fruit cake,' Gran said, lightning quick, but that didn't make Mam smile either.

The girls were sent upstairs to unpack their things in the dingy box room. Ellen wept openly, out of sight of the adults. 'What about my friends?' she wanted to know.

'You'll still see them at school,' May said.

'Yes, but they'll all know we live here in this horrible place. They'll all know that we're paupers. I hate Daddy and I hate Mam and I hate you. I hate you all. You've ruined my life.'

Even at the time May knew that was unfair but she had no answer to the accusation. And she thought Ellen would cry it out of her system anyhow. May didn't like this new house either. It didn't feel good, like maybe it was haunted. She was terrified then and ran down to ask Granny if there were ghosts here, and was shooed outside for her nonsense. She kicked about the filthy yard and presently the rain began to lash down as she'd known it would. A horrible thought occurred to her. They had moved house, so how would Daddy know where to find them when he came to his senses? She was certain then that she would never see him again. May began to cry, in the rain, so no one could see her. She cried her heart out.

Pennick Library was situated above the town's Courthouse in an echoing nineteenth-century building, the folly of a man now unremembered but named each time Burleigh Hall was mentioned. Policemen, lawyers and accused jostled past each other in the entrance. The overpowering stench was of urine from the neglected public toilets nearby. As Simon passed through a dishevelled man grabbed his arm and hawed stale alcohol and regret into his face, begging him to make sure he wasn't 'banged up and forgotten'. He was still drunk, by the smell of him.

'Now, now, Ricky,' a copper chided, 'let the new librarian be.' When Simon looked surprised, he shrugged. 'Detective, arn' I?'

Ricky let go of him and was ushered inside.

Simon climbed the grand, sweeping marble staircase to the library proper, with its hushed atmosphere and pleasing familiar smell of books. He gave himself a moment to study his new domain. He loved the way that rows of books were always so orderly, no matter how different the sizes and colours of the spines: somehow harmony was reached when they lined the shelves together. He had visited this place before but today was special as now it was in his charge. Or might have been, if Mona Fletcher hadn't taken it upon herself to stay for an interim period, to 'settle him in', as she put it. When asked how long that would be exactly she was vague and muttered about pieces of string. He would have to scotch that, and soon. In the meantime he was mesmerised by the sight of the four black wires that adorned her upper lip, two on either side of her badly painted Cupid's bow. How could she not pluck them? he wondered. Were they incidental to her, or invisible? A man could become obsessed.

The library was laid out in a regular fashion but, as with all institutions of its kind, it bore the stamp of the people who ran it and those who frequented it. So there was a large crime section (fitting, given its location above the court, Simon thought), lots of easy reading and popular fiction (he was uneasy with the terms chick-lit and lad-lit, or even lite-lit for that matter), and a generous local history holding which was the part he was most looking forward to curating. The local Historical Society stored many of their more precious manuscripts here and ran cultural evenings from the public meeting room. Pennick was a town with an interesting if much-neglected past, he felt.

'We've had a run on Egyptology,' Mona told him, 'because of the Fultons going there.'

'Yes,' Simon acknowledged, nodding and desperate to show his grasp of local events. 'Kitty and her mum,' he said, shameless in his attempt to appear to know more than he did.

Mona blinked and the bristles quivered. It was hard to be sure if these were good or bad omens. Simon thought it best to be prepared for either eventuality.

'May has Alzheimer's so, as Kitty herself says, she'll enjoy it but probably won't remember that she did.'

They both smiled at this gallows humour then separated. Simon watched his predecessor make for a quiet nook behind Fiction M – N and knew she'd be close enough to keep tabs on him all day.

Most of his time would be spent in the Chief Librarian's office out back so he went there to unpack the box of essentials he had sent on ahead. His father's shaving mug now held pencils and pens; a photograph of his parents on their wedding day was placed by the telephone alongside a pointed, wooden letter opener his mother had picked up once in an Oxfam shop in Brighton. It would serve as a handy weapon if Mona were ever to lie in ambush, he reckoned. He was of the opinion that the more natural light an office had, the more important the occupant was. He had two large windows to himself here and was happy with his lot.

He spent the morning migrating files from the huge and outdated computer on his desk to the laptop which would serve in its place from now on. Coffee appeared at what seemed an appropriate time and he had little else to do with anyone or anything as he gradually immersed himself in his new environment. He enjoyed the patient stealth of the takeover, getting to know the system, but most of all he wanted to be out amongst the books and records. That must wait, however. A few more days wouldn't hurt. There were lifetimes of knowledge and scholarly endeavour waiting for him out there and his eventual discovery of them would be all the sweeter for this delay.

Kitty and May had to walk through two sister ships docked side by side, to get to theirs. On the first, May saw the reception desk and turned left for their cabin, but Kitty explained they were not yet on their boat. This must be like Mum's head, she thought, everything looking similar but not quite right. May's world was through the looking glass now. After another false attempt to turn for their room, May checked with Kitty on the last ship before a look of relief settled on her face and she darted for home.

All around them big cruisers were filled with curious holidaymakers. No one knows exactly where we are now, Kitty thought, but for a group of strangers we have just met. She was tempted to send Dan a witty text, to establish a link with somewhere else, but resisted. Besides, he'd be at home now, with Donna and out of bounds.

Kitty was wearing a recently bought turquoise pashmina and May a vivid green one. They both felt swanky and swell. Kitty had stared longingly at a djellabah in the textile shop, one of the long tunics worn by the local men, and would have liked to have bought it for Dan. Instead it was now bagged up and destined for her dad. The tourists hung over the ships' rails, catching garments tossed up to them in plastic bags from hawkers in the little boats surrounding the liners. If they liked what they caught, they kept the item and reused the bags to throw money back down to the vendors. The commerce was rapid, fun. Tonight was a special party night on the ship with dancing before and after dinner and they were all gearing up for a good time.

The cabin stewards had left towels on the beds, folded in the shape of a turtle. May was enchanted. The lad responsible knocked on the door to ask if the ladies liked their treat, on the off chance of baksheesh, but Kitty held politely firm. They'd be cleaned out if they rewarded every such gesture. May was upset when they were forced to take the creature apart to dry themselves after they had washed. Kitty distracted her with a cereal bar and felt guilty for treating her like a toddler, or worse. Still, the ruse worked and no tears were spilled, another minor victory. One step forward, Kitty thought, but who knows how many back there will be.

She looked at her own reflection in the small bathroom mirror. May's blue eyes, translated to hazel, stared back at her. She had inherited Granny Fulton's hair. Out of sight were the legs that took after her dad's, no bad thing as he had run cross-country in his youth and had a shapely calf and turn of the heel. Her hands might have been original to her, but somehow she didn't think so. She was nature's remembering, a commemoration in flesh of all the generations who had gone before. We are all variations on a theme, Kitty thought, genetic shadows.

She sat back on the bed while May brushed her hair, chattering of things she didn't know and couldn't recognise.

'Where's my pink dress?' Mum asks.

To the best of my knowledge she doesn't own a pink dress. It may not do to point this out. 'I haven't seen it,' I reply. Ever, I might add.

She frowns. Who knows what hoops her mind is going through, trying to figure this news out.

'I left it in the thing.'

No hint as to what 'the thing' is, but it's non-essential information anyhow so I won't let it bother me. She fusses about looking under cushions and pillows. She tries the loo. I can hear muffled swearing. She reappears, red faced and agitated. 'I don't know who told you to come here but you are no help at all,' she spits at me, then stops and gives me a good long look. 'If you've stolen it, you'll be in big trouble,' she warns.

I don't want to start an argument so I keep my peace.

'My daughter will deal with you when she gets home,' Mum says. For a moment time slows and I realise that this is the first time she has admitted, out loud, to not knowing me. I can feel my heart lurch painfully and an ache creeps into my limbs. I suddenly feel very tired and hollow. But I can't share that with her, my closest of the close. She means no harm. She just doesn't remember me. I try to speak very evenly. 'It'll turn up,' I say, though I cannot guarantee that it will. And it may not matter. By now the pink dress may be consigned to history, its memory tangled irretrievably in the proteins advancing through her brain.

Tears sparkle in her eyes. 'I want to wear it to the party,' she says.

'We'll find you another pretty thing.'

She snuffles and nods but I can't be sure she's heard or understood me.

A bell rang and drums began to beat in the ship. It was the summons to the lounge and the inmates spewed forth from their cabins in traditional garb. Kitty had earlier envisioned Liz in a bellydancer's costume, an image which had greatly unsettled her. Thankfully Liz had settled for a spangled skull cap and flowing robes, the safe option chosen by the majority of those on board, a Euro-pudding of nationalities with Germans, English and Italians most heavily represented, and in that order.

The captain made a speech and even told an Egyptian joke, first recorded in 1600BC. 'How do you entertain a bored Pharaoh?' he asked, and the ship's pursar obliged by saying, 'I don't know, how do you entertain a bored Pharaoh?' The captain smiled widely before announcing, 'Sail a boatload of young women draped only in fishing nets down the Nile and urge the Pharaoh to go and catch a fish.' The assembled company laughed. Kitty was unsure if this proved 'the old ones are best', but warmed to the man for tying in a bit of history too.

The captain then introduced every last head of department and, although it was a lengthy process, Kitty found it affecting to see how proud they all were of their ship and the experience it offered their guests. When his crew members were all identified and praised, the captain announced that there would now be some dancing. May took to the floor with the Merries. She whirled about in ever-quickening circles. She waved to Kitty and shouted, 'Look at me, Ellen, I'm dancing.' Then she laughed and whooped and twirled even faster. That's another first, Kitty thought. She called me Ellen, her sister's name. Suddenly her attention was back on the dance floor where the Norfolk dervish had collided with some Italian guests' drinks and much excited chatter accompanied the clean up. It was minor but attentively clocked by the ship's complement.

Kitty steadied May and took her away for a non-alcoholic cocktail. Her mother looked like a younger Kitty used to do, on a sugar high and nearly-in-trouble territory. We seem to have swapped, she thought. Some are born parents and others have it thrust upon them. They had just got their drinks at the bar when Kitty heard an English woman's voice pronounce 'nutter'.

She swivelled round to face the room and the Faraway entourage looked guiltily away. Throughout the lounge whispers were exchanged behind discreetly raised hands. She smarted for her mother and the way she was misjudged. She hated these people for the way they drew their easy, mean-spirited conclusions. Mum won't recall this in the morning, she thought, she's already forgotten it. She feels a primitive joy, without any need for explanation or guilt. The others will remember. They will inspect it and reach judgement. What use is memory if it only festers grudges?

I don't think my heart-rate even quickens much when we have our moments. I have learned to be calm and deal with whatever has arisen. Every day has its new crises, one after the other. They don't necessarily follow from or feed off each other. There is no progression and it's important to remember that; they are unconnected. But cumulatively they are wearing and I cannot afford to let them grind me down. I cannot lose my sense of proportion. This disease is not my fault but it is my problem.

After her diagnosis, when Mum wasn't sleeping well and consequently neither was I, the deprivation made me jittery and emotional. Tears sapped my energy. They still do. As a result, I have learned to cope without giving way. Panic is counter-productive. But scalding embarrassment can be a problem.

We have to sit with the Brits because we are with the same tour company. I cannot meet their eyes. Mum is oblivious for which I envy her. The meal tonight is even better than usual so that fills a void in conversation. Everyone concentrates hard on the food. When Mum goes for dessert

I hear Liz clear her throat and think, Here it comes, but it is Rita who speaks first.

'You have your hands more than full with your mother,' she begins.

I want to dissolve into my chair but keep my back ramrod straight waiting for the insult. A silence settles over the table with my anxiety screeching above it on a frequency I am sure they can all hear. The background is filled with Italian chatter and the more glottal tones of the Germans. They don't notice the tense atmosphere at our table but the waiter does and backs off. Rita's voice is maddeningly even.

'You're exhausted dealing with her by yourself and you're not having much of a holiday as a result.'

She's correct about me being wrecked but I am enjoying the trip. I love Egypt. I take a few deep breaths, conserving myself for her next shot, ready for whatever they have decided to do with the peskier members of the party.

'We've been talking about how we can help.'

That gives me proper pause. Help? I hold my breath.

'From now on, we will take her when you need a rest. Starting with tonight. Why don't I see her to your cabin to get ready for bed and you can have a quiet drink on the deck. By yourself.'

The last sentence seems to be an instruction to the others as well as to me. I am to be left alone. Fine. I am still stinging from the embarrassment of it all. I honestly don't know where to put myself, where to look even. But while I draw breath for a cutting reply, I realise that I haven't listened properly all evening. These people are offering their help to me. The whispers I thought so condemnatory were in fact discussions about how to ease my burden. One of them said 'mother' not 'nutter' earlier after the dancing incident. I feel such a prat, I want to cry. I want to cry anyhow, from gratitude and the sheer relief of discovering that there can be good in people even when you think they are conspiring against you. Where I saw malice, there was only concern.

Mags says, 'My gran went the same way, though she was a lot older.'

'I wish you could have known her before,' I say.

'We know her now and she's lovely,' Sue points out.

'Just a handful,' adds Mags.

I do cry a little then. 'Thank you. Thank you all so much . . . and, yes,' I say, as Mum plants herself down at the table again with her largest plate of goodies yet from the dessert buffet.

'My eyes are bigger than my belly,' she tells us.

These strangers all smile kindly upon her and I am chastened.

Later, Mum goes off to the cabin with Rita without a murmur: she's as familiar to her as I am, after all. I wonder if she still has some innate meter for gauging other people's goodness. I hope so because everyone is a potential stranger to Mum now and she'd be easy picking for a malevolent one.

I feel a tug inside, seeing her go, but she looks happy. As instructed, I take a glass of white wine to the top deck and luxuriate in the peace of the night.

The sky is a downy dark blue with stars sprinkled generously across it, more than I remember seeing in a long time. I feel I should make a wish then I remember this is old light they are shedding. Those twinkles are long burned out before their glitter reaches us. There's probably a spare and shiny bit of the Space Programme up there, durable and endlessly orbiting; it might be a better bet for giving my wish a chance of success.

I wonder what Dan is up to. Is he thinking of me, as I am of him? Are there stars in the sky over Pennick tonight? There are, of course, it's just a matter of being able to see them. Their remains are out there alongside the flotsam of our efforts to tame space; all that hardware waiting for the earth's magnetism to pull it down in flames. Everything crashes and burns in the end.

Donna miscarried and for a dark time I thought it was somehow deliberate. I am not proud to admit that. Where previously Dan and Donna's happiness had cut through me, now their mutual sorrow wounded me even deeper. I felt cheated too. It seemed to me that Donna had fooled Dan into marriage. But I tortured myself by remembering his declaration of love for Donna, now his wife. Wife: to my mind it was a horrible word, one that marked the end of everything. A service was held and we all turned up to grieve, though I wasn't in mourning for the mite in the tiny, white box. I could hardly bear to see Donna play the victim, all skeletal and sad, Dan a six-foot mirror for her to adore herself and her suffering. I could not feel for them and their pain. It was as if a malign spirit had taken over me and I was trapped within a wretched cocoon of regret and bitterness, full of these awful thoughts.

I might have left town then but I met a guy called Mark, through my job as a cashier at the big local supermarket. He was on a placement from London, climbing the managerial ladder. Dan had taken time off to be with Donna and we weren't seeing one another as we had done. Our separation was liberating with Mark around. He was fun to be with, so we laughed and flirted and when he kissed me I almost thought, This would do. Finally I could see a way out of the Donna and Dan tangle. Even though I was still in love with Dan, reality had started to impinge and I knew I would have to extricate myself, however painful that might be.

And then one day Dan turned up at the allotment looking beautiful and forlorn. He was there to see me, to be with me. All my resolve crumbled in the face of his need. I wanted to believe that we could make this terrible situation work, but mostly I just wanted him. We made love and it was like our first time all over again, the sheer rightness of it knocking us both off kilter. Afterwards he whispered into my neck,

'What have we done?' Did he mean just then or the whole Donna and him thing? I didn't know and wasn't about to ask. I should have run away that very moment. I did not. 'I love you so much I could die of it,' I said instead.

He stopped wearing his wedding ring whenever he was with me after that. I knew it was a small gesture made for me, and I accepted it and loved him for it all the more. I knew he wore the ring at home because the indentation was always there, like a scar that has faded but is still visible.

Kitty watched the dawn light on the river with her mother. When she woke she found May already waiting with the curtains open, as if drawn by an elemental call to bear witness to a new day. Fanciful thoughts, Kitty knew. It was more probable that she liked the strong, shifting colours. Her knitting at home was equally vibrant, joyous in its dislocated way. Kitty wondered if May might be up to completing her patchwork bedspread when they got back, but suspected the art of making stitches was now beyond her. Perhaps Kitty would give it a go herself, try to finish what her mother had begun so purposefully before her mind had started to unravel itself.

They sat side by side on the bed and watched through the big picture window of their cabin. The river slid by. The sky set off strips of orange light against its deep night blue, then livid pink, to peach, and on to a pure bright blue, without flaw or blemish. They both sighed at the same time. If this was life at its most basic, Kitty had no argument with it.

If Ellen said it once to May she said it a thousand, maybe even a million, times: she couldn't wait to get out of that place. It smelled better now, so that was one good thing. And with their things around and about it didn't look as awful as it had. It was still the coldest place on earth, even when the sun was boiling down outside. Mam made friends with a neighbour, Ursula Freeney, and she came to mind them when they were at home while Mam was at work. Ursula had a stammer and that was funny, especially when she was cross about something because then she couldn't get a full word out at all. May peed herself once, she laughed so hard at one of the woman's tantrums, but then Ursula gave her a smack across the face. May's teeth dug into the inside of her cheek and she could taste blood. That wasn't so funny. Ellen smiled at it, mind you, but that was Ellen all over.

On the day of her next birthday Ellen blew the candles out on her cake and moved in with Granny Larkin. May thought her heart would break with the loneliness. She wanted her sister back, to tease her and show no mercy, for things to be normal again. Mam was really sad too, more so than usual. The house had an echo now, as well as the smells and the cold. May wished they could get a dog or a cat. Sometimes Ellen visited but you could tell it was because

Granny Larkin made her. She always brought cake so that was good but not enough to make everything all right. For one thing Ursula was still around.

A strange thing happened once: Mam just hugged May, out of nowhere. 'You're a very good girl,' she said. 'But you're so like him.'

May hoped she meant Daddy, not one of the dead boys, her brothers.

They gave it another month and then they moved in with Granny Larkin too. Then there were more smiles going around. May didn't miss Ursula one bit.

They visited a magnificent temple built by the great Queen Hatshepsut. Their guide was a man called Anwar who swung prayer beads and smelled of lamb, and expected them to finish his sentences, as a teacher would. He preferred to look the men in the eye, rather than the women, and Kitty could tell they were uncomfortable in case they got an answer wrong and were punished. 'The dog ate my homework,' she wanted to say, to make them laugh, but she didn't want to be rude to Anwar. He seemed reluctant to tell them too much about the queen's remarkable achievements. Perhaps he fears he'll have a feminist revolt on his hands, Kitty mused, and the men are outnumbered in our little party. Hatshepsut was the greatest of the female rulers, she knew, more powerful than Cleopatra even but now much less famous because Liz Taylor never played her in a movie. No one had, as far as Kitty could recall.

Hatshepsut's legacy was breathtaking: from the grand terraces of the temple, accessed by massive ramps, to its wonderful position on the plain. Surrounded by carefully tended trees and plants, it must have blown the peasants' minds when it was first built. Hatshepsut spent most of her life in men's clothing, playing the lads at their own game. Her successor, Tutmosis III ordered the destruction of all her name cartouches, the lozenges containing the hieroglyphic symbols of her name. He thought he had consigned her to oblivion but he had not managed to obliterate every trace. There were still enough to guarantee her immortality.

Kitty thought cartouches would be the perfect way to write her name and Dan's side by side, yet still keep them indecipherable and hidden. She might paint their symbols on the wall of her allotment shed or carve them into one of the mighty oaks that lined the pathway to work, like the other lovers' initials that lay entwined there. And no one would be any the wiser about their meaning but her.

Overhead the sky was dotted with hot-air balloons moving slowly across the heavens, striped and coloured silk crayoned against bluest blue. Little human figures hung over the sides, taking in the grandeur of the delta and its sacred places. Those on ground level couldn't help but point and stare.

Then it was on to the Valley of the Kings where they took a little train to the tombs from the entrance, which May called 'Puffin Billy' and the Egyptians a 'tuf-tuf'. The names seemed complimentary to the ear. Kitty thought of Dan again, a silly bit of information he loved to spout about the Von Trapp family: they did not escape on foot over the Alps but took a train to Italy. She glanced at her mother whose mind was likely throwing up all manner of trivia like this too, though in her case it was in the vain hope that another part of her brain could catch the memory and retain it. May's mind was guttering like a spent candle, desperate to endure and be of use but almost out of time.

They walked into the mountain and saw stars again, many and white against the darkness, painted on the low ceiling of a burial chamber, close enough to touch. Between them, Kitty imagined she saw the vacuum into which we must all go. The Pharaohs believed themselves girded against that emptiness, providing themselves in their earthly resting chambers with everything they would need in the after-life. Kitty stared into the celestial scene. Its beauty was heart-smashing. It's not a vacuum up there, she reminded herself, it is infinity.

We process, formally in a line, into the tomb of a minor queen whose mummy is displayed in a glass case. Like Snow White, I think to myself. There is a faded quality to this place that I like. The elderly man watching over it is expecting far less than his counterparts in the famous sites nearby. I put my hand into my baksheesh pocket and separate a few notes and coins. We are sorted.

The most unusual feature of this resting place is the tiny display to the right of the dead queen, again encased in glass. It is her unborn child, a handful of small bones now, separated from its mother. Mum stares at it and goes berserk.

She swings her head from side to side, checking where she is and not finding anything of comfort. She begins to holler, 'That's not my baby. My baby is alive. My baby isn't dead . . . Mam's baby died. Ellen's baby died. But my baby lived.'

Her anguished cries echo alarmingly off the walls of the enclosed space. The guardian is frightened. We all are. He reaches for her without ever meaning to make contact. I can see he simply wants her to leave, to stop her racket. She is heaving with sobs now. 'My Kitty is safe. My kitten didn't die.'

I try to calm her. 'I'm here, Mum. I'm fine. Look at me, I'm all grown up.'

She doesn't believe me, I can tell, but the alternative is too much even for her rambling mind to want to take on. She allows me to lead her off while she throws a last glance back at the skeleton foetus. The guardian is pressing himself against the walls and even the lack of baksheesh doesn't bother him. At the mouth of the tomb, Anwar is craning his neck to see what the noise is all about down here and wanting it to be someone else's group to blame for it. He clocks who is making the fuss and retreats, looking furious.

Outside, we rest on the dusty path. I keep my arms about

Mum, warding off the world and its offers of assistance. Her body is racked with convulsive sobs which eventually subside. Then she takes a jagged breath and asks, 'Why are we here?' looking around as if she's just noticed her surroundings and is quite intrigued by them. 'I'm thirsty,' she says then, and accepts a bottle of water from Rita. 'I know this place,' she continues. 'Egypt. I'm coming here with my daughter soon.'

SEVEN

Simon Hill was delighted to have stairs. He had rented a house that was not a bungalow, as his previous two rentals had been in the towns he'd grown bored of. Stairs, then, with their reassuringly regular treads and risers, were a symbol of a new beginning. Between the set at home and those of the marbled entrance hall at work he was on the up, and sometimes on the down, but all in a good way. Happiness made him whistle but he soon stopped as it was a tuneless affair and the situation deserved better.

Each day he tried different routes to the library, searching for the most interesting. The weather was grey and damp with a nip of wind to keep even the sleepiest head alert. He liked that. His favourite journey so far was quite circuitous: by some allotments, skirting a cemetery that looked ripe with local history, and over past the railway track before a sharp left turn through the small town square. It was neither up nor down, Pennick being a flat place. Again he was glad of his stairs.

Mona was on duty when he arrived. It didn't seem to matter how early he got there, she was ahead of him. She always instructed him to ignore her, saying she was just tying up some loose ends and pottering. As she was also a member of the library he couldn't very well bar her or ask her to leave. He often spied her ensconced in her alcove, happily reading, and his heart did melt a little towards her then. After a few days she appeared with his coffee, asking if there was anything that puzzled him, any way she could help.

'The huge crime section?' he said, without thinking, desperate not to have a conversational hiatus.

'Thrills,' she announced. 'Nothing much happens in Pennick these days and there's nothing like a good murder or serial killer to spice up the boredom. Better to have it all in a book than happening on the streets.'

It was the start of many illuminating chats. As gruff as her manner was, Simon found himself watching the clock and counting down the hours to another good conversation. Mona also made a mean cup of coffee and brought a caramel wafer bar for him, which he was certain he was becoming addicted to. He almost never clocked the bristles now.

Her accent was fascinating. It was soft, like all of the Norfolk voices he heard each day, but tempered by an education received elsewhere. He knew his own was a composite of every place he had lived. He had always adapted it enough to fit in but never to seem like he was taking the piss out of the natives. He didn't see himself picking up the Pennick drawl – or Panic drawl as it was pronounced locally. That was an oxymoron if ever he'd heard one. Oxford had smartened his diction and his parents had been proud to tell him he sounded posh to their ears.

'I never married,' Mona told him. 'Could have, of course. But I didn't need legal sanction. Never found the "right one" either. Or haven't yet. And I've never lacked for sex so I didn't see the point. You?'

'Funnily enough, just the same.'

It made him wonder if they looked alike, both dressed as fogeys and sporting their light 'taches and academic minds. Was this in any way attractive? Was he, in fact, the equivalent of an old maid? It seemed so. But, resting back in his swivel chair and laughing with his new friend, he found he didn't actually mind.

'The Historical Society's monthly meeting is upon us so you'll be given a formal introduction at that. You can get properly stuck into scrutinising our past from then on.'

'I look forward to it,' he said, and meant it.

'The ladies of the WI are also gagging for us to send them a new speaker with fresh stories so I'm forewarning you now.'

'I take it I have no choice but to do a talk?'

'Correct. And it will be talks, plural. They'll love you.'

Again, that seemed a kind of warning, but a gentle one and delivered with a twinkle. He liked this place, he decided.

*   *   *

They were sitting on the bed of the cabin, this time looking at the swans the stewards had made from towels, when May said, 'I'm so glad we're sharing again, Ellen. I was lonely without you.'

Kitty's heart turned about itself. She wasn't sure how to handle this but thought she should ask, 'What about Kitty?'

May shook her head, not comprehending or perhaps not wanting to. It was hard to tell. 'She's not you, Ellen,' she said, and smiled.

Kitty's world started closing in. Mum means no harm, she kept reminding herself, but it was crushing all the same. At least she had taken her for a beloved sister and not a stranger. She turned away to hide her disappointment.

'What's wrong, Kitty?' May asked.

'Nothing,' she replied, and for a moment it was true again and she was suddenly happy.

'Did you feed Pegasus?'

'I'll do that now,' she said, and moved off to the tiny loo to be alone with her worries about what would become of them.

They had one last day before leaving the boat and heading for the Red Sea. The cruiser was unusually quiet as the Italians and Germans had already left, en route for another leg of their holidays. Today they took a felucca to a tropical garden on a nearby island. The sails on this most traditional of boats picked up the merest breath of air. The sheer craft of the boatman was mesmerising, the skill of centuries handed down from father to son . . . and maybe even to a few girls along the way, Kitty hoped.

They admired the plants and May made everyone laugh by declaring the worst enemy of the public garden was an old lady with a large handbag. She looked at her smiling companions as if they were crazy to find amusement in this obvious fact.

She wanted to bring various wild cats they encountered home with her. 'Will the bus take long?' she asked, fretting about the time the creatures would have to be in boxes.

'A fair while,' Kitty said.

'We'd best try a train then. Dan will look after us.'

Oh, but will he? Kitty wondered. Can he?

May was moving up into Sister Vincent's class at school. It was exciting that she was growing up but Vincent had a bad name and was fond of the switch. Ellen told her to keep her head down because she wouldn't want to see the nun in a temper. When May came home and told Mam who she had for the next year, her mother went all quiet.

'Did she teach you too?' May asked.

'Yes,' was all the reply she got.

She knew better than to push it.

Later, lying in bed, she heard her mother's voice raised in the kitchen. 'If that bitch touches one hair on my daughter's head, I'll do for her, so help me God I will.'

My daughter. May liked the sound of that.

141

Sister Vincent was as mean as everyone said. She was scary to look at, too, with a face like a skull thinly covered in skin and only it and her hands showing from under her habit, and sometimes her shiny, black shoes if she walked quickly. Her hands were like a skeleton's, too, bony and sharp. When she poked you in the chest you knew all about it and had an angry, red mark afterwards to show for it. That hurt, but it was a badge of honour to be shown off in the yard at break-time.

Vinnie loved chanting prayers beseeching for mercy, even if she showed none herself. *'Hail, Holy Queen,'* she'd start, and they'd all chime in. *'Hail, our life, our sweetness and our hope.'* May found it boring. She wanted to learn things, lots of things. She wanted to read stories and poems.

'To thee do we cry, poor banished children of Eve.' Vinnie particularly liked to pick on the orphans in the class, especially a girl called Rose. *'To thee do we send up our sighs.'* She made Rose cut all her hair off, claiming she had nits. They all had nits, sure the dogs on the street knew that, but none of the rest of them had to have their heads shaved like Rose.

'Mourning and weeping in this valley of tears.' May asked at home if she could have hers done too so Rose wouldn't feel so bad. *'Turn then, O precious advocate, thine eyes of mercy on us.'* Mam asked all about the orphan and told May she must stick up for anyone being bullied or even worse off than herself. May didn't think anyone was as poor as they

were, but when she said that Mam snapped at her that she had a mam and a granny and Rose had no one.

'O clement, O loving, O sweet Virgin Mary.'

The next time Vincent picked on Rose, May stood up and said, 'Don't you touch a hair on her head again, you bad bitch, or my mam will be dug out of you, so help her God she will.'

Vincent scored her hands with five hard swipes of the switch each, and said she'd tan her hide for her too if she ever heard such language again. She said May would roast in Hell, no shadow of a doubt about that, but it was no wonder given where she was got from. Then Mam came to visit the school and after that Vincent never said a cross word to either May or Rose again. She still continued her devotion to Our Lady and no day passed without loads of Hail Marys and a round of hymns. *'Hail, Queen of Heav'n, the ocean star,'* they'd sing, *'guide of the wand'rer here below.'* May liked the hymns better than the prayers. She was partial to a good tune.

Rose got consumption and died a while later. May didn't think Sister Vincent was to blame for that, but she wasn't sure. The class sang at her funeral and Vinnie had the cheek to cry.

Hurghada has miles of bright beach and a sparkling sea to invite us in but the sight fills me with dread. I cannot forget Mum's remark of a week ago. Today she is dancing with excitement, though. There is no reason to suspect she even remembers the promise she thinks I made her then. All she wants is to get out into that water and enjoy it. I watch her splash round in delight and she waves back to me with the biggest smile I have seen on her face in ages. Back on the sand again she plays with children who react to her with such acceptance it makes my heart lift oddly. The parents aren't so sure about Mum. They keep watch discreetly, ready to spring to their kids' rescue if need be. I try to signal to them that there's nothing to worry about but, as usual, it makes Mum seem like an imbecile so I stop.

I can't blame the parents for their suspicion; we live in times when you cannot risk taking your eyes off a child for a moment. I want to tell them that I know how they feel, that I am the same. I too watch everyone for signs of imminent harm. I continually scout our surroundings for danger. The whole place is crawling with hucksters and pickpockets and people simply trying to better their lives by making some money for their families. I have to look out for mine first, so they'll have to back off and leave us be. *La, shukran*.

Mum eats an ice cream surrounded by her new friends. It's as if she has never encountered one before. Her face screws up when it is unexpectedly cold but she perseveres because it tastes so delicious, smacking her lips and declaring, 'Fuck me, that's good,' which betrays her age a tad, I feel.

Liz stands and stares at the sea for long periods of time without going in, which is a puzzle. I ask Rita about it.

'Her son is finishing a tour of duty in Afghanistan. It's always worst for her the nearer his return gets, as if there's more chance now that something will happen to him. I think she wants to be as close to him as possible in case he needs her, or as if it'll bring him luck.'

I like to think that explains a lot about Liz but I don't know her very well so I withhold any judgement. It would only be ill informed. Maybe I just want it to have a significance it actually doesn't. I see people noticing Mum and making assumptions so I try not to go there with anyone else, though it's impossible as I am only human. I suspect Liz is an unconscionable bossy boots whatever her situation.

I spend my time checking that Mum is wearing her hat against the sun and her sun block, which I say is tanning lotion so she doesn't know it's stopping her from getting burnt. She wants to get a tan, she tells me, and the surest way of doing that is to get burned and let it fade. Her pale Irish skin has a nice glow now and it will build but there is no way I am letting her follow the crazy plan she has formulated from somewhere in the faulty recesses of that head. Her logic is not what it used to be, though I secretly allow myself to acknowledge that, for all its drawbacks, it was a vaguely thought through notion.

We find a lovely seafront restaurant and settle in for the evening. Mum is off to our room with Edna. There is a tacit agreement that the women of our party take over these evening duties, although Liz never does, and the men are to help during the day. I am so grateful I feel like giving baksheesh to all of my new companions. Instead, I buy lots of drink. I couldn't care less how much it costs, it's worth it for the respite I am getting and the care and affection my mother is experiencing. We move on to talk of disease and death but I am not so paranoid as to believe that it is because of Mum. Who doesn't want to discuss misfortune and our short time on this earth, given a jar or three?

Sue lost her husband to cancer, watching him fade away over months, in great pain. Gradually he lost his dignity and, ultimately, his fight for survival, which she said was dogged. 'He really did not want to die. I didn't want him to. But die he did.' She shrugs. 'That's life.' I can see there is a raw part within her that will never truly heal, that can never forgive life for dealing her such a hand.

Mum is fading, too, but not in any pain so far, and for that I am truly grateful. I've heard of sufferers losing their ability to swallow when their brain shuts down the gag reflex. Eventually they die from hunger and thirst, through no fault of their family or carers. It's a tough disease to call; even tougher to deal with.

Mags's husband went suddenly from a massive, debilitating stroke. 'His circuitry just blew, like his mental wiring shorted and failed.' It's as if she's describing an execution in the electric chair. 'He was built, though, so it took him weeks to die because the rest of him was so physically strong.'

Mum's brain is dying, bit by bit, but I thank our lucky

genes that we are an otherwise hardy family and she has experienced little illness before this.

I look at the faces around the table and I know these stories make us realise just how precious our lives are and that we probably only get one shot, one ride on the carousel. I want my turn to count but with that aspiration comes a dark place: the idea that I am wasting not only my time but Dan's too. We have no future, yet to imagine any future without him is as awful as trying to get my head around the fact that Mum's days are curtailed. It's interesting that not one of us tonight has suggested there might be something beyond the grave. No resurrection for us, no eternal life hereafter.

Our days are lazy now. We have a big breakfast and get into our beach gear. I have bought Mum a bucket and spade and she's getting full use out of them. She has her uncomplicated friendships at the beach. They speak different languages but have no trouble communicating. The parents now know we mean no harm; that my mother has her problems but they are no threat to others. She loves the sand and the sea, swimming happily or just splashing at the water's edge. She talks about her little people to me and says, 'I'm away with the fairies.' I don't know whether this is said to make me laugh as it would have been when she was more compos mentis, but I don't care either. It's good, it's all good. I realise that if she were to die now she would go happy. I might almost be happy myself. I brush off the thought; it's ridiculous and obscene. We have a long way to go yet.

When the parents bring their children in for their afternoon nap we take one too. It's a routine and Mum likes that. So do I. I have not been this relaxed in ages. We write postcards to the neighbours and I send a round robin one to the station. I don't put 'wish you were here', even as a jokey cliché, because I don't wish anyone else was here with us and that surprises me. I do, however, buy a plastic ruler in the hotel shop with the hieroglyphic symbols for the letters of the Roman alphabet carved out of it so that I can spell out two secret name cartouches. It makes me think I am, literally, a hopeless romantic.

And then, one mid-morning, just as I am thinking we'd do well to shelter from the worst of the sun, I cannot find Mum. I have taken my eye off her for the briefest moment and she has disappeared. I get up and start to pace the sand, searching. She is not with the children but I don't want to panic anyone by asking where she's got to. Remy, the little French boy, notices me, and gestures to the sea. I go to the waterline but still I cannot see her. My eyes are squeezed tight against the glare, even behind my dark glasses. I am glad of them as I hope they are hiding my increasing distress. I scan the water but there are too many bobbing heads and much confusion.

I go over to Liz, standing in her usual sentinel position on the shore. I follow the line of her gaze and see Mum's head above the water as she forges on. Liz says, 'She's gone out further than usual today.' Anxiety creeps into her features. 'Should I have called her back?'

'No,' I say.

I hope she believes me. It is not this stranger's duty to look after May Fulton, it is mine. I call to Mum then, waving my arms. I whoop. I try to wolf-whistle, which is pathetic as I have never been able to do this, so why should I suddenly gain the ability now? Mum is still moving away from me. I have no choice but to follow.

I learned to swim nearly as soon as I could walk and I have always loved it. It's my form of exercise, along with keeping the allotment and sex with Dan. Christ, what's made me think of that? I keep my head above water, setting Mum in my sights, and force my arms and legs to work faster than they should. It is the wrong thing to do. Soon they tire and I feel the burn of lactic acid in my muscles. I ease up.

My breath is hot and ragged in my chest and my mind churning with the thought that this might be the end. I cannot allow that. She may have decided on a course, but what about me? Don't I have a say? 'I matter in all this,' I want to scream. I think I may actually have done just that. Today is not the day to die, for either of us. I won't allow it. My mother is still in there and I want her with me. If that's selfish, so be it. And who's to know which mother is swimming out too far right now. Is it the woman who reared me, or the kid who's trying to take over?

I'm gaining on her fast now. When I am close, I yell, 'Mum, over here.' She turns and waves but continues out to sea.

Is this deliberate? I go after her and am quickly beside her. 'You should come back now,' I say.

She stops and treads water. 'Why?' she wants to know.

'Because I want you to.'

She stares me down for a moment then turns for shore and calmly starts into a breaststroke.

'Race you,' I say. Anything to get her out of the water and back on the safety of dry sand.

She ignores that and takes her own sweet time about returning. At the end she lets the gentle waves deliver her to the shore, waiting for each thrust and eddy to inch her closer, like it's a little game she's playing. She rides in on the water. Allows it to see her safely back to land, not me. She walks up the beach without looking back. I drag myself after her, or try to. When I get out of the water I am staggering. My legs refuse to stop shaking. I sit, exhausted, with my head between my knees. My throat burns from the seawater I have swallowed. For all the boasting and certainty that I am unflappable, my heart-rate rose that time for sure. I get up and walk to where the Merries are standing guard over our things. Mum is drying herself off.

'You'd better put on some more lotion,' I say, as lightly as I can manage with a pounding heart and a wavering voice.

She snaps. 'Stop fussing over me,' she shouts. 'Fuss. Fuss. Fuss. It's driving me mad.' She sulks under an umbrella, her bottom lip ever so slightly pouted.

I want to reach across and smack her.

EIGHT

We don't say goodbye to our new comrades in Egypt and so the journey home is an odd mixture of homecoming and parting. We know we will split up at Heathrow and this lends a surreal air to the end of our trip. I know it's unlikely we'll see these people again. It would be unnatural to so I won't make any false promises to keep up, to stay in touch. They have shown us kindness and for that I will remember them. I hope for their happiness, as they have tried to ensure ours. I know they will speak to people we will never meet of the pair of Norfolk women they met in Egypt and describe the mother's illness and funny episodes. I am worried about that. I want us to be represented fairly, don't want us to be a comic story, lightly dismissed. Even Anwar, our erstwhile guide, will probably refer sometimes to the crazy English woman who went mad in a tomb. But we are not material for gossip, I want to protest, though we are that too, of course, even in Pennick.

I have Mum beside me, seated in the middle of the row while I take the window seat. I don't want her getting freaked by being high in the sky, although it doesn't seem to bother her. She eats her meal with relish, loving the way everything is squeezed on to the tray and looking cute. She watches the family movie then dozes, so the flight is uneventful. As we come into land I see the brown and green fields of Blighty, with their straight sides and haphazard shapes and sizes.

The first surprise is that Dad is waiting for us in Arrivals. I immediately assume someone is dead but I'm wrong. He has come to drive us home, as a treat. We will arrive in town by car, not train. I will not see Dan. I don't know how I feel about that.

'Look at you both, so tanned,' he says, and Mum links arms with him, giggling. I am happy to hand her over.

I introduce him to our travel companions and I can see the spark of interest this kindles. They know now there are details about our lives that they have missed. We never mentioned a husband or a father still alive. They made certain assumptions and we neglected to correct them. They'll have that to wonder about, our parting gift. We hug them awkwardly and Liz tries to squeeze in a few questions about Dad. She's out of luck. We wave to the others as we leave and the airport door slides shut on that part of our lives.

Mum is hanging off Dad's arm still. She says, 'Alf, you need a haircut.' Alf was my grandfather's name, my dad's father. Dad laughs it off and agrees that his hair is too long.

I leave them to take the front seats and try to grab some sleep in the back of the battered Peugeot. Instead, I am struck by how chilly the air is here and ask Dad to turn the heating up full blast. The countryside looks dull and parochial, not what I've become accustomed to. It seems to sneak by. Rain begins to spit and I imagine Jed's rheumatics will be playing up big time. I wonder if Egyptians ever get that sort of ache in their bones or whether it's impossible when every day is sunny and blue-skied. They don't have our damp. I'd almost forgotten it myself. My eyes become accustomed to the new palette and soon I can see that there are many fierce greens and browns out there, a variety of greys, and . . . I doze off, because next thing Dad is announcing we're home.

Here's our familiar redbrick street, though there are small changes to it. Fred Curtis has painted his front door yellow. It glows in the dark and I wonder if he'll still love its luminosity come summer. However, it scores higher than the gloss brown with cream trim he's had till now. Craig Melba's bike is lashed to the lamp-post, looking dejected, its front tyre punctured. Poor Craig seems to invite mishap. We pile out of the car on unsteady legs and see our breath cloud in the air. A light is on in our front room, welcoming against the early darkness. I wonder if Dan is in there too. He is not. He has made a lovely job of neatening the place, though, and the chemical smell has dissipated. He has left just the very essential Post-its on the walls and a new one on the cover of the household diary to say he hopes we had a good time, listing groceries laid in for us, and sighed simply with the letter D. No 'x' after it. No flowers, either, but it's the wrong time of year for those at the allotment and we are not wealthy people who can be indulging in such frivolities in the supermarket. Ah, well. I put the kettle on for tea, something I have not done in a fortnight.

Mum stares at the place, mesmerised. 'It's nicer than Granny Larkin's,' she says.

Dad looks quizzical but I shake my head. I will tell him anything he needs to know later. 'Will you stay?' I ask.

'Yes. We can have a chat.'

We treat ourselves to a Chinese takeaway and then I see Mum upstairs. She bounces on her bed. 'I get my own room,' she says, thrilled. She gets off and goes to the wardrobe to root around. She is looking for something specific but doesn't tell me what. She is disappointed and empty handed after her search.

Dad has opened a bottle of wine. 'She's worse, isn't she?' he says when I rejoin him.

There is no point in stalling this. 'Yes,' I admit, and feel like a traitor. I try some mitigation and, as it's the truth, it softens my guilt. 'We had a wonderful holiday, Dad, really special. Mind you, it's just as well I didn't leave it any longer to go or it might have been wasted on her. As it was, she remembered lots about Ancient Egypt, which was a bit astonishing but one in the eye for Alzheimer's, and she adored the beach.'

I take a long slug of a rich, peppery Shiraz that he gets for special occasions. I suppose this is one. It's a big moment. We are home after our awfully big adventure. Now we must face our grim future. After all, it's not as if it's not going to happen.

My father has the easiest manner about him of anyone I know. He makes it possible to talk of difficult things and always makes them seem approachable. I wish I'd had this same ease with him all along but growing up brings with it the grandiose and idiotic idea that it's you against the world and we all waste a lot of time shedding that baggage. He waits for me to go on. There is no rush.

'Mum's away in her own world nearly all the time now. She's happy there, in that place. It's only when she comes back, has some lucidity, that she's unhappy. She's frightened then.'

'I hate to think of that.' His voice is strained.

'You and me both. And I hate having to second-guess how she feels. I can't be sure I'm making the right decisions because I can't nail this bugger down. I don't have all the information. I don't have access to the thoughts in her head.'

Our eyes meet and I know he will say, 'Neither does she.' When he does, we both smile tightly.

'Tell me now, did *you* have a good holiday?' It's so like him to make sure I talk about me too.

'Oh, Dad, I loved it. I loved the country, the history, the architecture, the art – the lot.' And then I am off and blathering, I'm sure, all the time encouraged by his gentle smile.

Later, he has to bring us back to the present. 'We will have to think about managing this new phase,' he says.

The statement sits at the table with us, making room for itself, elbowing its way to the centre of my attention.

'I don't think it's time for a nursing home, yet, if that's what you mean. We can organise more help here. This is a lot better than sheltered accommodation, for instance. Everyone around here knows her and cares about her. This is the best place for Mum right now.'

I know I am just buying time. I am not ready to let her go. I may never be.

'It's up to you,' he says. 'But when the tough decision has to be made . . .'

'I know. But that time is not here yet, Dad. It's a fair while off yet.'

I hope I am not fooling myself too much.

Sleeping in her own bed made Kitty long for Dan more than when she had been away. It was to do with proximity, she supposed, the fact that he was close by and attainable. She had a troubled night but rose early to get her mother up for the day and take a tour by her allotment before work. Her father would stay with May until the next home shift took over and return that evening to help draw up a roster to deal with this next phase. He threatened to wear his djellabah for the entire day. May couldn't stop laughing at the idea of this man in a dress and nearly choked on her toast. Kitty told him he'd freeze.

She rushed along the streets, yellow street lights illuminating the familiar journey. As street gave way to mud path she heard the crackle of frost underfoot. She waved to Glenda Parfitt, on horseback, as she returned from her early-morning exercise. Andrew Faber and his wife's nurse walked by with their dogs. Everything was in its usual place. And so she was surprised to see Dan's shed in darkness as she neared the allotments. The sky brightened and still there was no sign of him. She had been so sure he would be here. She checked over her vegetable drills and plant beds. She loitered, chilled to the marrow, nose dripping. She should have dug a hole, anything to burn off the rising sense of shame she felt. In her absence the trees had lost the last of their leaves and were naked and pale. Finally, she set off for the station, astounded at the depths of her self-delusion. She had no right to expect anything of that man.

There was a chill hanging about the office even though the radiators were on full blast. Her autumn roses were now a faded brown, crisp in their vase. As she binned them a thorn bit into the soft pad of her thumb, brittle and angry after a fortnight's drought. She sucked on it and tried not to cry. Her world felt small and cold. She thought of the majesty of Egypt, the great sweeping vista of life and history there that had spoiled her for a three-up-two-down home, the frosty walk to work and an office whose magnolia walls wept with heat but would not share it. Dust lingered on every other surface as far as she could see. This was her desert sand, waiting its chance to claim the office. She felt grubby.

She made some coffee and settled in to see what Margo had been up to while she was in charge. The girl's handwriting was appalling, Kitty discovered, especially, and perhaps deliberately, in the Lost and Found book. The shelves were a jumble of items old and new and Kitty postponed their re-ordering in the face of the ordinary office work that needed to be got back on track. She must have been immersed half an hour before Dan arrived, trailing Benny from the night shift.

'Welcome back,' he called. 'You look great.'

He did not. He looked wretched. Kitty wondered if it was because he'd missed her but something in his demeanour forbade her to decide that this was the case. He gave her a light kiss on the cheek and she breathed in his familiar scent. It made her tingle. She had thought he might brush her arm or touch her hand but he did not. In fact, he took himself out of her immediate orbit.

Benny complimented her on her tan and asked how May had enjoyed the trip. She answered and described it all and so the required pleasantries were exchanged between colleagues. Go home, Benny, she wanted to say, but he was clearly glad she was back and wanted to know all about her adventures. Dan managed to avoid her eyes, no matter how wily her glances. What was wrong?

She sold tickets to a couple of old dears on their way to Crockton. A lot of the older clientele avoided the machine, preferring the human contact and a chat. Kitty knew that she might be about the only one an elderly person spoke to throughout a whole day. She tried to give of her time generously without becoming a branch of Social Services. Normally. Today she knew these customers were just the excuse Dan was looking for to escape. While the ladies were explaining that they were off to visit a friend who had broken her hip, he took his opportunity to sneak out.

Trains do not pause for breaks, like elevenses, so neither do we. Coffee is had on the run. Dan ducks in to get a proper cup as the stuff from the vending machine on the concourse is truly vile and very sweet. The Romanians who have settled here in the last few years love it, as do Mr and Mrs Shevchenko whose ancestors were Russian though they are as English as I am. More so, probably. The Shevchenko family have been here since just after the First World War, the ancestral sweet tooth abiding throughout the generations, however.

I glance at the messy shelves of lost items. 'Has that box of ashes been collected?'

'No. Margo moved it out of sight. Said it freaked her. It's a Mr Hill, by the way. That's who's in there.'

'How do you know?'

'His son is the new librarian. I said he should wait till you got back so that the handover would be done properly. I didn't want Margo telling him how gross it was to share an office with his dad's remains.'

Dan's shuffling around on the balls of his feet as if there's more he'd like to say but can't. If I didn't know him better it would be almost comical. There's something on his mind and I don't think I'm going to like it. He meets my eye but bottles it.

'Right, I'd best get on with things,' he says.

I sigh. I can wait.

'I'm glad you're back, Kitty.'

'Me too,' I say as he leaves, cold blasting in through the door. 'I think,' I add, for the benefit of the empty room.

A misty rain wreathed Dan Gibbs's face like a veil, trying to suffocate him as he stood on platform two. He wished it would. He felt ineffective and a shit. He was weak. He hadn't been able to tell Kitty the news. He had stored it up for two weeks, yet still he could not put it into a simple sentence and say it to her. He would have to summon his courage and set things to rights, if that could ever be done at all. And he had to do it soon. If she heard from anyone else it would be unforgivable. Today, then. He would have to tell her today. He groaned aloud which earned him the scrutiny of the resident train spotters. Hal, Fergie and Little Maurice were making notes and taking photographs on the east side of platform four. They stood by their top-heavy satchels like ladettes dancing around their handbags and jackets in a disco. He stared them down. They scribbled some more; about him, for all he knew or cared. Hal even spoke into his Dictaphone. Dan resisted the urge to yell across that he didn't believe that thing even worked. He wanted to kick something hard but they would have seen that too. He skulked off to a sidings where he could fling his arms around and make as much noise as he liked without being seen or heard, an outcast in his own station.

When he had spent his pent-up energy he sat in the rain, breathing heavily and wondering where to find some courage. He noticed Roly spying on him from the door of a nearby shed. Even the bloody cats were judgementalists these days. Or could be the cat thought he was mad not to take shelter from the weather.

I am rummaging for a rubber band in the bottom drawer when I come across the little package I dug up at the allotment before I left on my holiday. It's some sort of object wrapped in a now filthy linen pouch. Someone took the trouble to protect it so I am gentle as I unwrap it. I see it's ivory coloured through the mud and root about for a cloth to cleanse it of its earthy shroud. It's a complicated piece, from the details that emerge, but sturdy, and eventually I realise I can dip it in warm water without doing it damage.

It's a small sailing boat, a toy probably. It is quite the most elaborate thing I have unearthed on my patch. I place it on the desk like a curious paperweight but have no idea what I will do with it. Perhaps just to admire it is the best thing.

Edie Forbes arrives, sure that her glasses case is here because last Tuesday, when she was on her way to Trufford, she took her specs out of it to read the sign and left them on but didn't put the case back into her handbag. I consult the book and try to decipher Margo's hieroglyphics. There is a chance the missing item has been cast into the maw of the shelves and now is as good a time as any to wrestle with them and try to restore order. Edie wants to know did I bring her back a sheik from my travels?

I find Mr Hill and put him back in pride of place. Edie is saying it's a bit suspicious that when people dream of their past lives they are always Egyptian royalty and never one of the poor slaves.

'A cat would have had a good life in the time of the Pharaohs,' I say. 'They revered them. We saw some in the museum in Cairo that were mummified.'

'They've got one of those in a bar in Bury St Edmunds,' Edie says. 'Supposed to be the smallest pub in Britain.'

Lunchtime brought the arrival of the tall stranger. He seemed to know where he was going although Kitty had never seen him before at the station. A rush for the 13.12 to Fetchley meant he had to bide his time before approaching her. One or two of the commuters nodded at him, recognising him from somewhere. When the small throng had cleared he approached, looking ill at ease. He was. No one had told him quite how beautiful Miss Kitty Fulton was. He was unprepared for it. It was her oval green eyes that stopped him in his tracks and now he was having to look into them while trying to make sense of his words. She smiled to hear what he wanted and he promptly lost his powers of speech. She ushered him into the office and he caught a faint trace of citrus fragrance as he passed her, tangy and alive. The air hummed about her. She handed him the box containing his father's earthly remains and he found himself checking out her hands. No wedding or engagement rings. Good.

'I feel like such a dolt . . .'

'Don't. You would be amazed the things people forget – impossible things, you'd have thought. He is the most exotic thing we've had so far, mind you.'

'Thank you for taking such good care of him.'

'It was our pleasure.'

There was not a lot more to say but Simon did not want to leave so he asked, 'How was Egypt?'

'Glorious and ancient. Sunny. I loved it.'

'I've never been.' He could have kicked himself for putting a full stop to what might have been a conversational topic. He was beginning to sweat lightly and was terrified it would translate to a pong of BO.

'You're the new librarian, I hear. What a great job. I love

books and reading.' Kitty put a hand up to her face and laughed. 'Is that a really, terribly banal thing to say?'

'Not at all, it's music to my ears.' Like your voice, he thought. Then winced inwardly. What the hell was he doing, thinking and speaking in such twittering meaningless platitudes? He was coming across like a idiot. He was saved when he noticed an object on her desk. Something about it rang a bell in his memory, stirred a notion and put him on alert. He pointed and asked, 'What is that, if you don't mind my asking?'

'It's some sort of toy I dug up at my allotment.' She held it up and handed it to him. He put the box of ashes down on her desk and turned the ship round and round in his fingers.

'Are those the plots on the way here, over by the graveyard?'

'Yes. I'm forever finding bits and pieces but this seems special. It was wrapped in linen, deliberately I'd have said. It meant something to someone.'

'It reminds me of an item I saw in a book at the library recently. Let me hunt that out and then, if it's all right with you, I might take a further look at it?'

'Of course. It's probably just a kid's toy, though.'

'Yes,' he said, but didn't sound convinced. 'I'll let you get back to work. Lovely to meet you.' He stopped short and they both realised at the same time that they had not been introduced. Laughing, they shook hands and exchanged names. He looked into those eyes again and had to drag himself away to the door.

'Don't forget your dad,' she said, pointing at the lacquered box.

He had almost forsaken the old guy a second time.

I like him from the off. He's lanky and gauche in an academic way, the sort of awkward stance that makes his hair fall on to his face distractedly. His smile is shy but crinkles his eyes and makes him look kind. He has beautiful hands, long fingered and elegant. He's handsome. I don't notice men much, probably because I'm not interested in doing that. If I were I'd have joined a wine club or gone dancing or whatever. I have no need to, though. I have Dan, or a part-share in him. It's all I've ever known. I think it's enough.

I spend the afternoon correcting Margo's errors and omissions, selling tickets, reporting on my holiday to interested travellers, and checking on Mum by phone on the hour as usual. I wonder where Dan's got to as we get to clocking-off time. I am now certain he's been avoiding me all day. He appears, as if on cue, looking haggard. Somehow, I know he won't invite me for a half of lager across the road at the imaginatively titled Railway Inn. Or any further than that.

'Kitty,' he begins, and then flounders. He has an underlying steel about him this time, however, as if he has psyched himself right up and will just say the words out loud so that he must then deal with the consequences, like it or not.

I know what's coming. I have always known. I have been waiting for this since I was sixteen years old. Something clicks inside me on to a setting that has been primed forever. This is the end. We've had close shaves before but now he's finally going to call it off. Time of death, as they say on the TV medical soaps.

'We need to talk,' he says. Things are never good when 'we need to talk'. Things never end well when 'we need to talk'. He can't seem to get past this and on to the very bad news, though.

'Oh, spit it out, Dan,' I say, exasperated. If he's trying to be dramatic, I'll be insulted. If he's having difficulty putting words to something awful, I'll thank him to get it over with quickly.

'Donna is pregnant.'

That's not the phrase I was anticipating but there you have it nonetheless. Time slows and in the eerie silence I pick up on the nuances outside the vacuum bubble of the office. The station carries on as if nothing is happening to us in here. Some boys laugh in oddly high-pitched hysteria, then suddenly stop. I hear change rattle down the chute of the ticket machine. A child shouts at a parent, 'I want it. I WANT IT!' A truck growls past and the window on to the road shudders.

Donna is pregnant.

This news is bound up in such treachery. Not just our combined histories. Not just the betrayal we have perpetrated as a pair, but a betrayal beyond even that. There is an unspoken fact and one to which we will still not give voice because its result is now known: even as we have been lovers all these years, so have they. Donna and Dan. I would have been a madwoman, and fatally naïve, to suppose they were not, but as long as we never spoke of it there was refuge available for my foolish conscience. And a hiding place for him.

Donna is pregnant.

Time and motion hang suspended as I stare at him. I wonder what expression my face has settled into. I cannot register much about myself at that moment. What I do feel is such agony that I cannot isolate it. And time, I know, far from standing still is racking up the minutes, which will lead to hours and days, in spite of my resistance, since he has told me this. And so I'm not sure if one minute or thirty have passed when I say, 'Congratulations.'

Dan looks stung, as if I have slapped his face. If I was sarcastic I didn't mean to be. I am unable to put expression into anything I say. My voice sounds slight and far away but I speak the words that will save us all, reluctant as I am to do so.

'Let that be an end to it, so. We are finished.'

It is said and there will be no going back this time. I don't know what to do next, nor does he. This is not the way either of us might have imagined the end. And I have fantasised about it forever, hoping to look beautiful and tragic when the time came, imagining small speeches of great value that we would bestow on one another for the journey ahead without the beloved other, leaving the best possible last impression to be savoured later and at length, the proof that we were, and are, noble and stoic and other good things for humans to be in their moral universe. It's not like that, here, in the stuffy office of Pennick Railway Station, where a rattling tap on the window tells me someone can't figure out the ticket machine and they have somewhere to go, a place to be, where (quite possibly) someone they love will want to love them back.

My heart has slipped its anchor and I want to lie down and sleep but never wake up. I am suddenly exhausted, drained of all energy and will. Everything is so hopeless that I cannot see the point of fighting it any more. I have lost Dan and I am losing my mother, which leaves me with nothing. I can't think of anything more that could top this. Disappointingly, I don't fall apart there and then. I can't even squeeze out tears. It's as if I don't have the resources to do that, the normal response to tragedy. The body has some strange mechanisms for coping. I go through the motions of selling the ticket and explaining the change the man will have to make two stops down the line. Yes, the rain is awful but at least it's not as cold as it was earlier. With any luck winter will be mild this year. Thanks, I got the tan on my holidays. Oh, yes, I would recommend Egypt. Ten more minutes have passed and no one has died, more's the pity. I turn to face Dan again but he has gone.

I don't remember the journey home. I am on the street when Hannah, our neighbour and sometime Mum-minder, pulls me into her house. She is laughing. 'This is the best yet,' she tells me, and I prepare my face to smile and appreciate the story. Turns out she's right, it is a good one. Earlier Mum let herself into this house, a mirror image of our own. She made a cup of tea and had a Kit-Kat then rearranged the kitchen to look just like ours. 'I have no idea why that girl changed it around,' she told a startled Hannah when she got home. Then she got into bed and had a snooze. 'Let yourself out,' she said to Hannah as she disappeared up the other woman's stairs.

Dad is still laughing about it when I go through our door. Mum is oblivious, watching a makeover show on TV. She's clucking about the amount of white in the house and saying 'Use some colour' to the television set.

'This man is from the council,' she tells me, indicating Dad. 'He wants to talk to you about the rent.'

'You look weary,' he says. 'Are you feeling all right?'

'Yes, it's just first-day-back-at-work-after-a-holiday syndrome,' I tell him. I notice he doesn't look so hot himself but we are all under strains of our own every day and he'll tell me if it's something I need to know about.

We eat a nice dinner he's made and Mum settles back in front of the television while we discuss her future. We make some decisions about seeking a professional carer and looking for grants for whatever we might need, and it passes the time at least although it's hardly a laugh a minute.

'Are you sure nothing's wrong?' Dad asks.

'No. Just something at work that's been coming a while, but it'll sort itself out.'

I am amazed how plausible this sounds and how reassuring my voice is. I wish I could be as confident of this sunny outcome. My world is torn asunder. It's never going to be right again.

We take an early night and as I lie in bed I begin to picture Dan and me in better days. I realise there have never been ideal times. How could there have been? I long for his touch on my skin and his breath on my body. It occurs to me that I may never feel those again and I am suddenly gutted that I didn't know our last time of making love had been just that. I might have tried to make it even more special had I known. Or perhaps that would have been the wrong thing to do. It doesn't matter now as the moment has passed me by and cannot be regained. I thrust my face into the pillow and wail my anguish. No one hears. No one cares. No one knows.

That night I have a childhood dream that has not surfaced in years. It's the one where I am sitting on my bed and a hand reaches out from beneath and grabs my ankle. It is the stuff of a horror movie, a universal fear made spectral flesh.

I wake in the morning wrecked and wasted. My pillow is wet so I have probably cried all night in my shaken sleep.

Actually it feels as if my soul is sore, not just my stiff, strained body. My eyes are set in dark hollows, like a junkie's. And I will have to go through my own emotional DTs. I look under the bed, half hoping to see the bogeyman, but there are only tumbleweeds of dust and threads and a jungle of shoes that needs sorting.

'You look terrible,' Mum tells me when I appear.

'I think I'm coming down with something.'

I already have and it's a bad case of Daniel Gibbs. I've been able to manage it until now but I know I am headed into withdrawal and I'm terrified and worn out.

I want to be angry; that would be useful.

Mum says, 'We should go to Egypt like we've always said we would.'

Right.

Simon Hill would have liked to have been on Kitty's doorstep first thing but he knew that would look foolish and probably also unattractive. Instant neediness was a turn-off. To be over-eager was also not ideal. Actually it might appear creepy. Besides he was trawling records to check on his theory about the boat. He had made one small effort to see Kitty, which was to take the route to work by the allotments. He was un-surprised to find them deserted as the rain was lashing the area like a punishment for some slight. He was sodden by the time he reached work, but invigorated. Lawyers in gowns and wigs stood about as if this fancy dress was all the rage.

Drunks nursed hangovers and frowns. Policemen were smiling.

When Simon had applied for the post at Pennick Library he did some research into the town. It was commonly known as a sleepy hollow but, if that was true now, it wasn't always so. He couldn't yet give a proper opinion of his own as his only previous connection with the place had been a passing acquaintance with its railway station. Just one sentence in a précis of the town's history had piqued his interest then and it was rewakened when he'd seen the tiny ship on Kitty's desk. Pennick had once served as a Parole Town. He used the opportunity now to dig through the library's musty books and chronicles and when he found the years he needed he actually said 'Aha!' aloud. It was a mild eureka moment and he felt justified in his exclamation.

Now he needed to see the object again and examine it properly. He called Pennick railway station. Kitty sounded tired and distracted but agreed to see him that lunchtime. She warned him that there was no such thing as a formal break at the station which disappointed him as he very much wanted to be her focus. He promised not to get in her way.

She had been underwhelmed to hear from him and that bothered him a lot. He wanted to appear new and exciting to her. He wanted to make her laugh. He suddenly thought that she might have a lover; in fact the town was full of lunatics if this beautiful woman did not have admirers queuing out the door. If she had a significant other, a description he loathed, his attentions would be unwelcome. There wasn't much he could do about any of this from afar. He needed to get close to Kitty Fulton. To this end he had the boat. Was that enough?

He powered up his computer, typed in the word 'Alzheimer' and read for an hour.

The postman brings a padded envelope with a typed label amongst the rest of his delivery for the station. It is addressed to me. There is no accompanying note but the contents are so profoundly shocking to me that I whimper aloud. I am staring down at the broken pieces of a girl's brush and comb set. Donna has known all along. And not just about the ruined birthday gift. This is her warning. She is setting down her marker and challenging me, but to what I cannot quite say. I don't know what Donna expects of me, exactly, though I know she wants me to back right off, I get that part of the message. This manifestation of her knowledge of our situation shakes me. I sit and stare at the plastic pieces. I have not touched them since the day I broke them apart. I cannot touch them now. Their silent, jagged accusation is cutting me. I am mesmerised and a little frightened too. It is another layer of misery to file away, another level of hurt, and not just for me.

What a fitting start to a morning of agony. Dan is avoiding me, which is to be expected, but it is Donna's presence that bothers me more because she might as well be physically in the office with me. Every time I look at the broken vanity set, I wince. I could hide it away, should do, but I will know exactly where it is. After a mental tussle, I settle for placing it on a Lost and Found shelf and log it into the book. It seems a fitting gesture. A lost friendship and a broken thing, found again. All unwanted, like me.

The wind and rain are howling outside, raging against us all. The commuters are damp and cranky and several umbrellas are reclaimed. I find the noise comforting. The natural world seems to have taken on my pain and is running with it. It's an acknowledgement of sorts or, at least, it suits my mood. I have to keep the lights on all day against the darkness. A spotty lad comes to take the turquoise wind-cheater away. I don't think it will give him much protection against the angry weather but at least the garment has gone home.

Simon Hill will be a distraction at lunch hour. Although it will kill me to have to talk sensibly to someone, particularly a stranger, his presence will fill a void. A baby's soother is handed in, well worn and clearly a favourite; there'll be hell to pay on that journey.

Roly takes refuge on a shelf. He's a macho cat but this weather is too much even for him and not worth trying to show off in. He lets me stroke his head as I pass. I know better than to spend too long giving him affection as there is only so much he will allow from anyone. I will try to profit from his example. I have been a doormat for too long. If this

is the beginning of anger, I want to nurture it. I need a right-
eous flame to sustain me. I feel hollow and alone. I wonder
if I have been a coward all my life, a passive onlooker who
has chosen to take the simplest course and roll with the
punches. I am probably getting all I deserve.

I carry out the mundanities of my work. In the lulls
between trains I am jolted by sudden onsets of fear. The
future is rattling down the line, whether I like it or not, and
the terror-jolts are reminders of it. Like the hand of the
hidden creature beneath the bed. I will deal with what I
can and time will look after the rest as it ticks on, relentless, winding down till we all land in the dirt like Newton's
apple hitting the ground, though we will go further in.

I am soon ashamed of such florid imaginings and relieved
to see the gangling shape of Simon Hill approach.

Kitty looked tired and wan, he thought, but she explained
she was adjusting to the awful climate again and that covered
it. It was a filthy day. He had brought a small bag of tricks
with him, including a magnifying glass, and quickly got to
work. He looked the boat up and down then brushed it to
try to loosen the last of the dirt away.

'I think it's made of bone,' he said. 'Perhaps chicken bone.
I've been looking at pictures of other items like it this
morning. I wonder if we mightn't find some initials.'

Kitty filled a bowl with lukewarm, soapy water and Simon
carefully washed the boat. He prodded it with cotton buds,

then dried it very gently. Although it had spent many years in the ground Kitty was suddenly worried that it might break in her care and she would have thwarted history somehow.

'Did you know that Pennick was a Parole Town?' Simon was asking her. She shook her head and murmured she did not. He was delighted with her answer. He had information to share.

'At the beginning of the nineteenth century several English towns were selected to act as open prisons for French soldiers captured during the Napoleonic Wars. Pennick was one for a short while but it was too close to the sea and there were a lot of escapes so it was decommissioned after only eighteen months. The basic idea was that the officer class who'd been captured could be trusted to live openly with the populace, observing a curfew and never straying further than a mile from the town centre. That's where the term "milestone" comes from because they marked the boundaries. If I'm not mistaken I passed one near your allotments. Many of the soldiers made items like this to sell for extra cash or to give to sweethearts, but few have survived.'

Now he had the magnifying glass held above the base of the ship. 'I'd say those are the letters FVAC.'

He handed Kitty the glass and sure enough she saw the initials.

'Now we can set about finding the name or names they correspond to.'

An extra flicker of interest stirred inside Kitty. She felt it sometimes when she took in the most unusual lost items and resolved to get them back where they belonged. She raised the little object and kissed it gently before placing it on her desk again.

'As a matter of interest,' Simon continued, 'are there any oak trees near your vegetable plot?'

'Yes,' she said.

'Honour oaks,' he told her. 'They were another marker the prisoners must observe and not pass by.'

'I had absolutely no idea about any of this.'

'It's unusual for a town and it wasn't for very long so I'm not surprised.'

'What should we do next?'

Simon could not help but smile. Kitty had joined the quest.

The rat-tat-tat of coin on glass jolted them both. Martha D'Arcy needed a ticket to Selscott and it wasn't listed as an option on the concourse machine.

NINE

When I look back, I wonder if I should have spotted the signs. Dad looked tired, but when you are used to seeing that you don't pick up on it or find it remarkable. I assumed he was working too hard, or sleeping badly, all things I under-stood very well. The call to say he has been rushed to hospital is unexpected and by the time I get there he is gone. The nurse calls it 'passed away'. I miss his death by moments. He is still warm to my touch as I cry over his body. I am rent ragged to see this man I adore so still and unrespon-sive. He is no longer himself. His big, generous heart has let him down. My own is full of shards that tear me every time I take a breath. This human shell on the hospital bed has his appearance and wears his familiar expression but it is not truly my dad. His life-song is missing.

The room is unnaturally bright courtesy of fluorescent strip lighting. It always seems to sap any other energy around it, suck it up and give nothing back. It hurts my eyes and makes Dad look even paler than he might. The staff have left me alone with him and the room is eerily quiet, but for my jagged breathing and snuffled tears. I want to talk to him but I am all out of words. I would give a leg to have a beeping cardiac machine tap out its hopeful rhythm. It stands silent by the bed. Outside, life clatters on. I hear voices, laughter, and the squeak of a trolley pushed by.

I am suddenly beset with worry that my father was afraid as he realised what was happening. He was alone, on the street, at the mercy of strangers. They did their best for him, as we must all hope we will if called upon. Guiltily, I think of figures slumped in doorways that I never approached, assuming they were drunk or homeless and none of my affair. I brush his tousled hair with my hand and say, 'Oh, Dad. Oh, Dad,' because no words can cope with the magnitude of this moment or offer any consolation.

I can never speak to him again or seek his advice. I can tell him news but he will not respond. There can be no discussion any more, just my one-sided conversation with the most important bit, his opinion, missing. I know he didn't mean to abandon me but that's what he has been forced to do. I worry about where he has got to. Will someone look out for him? Are his affairs in order that he may have calm passage on this next leg of his journey?

There is a further, extraordinary problem too: I have to make this real for Mum. How can I explain the event to her, meaningfully, now that her lexicon is diminished? The nurse has returned, wants to know what I'd like to do now. She means what undertaker will come for my father's body. His remains. I don't want to part with him or have any truck with seeing him go. When he leaves the hospital he is officially beyond help, there is no hope of getting him back to rights. I want to accuse a doctor of not trying hard enough to save him. I want blame and I want it now; that would be of some use, not the offer of a cup of tea and a chat with a counsellor I have never met before. I don't want standard help. This is a specific case. My father has died, not someone else's. It makes this case unique.

I do not know where to start with the arrangements. The nurse hands me a black, plastic sack with the clothes inside that were torn from his body while the medics tried to save him. I sign for his wallet and the watch I gave him five years ago for his birthday. I slip it on to my wrist, wanting him close, hoping it will help me to do the right thing. This is foreign territory.

I leave the room and find Miss Marshall crying outside on an orange seat in the corridor. She is my father's right-hand woman in the publishing firm. She probably knows him better than I do. Or she did. It is so strange to need a past tense now. With Mum everything is in the present. There is only now and then it is forgotten and we move on to more now and repeat the process. But always in the now. Any of her deep history is unavailable to me, buried in her and unlikely to be shared. She remembers things from long ago because they've had fifty or sixty years to embed, recalled afresh each year and therefore strongly entrenched in her consciousness. Things that happened an hour ago haven't a hope.

I have always thought Miss Marshall a little stern and wooden but now she flings herself at me. We hug. She is trembling, overcome.

'I should have been with him,' she sobs.

'Maybe he wanted to go alone,' I say, trying to comfort her, to give her that straw to clutch at.

'He was tired and we'd run out of coffee so he went to get some. If only I had bought a jar this morning. I should have known to . . .'

'It's not your fault,' I tell her. 'It's no one's fault.' I don't know if I believe this. I still want someone or something tangible to blame. I need something to hold, to examine and fling against a wall. And I don't want a medical explanation; I want a moral one. The world is no better a place because my father has been taken from it. It is a pointless act of karmic cruelty and we are left to deal with the fallout.

Kitty's mobile had taken a message. It was from Dan, wondering how her father was. She listened to it once, and only just resisted the urge to smash the phone to pieces against the door of the undertaker's. Later, after she had chosen her father's coffin and the wording of a funeral notice for the local paper, she texted Dan the information he sought. She could not, and would not, talk to him. Those days were gone. She stood outside Jensen's and thought of the box of ashes left at the station. It had led her here today, looking for help. She knew the firm to be discreet and professional.

Dan Gibbs read the plain message and knew it meant so much more than the sum of its words. His misery expanded. He loved this woman but that was of no use to anyone any more. He could not join her on this journey or be of any help from the fringes. He had his own mess of duties and conflicts. The one useful thing he did was to call his niece Margo and ask her back to work at the station in the interim.

In Norwich, rain began to sheet across the town. Kitty was glad of it. It set a tone and she wanted fitting tribute to the events taking place here. Miss Marshall insisted she be called Marie now though Kitty could not imagine ever doing that. She offered to drive her home and Kitty all but said, 'Dad can take me.' Her hand shot to her mouth, as if to push the words back in. Her face suddenly ached with the tears forming behind her sinuses. She thought it might burst under the pressure. She let Miss Marshall see her to the station where she boarded a train to Pennick, unable to believe that the other passengers were oblivious to her distress.

A man sitting opposite finished a damp-looking sandwich and began to clear his teeth in short bursts of breath. 'Tseh, tseh, tseh.' He kept at it, sucking air back through his mouth.

'Tseh, tseh, tseh.' He ran his tongue along the front of the teeth, over and back, over and back. Then the sucking sound again. 'Tseh, tseh, tseh.' Eventually she could take no more and snarled, 'Will you stop that awful noise.' No 'please' in the request, no 'thank you' when he did as he was bidden. She could have torn his head off with her bare hands by then and not regretted it. He got the message, as did the other passengers. They felt her mood then.

Kitty was the only one to alight at Pennick, the commuters having returned from their daily grind, the pensioners from their jaunts and teenagers from their adventures or school. She went to the office and tidied her desk. At the door, hand on light switch, she remembered what she had come in for. She returned to the desk, wrapped the Frenchman's boat carefully in a clean dishcloth, placed it in her handbag and left.

Dan Gibbs watched her come and go from the rear of platform four and cursed himself for being an idiot all his life.

Mum goes a little nuts when I say, 'I have bad news. Dad is dead.' It is to be expected. She cries and pulls at her hair. She paces the room. I cannot make out what she's saying and, in any case, it may make no sense. After hunching herself into a ball in an armchair, she tilts her head back and rages at me.

'How can Dad be dead?' she wants to know.

'It was a heart attack,' I explain.

She screams, 'I don't want him to be dead.'

I want to yell back 'Neither do I' but my rage and sorrow should not be directed at or used against her.

She begins to rock in the seat and moan and I gradually make out the words 'my daddy' and 'dead'. I have an awful realisation of the hash I have made of explaining the situation to her. I hang my head, ashamed of such a mistake and sorry to have caused her this unnecessary extra suffering; she thinks I am talking about *her* father, the one who abandoned the family when she was a child and was never heard of again. She always spoke about him in a soft tone that underlined how much she'd loved him. It had not occurred to me that there would be this confusion. I have made a balls of the task and the situation is now a lot worse than it might have been. I review my options. I need to correct this, and fast.

'No, May,' I say, thinking that using her name will broaden the picture beyond our little family, lend a helpful distance. '*My* dad is dead.'

She is slightly taken aback. 'Why are you telling me?'

'You knew him.'

'Did I?' She really doesn't trust this information and clearly doesn't like the look of me. I have done nothing but bamboozle and upset her since I came through her front door.

'Yes, May, you knew him. His name was Stephen.' I reach

187

for a framed photo of the three of us and point at my dad. 'That man there.'

She decides to ignore this. Perhaps she doesn't recognise him.

'Why did you say my daddy was dead?'

'It was a misunderstanding.'

'A what?'

'A mistake.'

'It was a rotten thing to do.'

She's not wrong there.

'My daughter is going to be very angry with you,' she tells me, with considerable menace. Her face is twisted with fury. 'You can go now,' she adds, imperiously waving her hand to gesture me away, horrid creature that I am.

She picks up the photograph and proceeds to have a conversation with it, as if there are three people talking though only she can make out what's being said. 'Really, dear,' she says to my image, and laughs. 'What do you make of that, Stephen?' she asks the representation of my dead dad. Then she bursts into tears. I suppose it's progress.

I go to make us some pasta, knowing I won't have any but Mum must eat. At the kitchen sink I quietly, gently, vomit up the contents of my depleted stomach. It doesn't help much. I remember Dad holding my hair back once as I threw up too much ice cream and chocolate into this sink. 'It's all right, sweetheart,' he'd said. 'Let it all out.' I start to cry, aching for this moment magically to become then, to feel his comfort and hear his voice. He can't help me now.

A small voice calls from the door, 'Ellen, is it true that Daddy is dead?'

News travelled fast in a small town and it didn't take long for Simon Hill to hear of the death. He was not sure whether he'd known Kitty long enough to call in person and offer his condolences. Probably not. He rang her, to commiserate but also anxious to talk and keep in touch. He wanted to help if he could. She sounded glad to hear from him. He offered to keep her company and, to his astonishment, she agreed. He spent twenty minutes changing clothes, like a teenager, inappropriate as it was for such a sad occasion. He battled with the right choice of wine, too, wanting to bring a bottle that struck a balance between good and not-over-the-top. He sat still for a moment then and realised what a jerk all of this calculation made him. He was acting like a predator, for crying out loud. He changed back into what he had worn for the day and mussed up his hair again, but stayed with the wine he'd chosen.

He arrived on Kitty's front step, breathless and disconcerted. She looked heartbreakingly beautiful, he thought, as she answered the door. The deep hollows under her extraordinary eyes counterpointed them, and her hair, dragged back into a severe bun, brought her cheekbones into focus more than usual. Black clothing set off her milky skin and emphasised her curves. Grief might be hell on earth but it suited Kitty Fulton, at least externally. She smiled weakly and welcomed him in.

The house was packed. This is what we do, it seemed to say. We are a community: we gather, we comfort, we bring food and drink. Simon held out his offering, tongue-tied. For one flash-mad moment he felt he should have allowed himself to dress up more for the occasion and immediately wanted to kick himself for more of his arrant shallowness. A much-loved man had died and good people were hurting. He also wished there weren't so many of them here, and again cursed his fickle heart; this was not a fucking date, for chrissake. Kitty took the bottle and said, 'You're very generous and this is far too good.' She looked into his eyes a little longer than necessary, or so he thought; so he hoped. He was a total heel, he knew, for these calculations. 'Thank you for coming along.'

'I'm sorry for your loss.' It seemed depressingly inadequate.

She smiled as if she understood that this was the phrase required at this juncture, this was what was said until more meaningful words were available, until they were allowed to speak in a more intimate language. I don't know her well enough for that yet, he reminded himself, but I hope to. He couldn't hug her by way of comfort and a handshake would now be too late and lame. He had rarely felt so gawky and tall and out of place. They stood there awkwardly a moment longer, each hoping the other knew what to do next. Eventually, Kitty moved off and he followed.

Simon was given a lot of names to put with as many faces as they made their way through to the small kitchen. He imagined he recognised some of them from the library, and everyone seemed to know who he was. He thought of his last posting, where he had been when his father had died. No one had called around to his home – he'd discouraged it – and the few who had wanted to offer condolences were told to meet him at his local pub. This was a world away.

He was last to leave, though the hour was not late. He found himself sitting in an armchair that was far too comfortable in front of a real fire. May looked him over and decided she liked him. She had a charming Irish burr as she repeated his name. In fact, she said a lot of what he did over again.

'Is this a party?' she asked him.

'Sort of.'

'Sort of.' A nod. 'Do I know you?'

'We just met. I'm Simon.'

'Simon. Si . . . Are you nice?'

Such a difficult question to answer. 'I hope so.'

She nodded. 'I hope so.'

She checked who was looking then leaned toward him and whispered loudly, 'Kitty is having an affair.'

He noticed her daughter stiffen.

'With a married man.'

Kitty reddened. 'You know about my mum,' she broke in.

'Yes, I had heard.'

'Well . . .' she shrugged and trailed off.

'The court case starts tomorrow,' May told him. 'The television cameras are parked outside. Ask Dan, he'll tell you all.'

Simon gave Kitty an understanding smile as he hauled himself out of the chair and took his leave. Poor May was obviously very far gone. He kissed Kitty on the cheek as he bade her goodnight and promised to keep her up to date with his researches into the Napoleonic ship. It would be a welcome distraction, she told him. He stepped out into the street and walked hurriedly away, ashamed of the carnal longings he felt and how fickle they showed him to be.

Mum is having bad dreams and worse days. When she is calm she is worried; when she's agitated she cannot be reasoned with. I refuse to take the easy route and have her sedated. She is entitled to her grief as much as I am, and even if she does not entirely grasp where it has come from, that in no way lessens her pain. She may be reliving the hell of her own father dying, which happened at a remove. He never returned to the family home and the news that he had passed away arrived anecdotally, years after he was gone. She once told me she always wondered if he truly was dead or if it had been misreported. There was no way of checking at the time. Later, I think she didn't want to pursue it, preferring to believe he might still be out there somewhere, remembering her now and again, maybe even loving her from afar. Now I have delivered a terrible blow.

I wish I could help her more. I remind her each day that we will bury Stephen in a week. It's a sadder variant of telling her in advance about our holiday. That seems a lifetime ago. Such carefree, lazy days.

The language I use to keep it simple for her negates much of a daughterly claim to him on my part, in case that sets her off again. In its way, dealing with her fills the terrible, slow time as we await our turn at the church to say farewell to my father. Sorrow has its own relentless pace. This is only slightly different from how I felt when I lost Dan. It has that same dreamlike quality. I am functioning: I speak, I make decisions, I fulfil my duties. But I wait to be pierced by sharp pain at any moment. I feel horribly afraid all of the time.

I worry now that I disappointed Dad. I never went to Cambridge, as he did, or any university for that matter. I never showed any ambition. I had no interest in a lot of the things that made him tick. He must have wondered where they got me from. He worked hard at making his business succeed in a famously tough market. I never showed any get up and go, just faded into fat-arsed sloth in a dead-end job. I worry I didn't tell him enough that I loved him.

I am stunned by the expressions of solidarity from people who are virtual strangers to me but who knew Dad well, worked for him, were published by him. Many knew Mum in her heyday. The types crawling out of their woodwork are so various as to make me feel even more humble. Dad's literary and scholarly net was a mighty catchment area.

Miss Marshall helps me choose readers for the funeral. We will have a mixture of liturgical tracts and secular poetry. Everyone wants to be a part of it; the trouble is whittling down the number of speakers. We'd need days if we allowed everyone their moment.

'Why am I so sad?' Mum asks me, for the umpteenth time.

'Because Stephen is dead.'

'Dead.' She tries to get her head around that concept. 'Oh,' she says, when it hits home. Tears are about to roll. 'Did I like him, dear?'

'Yes, very much.'

'That's sad.'

So sad, I want to tell her. Not least because, if you don't remember him, I might as well not exist. In your mind I don't, not as a daughter, or not all the time. What does that make me? Who does that make me? I have only one parent left and I am no one to her. I feel I am slowly disappearing. I too am being cancelled out by her greedy disease. It takes more than one when it comes.

May had her first accident that night. She came into Kitty's room and said, 'Ellen wet the bed. She's upset.'

They peeled off the sodden sheets and propped the mattress against the wall to dry. They changed May's pyjamas and she climbed into her daughter's bed, excited at the treat, the reason for it already receding from her mind or else

194

obliterated altogether. Kitty said a small prayer that this was a one-off. She wasn't sure she was up to a life of incontinence pads and rubber matting. The following morning her mattress was dry beneath them.

The house was filled with cards and flowers. May was delighted by it afresh, hour by hour, although it was explained they were not celebrating a happy day but a sad one. She told anyone who would listen that her daddy had been murdered. She began to have nightmares straight out of horror movies, which was when Kitty started to monitor her television consumption properly and control what she watched. The amount of violence on air at any time was gobsmacking. She was careful not to let May have too much to drink in the evenings, and loo breaks were regularly enforced. There was no more bed-wetting. They somehow got through to the day of the service and burial.

May's wardrobe didn't extend to much in the way of dark clothing. She went for colours, often very bright and clashing. Over the years the pieces had been adapted to leave her some independence, which meant elasticated waists, slip-on shoes or ones with Velcro fastenings, sweaters rather than cardigans. Fussy, fiddly clothes were too much of a challenge so now she looked as if she went for extreme comfort when, in fact, function was everything. Even her overcoat had a tie belt rather than one with a buckle. Kitty managed to get her into a largely navy ensemble with pink and white highlights to set it off. She was adamant about the pink scarf, it being her current favourite colour by a long shot. Kitty threw on her own winter coat and hat and grabbed a handbag. They were about to set forth when Jed appeared, holding a container of plants. It was a square pot filled with ornate coloured cabbages and variegated ivies, arranged to perfection, worthy of a television gardening programme.

'Fer yer daad,' he said gruffly, handing it over. 'An' yew both. Sorry fer yer troubles.' He coughed a bit, looking up and down the street to alleviate the embarrassment.

Kitty knew not to be effusive. Jed didn't do sentiment, or never admitted to it, although Kitty had seen him cry as he dug his plot over, glad of the exertion to mask this weakness, his loneliness. So she told him the truth. 'It's the most beautiful thing, Jed. I don't know how to thank you.'

'Ollust liked yer daad. Ollust good fer a mardle.' It was true they'd chatted, and laughed quietly too, man to man, whenever her father visited the allotment. Stephen had loved the broad beans she grew and liked to help harvest them. He'd made the same jokes every year about Norfolk Broads, both fens and women. Every year Kitty had smacked him gently with her gardening gloves, telling him they were the worst puns ever. Another thing she could never again do.

She thought her father might have liked to publish a book about Jed and his ilk, to record their disappearing ways and speech. Only the older people had that particular strangled drawl now. Jed called it his 'drant'. Everyone else's speech was becoming standardised. Her father had loved language and now would never speak again. She gulped back an involuntary moan.

'Yer goin ter church?'

'Yes.'

'We'll walk tergether.'

Jed took the outside of the path, to be their protector in the most old-fashioned and touching way. They walked along in silence, Kitty linking arms with May, and as they did other neighbours joined until they had the makings of a protest march. I am glad we never got a car, Kitty thought.

I have made a selfish decision but cannot regret it. I have decided to bury Dad locally. I want him close. I need him to be near me as we face further into the unknown. Somewhere in the back of my mind I hear him laugh at a poem scanning he once read me of a Donald Rumsfeld speech about known knowns and unknown knowns and unknown unknowns. I thought he would be sick with merriment that day. The memory tears through me and I cough into my hand to mask any other sound I may have made, remembering it. So, we are on our way to St Boniface's for his service. Afterwards we take the short walk to the cemetery and then home to serve tea and sandwiches and tell fond stories. I picture the station, trains disgorging more mourners. The Fultons are good for business today. The other passengers will wonder whose funeral these people are attending so, in their unwitting way, they too will think of my father. I feel it is only fitting.

We arrive in a neighbourly entourage at the little church and I am astonished to find it full to bursting. I wish Dad were here to see his turn-out. He'd probably laugh and say something self-deprecating like, 'I must owe more money than I thought.' The Vicar resists the opportunity to talk about anyone or anything but Dad in his address and I am grateful to him for this. There is a comfort in the liturgy too. It's inclusive and communal. This surprises me, in a good way. I have no system of belief, I barely have hope any more, but this soothes me. It is helping.

The sight of so many different people moved by the passing of a decent man is unbearably touching. It gets to Mum who starts to giggle.

'Sister Vincent's not here, is she?' she whispers.

'No,' I say.

'Pity. She'd definitely go to hell if she set foot here in a Protestant church. The bad bitch.' That sets her off again but there is a choking note to the sound now. She blows her nose.

A large hairy poet has to stop speaking during his reading to catch his breath and staunch his sorrow. He looks like a labourer or farmhand, with his huge features and haphazard clothes, but to hear him speak is to be transported. His rich voice catches occasionally as he reads a poem he has written in tribute to my father. Miss Marshall remains behind dark glasses but holds a tissue under her nose for the duration to catch her tears. The soloist's voice wobbles at the start of 'Abide With Me'. Many people reach out to touch the coffin as it leaves the church to begin its final journey to the graveyard, and it affects me so much I worry I won't be able to stay upright. Mum is sobbing freely now.

'Tell me again who is dead,' she asks me.

'Stephen. My dad.'

She stops in her tracks, aghast. 'But he has my memories. He was minding them for me. What will I do? How will I manage?'

'It's all right,' I assure her. 'I have those for you now. Please don't worry. I have your memories.'

'Promise?'

'Promise.'

Simon nodded at the Station Master as he took a place opposite him by the side of the open grave where Kitty and May were standing. Dan Gibbs was accompanied by a pale, pregnant blonde. They both wore wedding bands and Simon assumed that this was Mrs Gibbs. Neither of the pair could take their eyes off Kitty. He could see why. In her dark coat and large beret she looked like a forties film star. He remembered seeing hanks of yarn at her house and wondered which of the women had knitted the hat. He didn't know a lot about fashion but it looked like a couture item to his untrained eye. Whoever made it should have gone into business.

Kitty and May stepped forward and each threw some

earth down on to the coffin. Boards were laid across the grave and dressed with many floral tributes, and the invitation circulated to go back to their house for refreshments. Simon hovered at Kitty's back, ready to help with anything that was needed. He wasn't sure if she had actually noticed him at all so far. He was joined by a gnarled old codger, also looking out for the women. The older man watched Dan Gibbs with hawk-like scrutiny, something Simon felt to be significant. He filed it away in his librarian's system. Scrawny Mrs Gibbs looked over at Kitty with barely concealed envy. He wondered if she was jealous of her quite numinous beauty. Then he recalled May's words about Kitty having an affair with a married man and wondered if perhaps they might not have been the ravings of a demented woman. His stomach gave a strange heave.

Kitty turned and smiled at him. Another lurch, more pleasant this time. 'Simon,' she said, and reached for his hand, but not to shake it, to hold it. Do not look surprised or act awkwardly, he warned himself. They walked from the graveyard like that, as if it was the most natural thing in the world. For Simon it felt like a thrillingly intimate gesture. He prayed his hands would not turn clammy as his brain told them this was in no way regular or familiar and was, in fact, potentially filled with new and deep significance.

I wish I didn't have to look straight into Donna's face for the burial but she has planted herself and Dan right across from me. She holds her hands over her bump which I am certain she is thrusting forward for all to see, but especially me. Dan cannot meet my eye but I know he is watching me closely. I concentrate on Dad and handling this last rite with dignity for him. I think of the small, customised job I had done to his coffin. What no one knows is that I got an illustrator who'd worked with him to paint silver stars on a navy night sky on the inside of the lid, to light his way to his next incarnation or maybe just to please him where he lies.

I hope he will have another opportunity at an existence, if he'd like it. He deserves many lives and I know he will be wonderful in all of them. God speed, I say, in my mind. I don't know how else to put it, or whoever and whatever to invoke that might loosely be said to be in charge of this glorious mess we call life. If there is continuity, my father should be part of it. He is one of the good guys. If these are foolish thoughts so be it, as long as they can lend me comfort in my shattered world and help me move forward. I have to motor on for two as Mum will need all the help I can give her.

The Vicar speaks about remembrance. 'Lord, You have called Your servant Stephen to You. His mortal body has left us but we remember his kindness and love. His family will cherish precious memories and, even as You welcome him to Your heavenly kingdom and grant him eternal life, so shall he live on in the minds of those who loved him here on earth.'

He has no way of knowing that memory is the central problem in our household. I zone out for a moment, wondering about the things I cannot remember about my dad, things I can never know because he never told me, memories never shared that have gone with him to the grave. If he never passed these on to me, did they matter in the first place? Do we lose anything by never having it at all? Is Mum's condition so different? She is simply living in advance that aspect of death: the forgetting, the oblivion. I turn my attention to the Vicar who is quoting from the book he's holding. '"Remember me",' he reads aloud. Poor old Hamlet got that same instruction from his father's ghost and was never the better for it, not that I am comparing myself with Hamlet, because I am not. Mum turns and whispers, 'Remember me,' but I am unsure if she's telling me to or repeating the words she's just heard. I squeeze her hand and say, 'I will.' I am, I want to add. I am remembering you every day.

The air is icy, the light crystal as if all is clear and logical. A robin sits on a nearby headstone. I see Jed nod to himself. He believes these birds are lost friends returned to visit. I'd like to think this one is Dad and that he's pleased with how the day is going. I want him to be proud of us. Many people crowd around to offer condolences. They are kind and say how lovely they found the service. It was beautiful, I am glad to agree.

I catch Donna looking at me with what can only pass for

jealousy. What . . . now? My father is dead. Surely there is nothing in that situation that she wants for herself. She is probably just furious not to be centre of attention, especially now that she's pregnant. Her needy crankiness makes my back ache with exhaustion.

We make for home and I find that I am walking hand in hand with Simon Hill. It feels comfortable but not in an over-familiar way. It's almost as if we have done this before, though we have not, and that's something to think about at another time. Right now my plate is full with other urgent matters. When we get to the house, I introduce him to Jed who is like a mother hen clucking after Mum and me.

'Jed made us a beautiful planter,' I tell Simon, and burst into tears.

TEN

When I wake each morning I have an average of three minutes before reality hits. One hundred and eighty precious seconds, then . . . my father is dead, Dan is gone, my mother is leaving me. This blow to the soul gets me, fresh and raw, every day. I have to be up before Mum to steal a march on her day as well as mine, which means I have no choice but to get out of bed. I don't allow myself to stew in my own misery first thing otherwise everything will fall apart. As it is, the house is returning to our usual warped normality. As each bunch of flowers dies and is added to the compost heap, I have fewer questions to answer about why they're there in the first place. I removed all the sympathy cards the day after the funeral and immediately the house looked a lot less festive and confusing. I try not to wear black from head to toe, much as I want to. The weather is vile and suits my mood.

Today is a big one as I'm to attend the reading of Dad's

will with Miss Marshall in the afternoon. It's a week since we buried him but it feels like a year has passed, and slowly at that. I don't want Mum along as it will only dredge up things she cannot understand and make her unhappy. Life is hard enough without that, for both of us. I did question my motives, wondering if I was excluding her to make my own lot easier, but after much mental flagellation I decided this was the best course. In the meantime I try hard to concentrate at the station office. I've been finding work a massive chore ever since I got back from Egypt but, considering everything that's happened, that's hardly surprising.

I returned to the station immediately after Dad's funeral, thinking it best to keep up some sort of routine. Dan and I skirt about each other, of necessity, like magnets repelling one another. Neither of us is finding this easy. Roly has taken up full-time residence and decides today is the day he will grace my knee with his furry bulk. It has been a slow gradual progression across the office, from the Lost and Found shelves, to a box of paper under my desk, then on to the desk itself. The day he began to head-butt me while he stood on the computer keypad, rewriting the accounts as he did so, I knew we were in business as pals. I have tried to explain to him that the computer's bits are not for him to roll about on or play with, but I am wasting my breath. It's pointless trying to reason with him a lot of the time. His progress has had an inexorability about it that has made me grin when I thought I might never smile again. 'You got your invisibility cloak on?' I tease as he mooches about. He ignores me, which means he thinks I can't see him, which in turn means that he's wearing it all right.

Here's an interesting thing: he doesn't much like Dan who says it's because he's not a cat person, more of a dog man. Could be. Roly is a smart cookie and he hasn't survived this long in the wild without knowing a thing or two. Perhaps he senses that Dan is not a fan and therefore stays away, not wanting to waste his feline time, or could it be that he sees something he doesn't approve of and is making a stand against it? Intriguing.

I really value Roly's friendship. I feel alone in the office now that lines have been drawn between Dan and me, and I don't see much of Benny in the way of things. I play the radio and chat with Roly and help the customers with their journeys, and somehow we make the day become evening and time to go home. It would be a lot harder without the cat's kindness. He is one of the few creatures who does not refer to me as 'poor Kitty'. I do not want that title. I am not a victim. I don't want to believe I am in any way to be pitied. Mind you, a neighbour told me I was brave last week and that was no better. I nearly laughed outright. I am not brave, I am merely getting on with it. And that's largely because I have no choice in the matter.

Roly was 'done' a few years ago when he took to spraying the station with honky tomcat hormones and dragging himself in with angry-looking cuts, torn ears and limps, from proving himself around the greater Pennick area. Steps were taken though Benny in particular was horrified by the plan. We got hold of a special trap from the Animal Welfare people and baited it with my chicken risotto which Roly is unable to resist. Benny was so upset by the incident he would not talk to me for a week. Roly made me feel horribly guilty too by worrying his stitches and walking about the station with a bloodied snout. But in time he began to let me pet him again and we took it from there. Today he is on my lap and purring so hard the noise is distorted. Maybe if I had chopped Dan's balls off he would have grown to adore me like the cat does. Instead, Donna did it and she got him.

The paper is full of the latest famous person to admit to having Alzheimer's so the radio is full of talk about it too. High-profile victims are gold dust. Everyone says what a disgrace it is that the health system denies younger sufferers free meds that would arrest the progress of the disease and, ultimately, delay their becoming a complete burden on the system. That is what's happening now. It defies logic but I have long ago stopped my ranting on that subject, too busy coping with the curse. There'll be a brouhaha for a few days, then everyone who is not personally affected will forget about it until next time. There is a reminder that Charlton Heston died with Alzheimer's and that makes for nice photo opportunities in the papers. I see a few shots of Ronald Reagan, too, another high-flyer who had it. The feel-good tag is news of a promising scientific discovery that the venom of a tropical cone snail may hold the key to treatments for heart failure, obesity and Alzheimer's. Too late for the Fultons and their Alzheimer's. Too late for Dad and his dicky heart. Where was this snail hiding when we needed him most?

Dan creeps in on eggshells. These are of his own strewing, not mine, I'm too wrung out to be nasty or vengeful to him. His long face is actually beginning to annoy me and I take it as a very good sign that I might eventually mend, in a century or so. Roly senses a shift in the atmosphere and takes off for the tartan rug handed in yesterday off the Kings Lynn connector. I remind Dan that I'll be gone from two o'clock and he winces like I've struck him. For God's sake, the man is falling apart; that's supposed to be my bag. OK, I'm fractious, I'll admit it. He'd do well to stay out of my way for the time being. I take the bad temper as a positive sign too. At least it shows I have some energy. I touch my dad's watch, which I still wear as a talisman, and, unbidden, the mourning cloud descends on me full strength. I wonder if I will ever be happy again.

The offices of Hartley & Benson had an oaky-panelled air of reliability and looked like they dated from the turn of a century long past, so it was a surprise to be introduced to a young blade wearing a trendy shirt and ironic cufflinks: Kitty had expected a waistcoated ancient with grey whiskers and a pipe. He was Jason Hartley, he explained, great-grandson of the original founder of the firm. She felt gratified to see him use a fountain pen at least. When they were sunk into further soft leather furnishings with a cup of tea each and some Digestives, Jason Hartley delivered the first in his list of surprise announcements. This was that May and Stephen Duke had actually been man and wife, married some thirty years ago.

A secretary brought in a cloth then to mop up Kitty's spilled tea, and some water to help clear her throat of the lump of biscuit swallowed on the sharp intake of breath when she'd heard that.

'Unexpected news,' young Mr Hartley observed.

Even Miss Marshall was surprised. 'I had no idea,' she told Kitty, anxious to clear up that point.

'Bloody hell,' was all Kitty could offer.

'There's more,' Jason Hartley warned.

Kitty nodded. 'I'll put the tea down.'

The business went to her. She was now the owner of Duke Publishing. A trust fund had been set up to meet May's medical bills. Various small personal bequests were made, including five thousand pounds for Miss Marshall plus a tiny Lowry drawing she'd always loved. A sealed letter had been left for Kitty. Her hand shook as she saw her name on it, written in her father's artistic scrawl. Jason Hartley suggested to Miss Marshall that they should leave Kitty to read it alone. He took her on a brief tour of the premises while her new boss was left to commune in private with her dead father.

My Dearest Kitten,

I'll race through the usual spiel about 'If you're reading this now I am no longer with you' and so on (whoever knew my life would imitate a movie in any way, eh?), but sadly that's what we are faced with. Sorry. I did not plan it this way. By now you will also know that your mother and I have been married a long time. We did that to safeguard your inheritance and I hope you don't mind. May and I were never going to manage living together, more's the pity, so we left your surname as Fulton, though I would have been most chuffed to call you Kitty Duke. It has a nice ring to it, I hope you'll agree.

Now you own Duke Publishing and I know that will be a shock. It has never been a huge aspect of your daily life, but I wonder if perhaps it ought to be. And that is a thought I'll leave you with. You may decide to sell it on, as is your prerogative, but do give some thought to running it yourself, even for a little while, to see how you like it. It's a well-oiled machine, with Marie Marshall doing all her surname suggests. Cameron Field is an excellent poetry editor and has great taste. Victor Long handles the academic side and is a safe pair of hands. All three are also your Board of Directors, and your wonderful mother would be with them too were it not for her cursed affliction. The firm is holding its own, in difficult times, with the academic list bringing in enough to underwrite the more literary side. There are some projects underway that I hope you will see to fruition before you make any momentous decision. Give it a try, Kit, won't you? You might like it.

And it may be time to get away from that station. I think you have given enough of your life to it. Also, I suspect you are more of a chip off the old blocks than you realise: between your mother's legacy and my own, I know there is talent in you that just needs a bit of bringing out. This is that opportunity.

I'll miss you and I know you will miss me, but please know that no father could have been prouder of his beautiful, kind and courageous daughter. I have been the blessed one.

With all my love,

Your Dad

When we were kids, Dan and I loved to sit and chat under a massive oak tree near the allotments. Donna thought just lazing around was boring and usually headed off early in a mood. We'd talk idly about what we wanted to be when we grew up. That never took Donna long. She would be a top model and divide her time between London and New York. She had little interest in hearing about our aspirations and would go off then to get ice creams or hook up with her older sisters if they let her. 'Include me out,' she'd say and flounce off. She was perfecting a hair toss at the time and this was good practice. We knew she'd be back and never worried that she had actually fallen out with us. Dan and I had no problem day-dreaming in each other's company, silently or aloud.

'I'd like to drive a train,' was a favourite opening gambit of his. It morphed into designing them for a few months when he was fourteen and I can't remember why it was that he dropped that idea. He was probably crap at drawing, or thought he was, I don't recall exactly. He had a habit of scotching his own notions before ever letting them fly. He was good at arguing with himself and putting himself down. It meant he did very little that was constructive towards achieving any goal, like trying to be an engineer. Perhaps that removed any chance of failure too. Of course, I say this with the benefit of hindsight.

Me: 'Where would you go?'

Dan: 'All over. First England and then on from there.'

Me: 'I could be a passenger. I want to see the world.' (I have no idea where the money was to come from, though I did nurture a brief yen to be an air stewardess. Maybe I was more practical than I realised.)

Dan: 'I'd better get a job on the Orient Express.'

Me: 'You could invite me to the engine cab and we'd whizz along and laugh a lot.'

Dan: 'When the relief driver took over in the evening, we could sit in the beautiful bar and drink cocktails.'

Me: 'And watch the world go by.'

Dan: 'And laugh.'

We never did get to be that 'coupla swells' and I can't remember the last time we shared a laugh, unfettered and ribsore. If ever we speak of our ambitions any more they seem paltry, prosaic. Dan uses a strange tense that sums up our wasted lives. It goes along the lines of 'I'd have liked to have been', full of regret and failure. To give Donna her due, at least she made a bolt for it. She got out, even if it didn't last. I suppose she would say that was worse in the long run, because she caught a glimpse of what might have been.

The letter is rustling in my trembling hand. I am now the owner of a thriving business. I don't deserve it. My heart wants to burst at Dad's generosity and it quakes at his belief in me. I feel nauseous.

I remember Donna's expression at the graveside. She looked like she hated me. She may do. Isn't it widely believed that we hate what we fear most? I feel a little better for that thought. A little ashamed too, but I'm used to that. Donna's really going to resent this latest turn up, perhaps even more than my relationship with Dan. This line of reasoning lets me know I am going to take on Dad's challenge. He thought I might be up for it and maybe I am. I hope so. There's a lot riding on it. Now I am scared as well as nauseous but, again, that's no new thing. I am not an erudite woman but I hope I am not a stupid one either. I rather think we are all about to find out.

✿ ✿ ✿

Simon had to admit he had become a little obsessed with the idea that Kitty was having an affair. He constantly reminded himself that this news had been delivered by a woman no longer in full possession of her mental faculties, but the more he thought about it, the more sense it made. And it stood to reason that the other party was Dan Gibbs. They worked together. They had known each other since childhood. Their allotments were close by. Why this last detail counted he was at a loss to know but it did, for him at least, in the building of a case for his theory. He made casual enquiries about the station and its personnel and, as far as he could glean, Dan was the only likely candidate. With each new clue he felt a little more ensnared. He could not let it alone. He worried it like a scab on a soft healing wound, giving himself further pain and making things worse. If it turned out that his conjectures were wrong he knew his new starting point would be a whole lot worse for the hard time he'd already given himself. He almost hoped it *was* Dan Gibbs with whom Kitty was having this affair, which might or might not be happening. He was prepared for that.

He wondered what qualities he had that might be to his advantage in any competition for Kitty's affections. He put together a list of attributes in his mind that could be seen as wholesome or attractive. He was easy-going, but that was more a trait than anything else. Other descriptions like 'tall' didn't hack it either in convincing the rest of humanity, and one person in particular, that he was worthy of attention.

He was easy on the eye as a package, he assumed, never having had any complaints in that department. He was slightly worried that 'easy' was turning up so often on this list. He certainly had been a pushover for women to get into bed up until now, not something he'd willingly boast about.

He thought of advertisements in Singles columns where a good sense of humour seemed important. He had a GSOH and he hoped he made people laugh occasionally too. That must count as a plus, he felt. He was smart, in an academic way, and clever enough in a streetwise one. He wore his intelligence lightly, after all it wasn't rocket science, and his job wasn't one that would save the world except incrementally, he hoped, by encouraging people to read and explore. He knew he'd been loyal to his family of two but they were dead now. He had never made such firm friends that he was asked for loyalty in a major way as opposed to just being there regularly, making up numbers almost. He was generous. He hoped he could be loving. He wondered if he could be trusted.

This exercise was a depressing one, he concluded, leaving him with a fairly poor sense of self-worth. He tried once more. I am kind to animals, he thought, and (more often than not) people. Surely that's a positive? Oh, hell, he was a work in progress, but who was not?

He resolved to win her attention, at least in part, with the results of his search into the Napoleonic boat. He was now certain that was what they had here. In fact, this research project was the most focused aspect of his life, the rest being mostly in turmoil because of Kitty Fulton. At the library he spent far too much time walking the floor in case she came to exchange a book. He also walked around the town unnecessarily, though it also meant he was a regular feature there now and had a lot more nodding acquaintances. He wandered past the allotments, in case he might catch a glimpse of her, and often chatted with Jed, which was interesting but tough as the old man had a vocabulary of which Simon had no previous knowledge. He was making inroads, though, and they were not as divided by a common language as they had been at the start. He had no real reason to visit the train station and longed to have a journey to make so that he could see her there.

Clearly, the best way to show himself off to Kitty Fulton was to accumulate as much information as possible about her little ship, make an appointment to discuss it with her, and thereupon mesmerise her with the scale of his discoveries.

Miss Marshall is very kind about my being her new boss. She is probably dismayed, though, and I, for one, would not blame her if she were.

'I think I should just take over as a kind of caretaker for the moment, if that's acceptable? I am not convinced I will ever be able to do the job my father did. In fact, it would be ridiculous to think I could. I know nothing about publishing or any of the areas you cover.'

'Kitty, I just run the office. I do the grunt work. I have very little to do with the literary side of things,' Miss Marshall says. 'Your father obviously thought this a good plan.'

I think I am still in shock. I suffer from bouts of trembling that are unpredictable and sometimes quite violent.

'Why don't we go back to the office?' Miss Marshall suggests. 'You can have a look around and let this sink in. You might even get a feel for the place.'

I'm flying blind here, as I have not the slightest notion where to begin, so I agree. I still cannot bring myself to call her Marie. It doesn't sit right with me.

In my head, we 'repair' to the office. I hope this doesn't mean I have flowery taste in vocabulary. I don't think I do, but I'm still having rushes of blood to the head and must let them roll over me till I get the hang of at least looking the part. If pushed, I'd say I like beauty without pretension. I don't mind flashy occasionally, as long as the embellishment is earned. Dad always told me his work was about personal taste a lot of the time; that much is subjective in the world of art. In a climate of fads and constant artsy change your own taste is about all you can rely on – and even then it's hard to trust yourself fully.

It's disconcerting to see his desk, left just as it was when he went to buy that final jar of coffee. I circle it tentatively before sitting down in his swivel chair. I catch the faintest suggestion of him. It runs through me like electricity. When I was a kid I loved to twirl around on this but today I settle for a milder side-to-side action. There is a framed photo of the three of us on holiday in the Lake District, years ago, in pride of place on the desk. It doesn't have a label explaining who we are so it looks different from the ones I see at home every day. Alongside it is a small black-and-white shot of me as a child. I feel such love emanating from his chosen display that I could break under the crushing emotion of it all. 'Oh, Dad,' I say, remembering the feel of him at the hospital just after he left the world. 'Oh, Dad.'

I am not up to going through his things properly today. I just want to let the atmosphere permeate through me. I'm afraid of all that working here entails, afraid that I will fail him. All that will have to wait a while. But not long, a voice tells me. No, not long. If there is one thing I do know, and have learned bitterly, it is that we don't have the luxury of 'long'. Time is fleeting and precious.

I do fiddle about with the top layer of papers and already I can see some of the unfinished business he meant to attend to. He went so suddenly that his desk diary is crammed for weeks ahead with events he will never now attend. It hits me then like a ten-ton truck that I will have to clear out his house too. I sit there winded, gripping the desk. The shakes return. I am in no mood for swinging in the chair now. I just want to sit here, feeling him all around me still, able to believe that he might come walking through the door at any moment, in spite of all knowledge to the contrary. Just a little longer, I tell myself, and hope he doesn't mind. I am afraid my dithering will hold his spirit back in the world he has forsaken so I resolve to put a time limit on my self-indulgence. Easier said than done.

And I'm not sure I really believe in spirits, hovering or gone elsewhere. I have always thought we die and that's that, but the comforting notion of an Other World appeals to me now and I imagine Anubis, the Egyptian jackal god of death, looking after my father there, figuring out why he has so many books of poetry with him rather than grain and fowl, or gold to pay the ferryman to the Underworld. I can only hope that dark sailor is a man of letters and the arts. I imagine a frieze, picturing Dad in formal profile on a funeral barque, bathed in a radiant light that speaks to me of happiness.

There is a note scribbled on a xeroxed page of poetry, slipped into the jotter, It says, 'Show Kitty, ref ancient graffiti'. The verse is by Byron, of all people. How like Dad to make no concession to my lack of scholarship.

    . . . approach this consecrated land
    And pass in peace along the magic waste:
    But spare its relics – let no busy hand
    Deface the scenes, already how defaced!

I wonder where in the world the poet is writing about. I must look it up. I only realise I am crying when Miss Marshall hands me a tissue.

✧ ✧ ✧

Kitty took the train home to Pennick, alighted at the familiar station and checked that no harm had befallen the office. Someone had left a schoolbag on the 16.26 from Fetchley, which would provide the perfect excuse not to do any homework. She looked inside and found it belonged to Amanda Pike. Unlucky for Amanda, then, that Kitty knew where she lived and delivered it to her door as it was on her way home. She wasn't being mean; it was a bulky item and they didn't have room for unnecessary clutter in the office. She saw neither Benny, Roly nor Dan, and was glad of that. She didn't know what to say to any of them. Big changes were in the offing and she needed time to think and plot her next move. These decisions were hers to make, for better or worse; she should not involve anyone else.

Val was waiting to hear her news. He had taken over supervisory duties when May returned from the day's outing to the local miniature pony centre. When Kitty told him she had inherited the business, he shrugged and said, 'Stands to reason.' Was she the only one to be surprised? Scratch surprised, she was shocked to her core and the shakes started up again.

'Glass of wine for you, my dear,' Val said, and went to make good on the offer.

'I want a pony,' May told her.

'We'll talk about it later.'

'You never let me have anything.'

Her mother sat on her favourite chair, pouting, but relaxed when Val presented her with a white wine spritzer.

'You don't want her rat-arsed and troublesome,' he said to Kitty.

'Amen to that.'

'Fizzy,' May said, tasting the drink and happy with it.

Val smiled indulgently at her. 'Chris Cant was freaked because he thought someone had shrunk the horses. May told him he was a stupid boy and that they were dogs.'

'Can we get a dog?' her mother piped up.

'We'll see.'

'Grumpy bum,' May said, smiling as if butter wouldn't melt.

ELEVEN

Kitty's always wanted what I had. She always has, and probably always will. Kind of strange, seeing as how she was so spoiled at every turn, but then she has that doe-eyed way about her that makes you feel she's being neglected when the opposite is true. Or that's how it seems to me. She's had it cushy. All I ever heard from her is, 'You're so lucky, you've got this, that and the other.' Well, let me tell you, luck doesn't come into it. Never has, never seems to want to.

She's always had this weird crush on me. And Dan, of course, but we'll deal with that later. When we were kids she'd follow me around like a stray pup. The more I tried to get rid of her, the more she stuck, so I sort of gave in, I suppose you could say, and let her be with me. Wasn't all bad, we had a laugh. But I did get sick of her taking up what little space we had spare in our house, mooning over everything we had – or didn't have, more like. She seemed to think it was great to live in a place like an asylum – didn't know squit about it. As kids we never had things of our own, everything was some kind of hand-me-down. Even if you liked your sister's best dress you knew it'd be knackered by the time it got to you, a whisper of what you had wanted. Shoes were the worst, if they survived an older sister, all dark stains from skinned heels and wonky if they walked to one side. Mostly the shoes didn't make it down the line, unless they were dressy, special occasion shoes, and thank fuck for that.

Everyone thought Kitty was harmless but then things started to happen and I began to wonder about that. She destroyed my birthday present once. Hadn't had it more than two hours before it was broken. I knew it wasn't any of my family; I had ways of checking. It had to be Kitty. Made sense, too. I waited for her to tell me, like she should have if she was really the best friend she was supposed to be. She never did. That should have told me all I needed to know. But I was a kid. I got over it and moved on. It was only later I got to realising its significance. But that's always the way. You know later what would have been really handy at the time and saved a shit-load of grief coming down. I mean, we could have avoided other things happening. And maybe I did know it was a memory I should hang on to because I didn't throw the broken bits away but kept them as a reminder of treachery at the hands of somebody close to me.

So, she had this crush on me, and for a short while when we were teens it got intense. That was a mad time. Whatever.

She took it all so seriously. I didn't mind finding a few things out but, to look at Kitty and her carry-on then, you'd think it was a major love affair or something. I mean, *really*. I wanted to say, Get over it, move on with your life. It's what I did and what I've always done. When you come nowhere in a big family, you have to make your mark or get swallowed up and overlooked. That's made me very independent and I have fought for everything I've achieved. I sometimes wonder if Kitty knows the meaning of hard work.

Dan saved me from a lot, though I don't think he entirely realised it at the time. He was the third member of our gang and the best one too. I might have killed Kitty if it hadn't been for him. He made the arrangement bearable.

Strange that someone as seemingly bland as Dan could have two women on the go. But he does. I think it's the fact that he is so open and encouraging and he really does believe everything he says at the very moment he's saying it. I think he's incapable of giving anyone bad news like 'I'm having an affair with your best friend' or 'I don't love you any more' or 'My wife is having our baby and I am committed to us'. Some would say this is cowardly but maybe it's a sort of warped kindness. I have known him so long I can hardly find it in myself to judge him any more. I wouldn't know where to start. Can't see the wood for the trees type of thing.

The Kitty, me and him thing goes way, way back. Sounds better in the French: a ménage à trois. The French always seem to make unsavoury things acceptable by the words they use. It is the very sound of romance, that language. We were all a bit in love with one another, I guess. Dan and me just went further. It seemed natural. Of course, I knew Kitty was mad about him too, a blind man could have spotted that, but I always knew he'd be mine if I wanted. And I did want him.

I'd always planned on leaving Hicksville. Pennick had nothing to offer, so I played out my time at school and waited for the day when I could split. I wanted to be a model. I had the looks, the drive. A Town Called Panic had nothing for me in that area so I had to get out. I had a few shots at making it but they didn't end up the way I'd thought they would. Turned out I was always going to be the country bumpkin. I remember hearing one photographer in a warehouse in the East End of London snigger and describe me as: 'Luscious. All Norfolk cow and milkiness.' Then the next minute he was mid-patter with his, 'The camera LOVES you, Donna, really, really LOVES you.' I was the wholesome summer fuck for a city boy on a farm holiday. 'All come-to-bed-eyes and *open*,' as I heard him say into the phone. Bastard. Sniffing constantly from too much coke and opportunity. Fuck him. And he did want me to by the end of the session, by the way. I made sure of that. 'Yeah, right, go fuck yourself, mister,' is what he got told then. I felt fat and useless and I knew I wasn't; I hadn't had a square meal in three years and I wasn't afraid of hard graft.

Kitty had her own opportunity to get out. She was bright

enough to do well and go to college. Instead she flunked her exams and stayed put. I always suspected she did it to be close to Dan, maybe even me too. She's never had much ambition. You couldn't describe her job at the station as any great shakes. But she seems content with little enough. Of course Dan got her that and she jumped at the chance to work alongside him every day. Took me ages to see what was going on there. I felt so belittled when I did but, by then, I had other things to worry about and it didn't seem like such a big fucking deal. Amazing how time can skew a situation.

Whenever I came home, after each and every knock back, Dan was there for me. I took a lot of my frustration out on him, but he was my rock. We became even closer. I got pregnant. Old story, I know, I know. That's when I knew I was a proper Pennick gal, all right, because we were never not getting married, if you know what I mean. We never considered any other alternative, actually. Never wanted to. I didn't mind that bit. I really didn't want to be knocked up, though. I could tell from Kitty's eyes that she thought I'd deliberately trapped Dan. Well, lady, I wanted to say, it takes two.

Maybe the baby sensed the resentment. Maybe I hadn't enough vitamins in me after the years of slimming or downright starvation. Maybe the world wasn't ready for him and he knew it. He didn't last. It was a he, as it happens. I thought that was the worst pain I would ever feel, but it wasn't. Kitty and Dan saw to that.

I was adrift after the miscarriage. Dan didn't know how to help me and, because I didn't know how to help myself, I couldn't steer him in any particular direction. I didn't care about anything. That's when he gave Kitty the job at the station. I felt so lonely. I never got the hunger back for my modelling career either. It didn't seem important any more. I wanted the baby very badly once I couldn't have him and I felt so terribly guilty, too, like I had killed him somehow with my body's poisonous resentment. I spent years trying to re-create him but until now it hasn't worked out.

In the meantime, I set up a small beauty business. I can't stay still for long. I don't want to be beholden to Dan for money either. I believe in having financial independence. And if I want something, I like to think I can get it for myself and not have to rely on handouts from someone else. That's the legacy of being the kid in the middle in a big family.

So, Dan and Kitty. What is there to say, really? They're in love, I suppose, but I know he loves me too, very, very much. I raged like a wild thing when I finally realised what was going on but always stopped short of confrontation. I'm not sure why that is. Maybe it's that we three have been together so long that it was kind of inappropriate to talk about what the other two were up to. I can't really explain it. And I suppose I always thought it would peter out. I quit wifely duties, from time to time, if that's the way to put it, but it was pointless because, hey, he was getting his oats elsewhere so it's not like it was total punishment for him.

And they have been so discreet all along. God, listen to me, practically condoning this unforgivable thing.

But I must have some forgiveness in me because I take my husband home every night.

The little things have hurt the most. The laughs they share at work that I will never hear about. Those bloody vegetable patches they've got. I have seen all of the things he's brought her back over the years from breaks and holidays we took. I'm not sure if he has actually done a 'wish you were here' postcard but I imagine he has, and meant it too, maybe. That's very hard for me to endure and it's best not to dwell on it. I want my marriage to work now. I'm fighting hard for it and I won't take no for an answer. Failure is not an option, as the Americans say.

Once, after a lovely weekend in a B&B in Devon, he brought back two oak saplings. I know where they both are: one is out in our back garden, in its own decorative pot, and the other is in Kitty's. He must really think I'm thick if he imagines I wouldn't notice that. I can only thank the Lord above they are not in matching frigging pots. I asked him one winter, for a joke, if ours was dead. He looked at me like I was the most stupid person ever to tread shoe leather. I wanted to scream at him, 'I did biology too. I know it's a fucking deciduous tree.' I didn't. I was too disappointed in his opinion of me, so I let it slide.

Like a lot of things.

I got a tattoo. 'Donna loves Dan', it says. I deliberately

wanted it that way round. It felt like inking his guilt on to my skin. I don't know what he really thinks of it, this self-branding, but I mean it and I don't care who sees it. I'm always ready to show it off.

Why have I put up with it all? Simple. I love him. I am devoted to him and always have been. Sometimes it hurts me to look at him and feel so strongly about him. There are times when I can't blame Kitty for being mad about him too; it makes perfect sense. But he is mine and I have officially had enough. It's no joke being the Other Woman in your own marriage. Laughable, yes. Bewildering. Awful. She'll have to back off now. We have to be given a proper chance to be a family. Did I mention I'm pregnant? I won't lose this baby through my own unhappiness. I want it to know that it is loved, respected: all the things I want for myself, really.

I sent her my broken birthday gift. Parting with the pieces after all these years was symbolic for me, a letting go. I know she'll get the message.

Her dad has died and I've never seen her look more beautiful. Grief suits Kitty. She had this otherworldly glow at the funeral. I think I must have been staring at her because the new librarian gave me some funny looks. I felt like vomiting my morning sickness all over him then and shouting, You haven't a clue, but he looked like he was putting a lot of things together that day and it wasn't making him too happy. I should have welcomed him to the club. The mum was out of it, of course, away with her dementia. Kitty's plate is full. But so is mine. I am making a fresh start and she'll have to as well. Without me. Without Dan.

TWELVE

I need time to think. So much has happened, I have staggered through one event and on to the next without any
real consideration for what each one means. I have to take
stock. I will ask Dan for compassionate leave and spend a
fortnight weighing up my options. This is what I decide in
my three precious minutes before reality hits me. I get out
of bed and immediately begin to backtrack. I decide to
work out the week, on the grounds that I have organised
Mum's routine till then and don't want to upset her by
changing it at short notice. Chances are she'd be oblivious,
but she has been more distracted and upset since Dad died
and I don't want to make it worse. We'll all suffer even
more if I do, not just her. So I'll stick to my original plan
for the rest of the week. Then I wonder if it's merely
cowardice prompting me and I am simply putting off
inevitable changes. But I am too tired to go into that. I will
stay at the station till Friday evening then take a step back

to consider my options. Ding-ding, time up, on into the day.

Mum appears to be hiding behind the sofa when I go downstairs.

'There are people here,' she tells me.

'Really?' There shouldn't be. We may operate an open-door policy, in general, but this is the earliest we've had visitors by a long shot. 'Where are they?' I ask.

'There,' she whispers loudly, indicating the fireplace, then makes a gesture to me to shush in case they hear us.

I don't see any intruders, friend or foe. 'They've gone now,' I say and make for the kitchen. I am in need of a bracing cup of tea.

'One of them is back!' she shrieks.

I return to see her hiding again. Still no invader to be seen. Still no evidence of anyone. 'Where?' I ask.

She points to the fireplace again, though higher, and I realise what has happened. We have a large mirror hanging there which gives a bit of extra depth to the room. It would appear to be multiplying the number of people within it now, too. I stand in front of it, point, and say, 'It's a mirror, Mum. It shows us to ourselves. That's me there.' She peeks out from behind the sofa, still unconvinced. Gradually she edges round the side and considers my reflection.

'She looks like you,' she says, which is a good start.

'Come stand beside me,' I urge, and slowly she does, her

eyes downcast. When she raises them, she shrieks again and dives away.

'Mum, it's a mirror. We are meant to be in there.' I hope I have put it in language she can fathom. 'Come back and I'll show you.'

She approaches again, gingerly, and I point at our reflections. 'There we are,' I say. 'There's me, and there's you.'

'That's not me,' she says, genuinely aghast. 'That's me.' She points at a photograph taken many decades ago of a fresh-faced girl sitting in a garden. She doesn't recognise the old lady in the mirror. Nor does she seem bothered by the fact that the May she recognises in the photo is in black and white.

Kitty followed her breath all the way to the allotment. She maintained a brisk pace, as exercise was the one sure salve for her grief. She always felt better after a good stretch of the legs. She breathed deeply, the icy cold slicing through her throat and lungs. It felt cleansing and good. She checked the plot over for form's sake, not expecting to find much as the earth continued its winter break. She had a great desire to dig a big trench but resisted it when her thoughts drifted to the idea that this was akin to digging a grave. She needed to think, not bury herself, as attractive as the latter notion was. The air cleared her head and left a blankish canvas ready for tainting with plans-in-progress.

Work was the nub of the latest dilemma. If she took on

the proper running of the publisher's, she would have to give up the station. Her father's letter was in her pocket and, without needing to read it again, she recalled his phrase 'you have given enough of your life to it'. He knew, she thought. Everyone seemed to know about her and Dan. She was so battered by the vagaries of the last weeks, months and years that she couldn't even feel mortified that her life was an open secret. She wondered if Dan realised their hidden closeness was probably common, but unmentioned, knowledge.

The allotment was redolent of their alternative universe. She was suddenly torn between the urgent desire to see him, to touch him, but also to run from the place in case he appeared. She would have to face him at work but that was different. The station was a carefully managed environment where both of them were restrained. They seldom touched intimately there. This stretch of allotments marked the boundaries of their romance and abandon. It was hardly the ice palace of Dr Zhivago. Still, they had loved and been happy here in their shadow world.

Dan would hold her in his arms and whisper, 'I love this. It's just you and me, and no one else need ever know.'

I am standing in a field in an area hardly anyone has heard of, wondering if I am a laughing stock to the whole town. Shame burns in my cheeks. What Dan and I did was wrong. I have always known that deep down. But somehow, because I was so in love, I rose above any troubling feelings of guilt and let the wrong continue. I convinced myself I had no option, that love was the only path I could follow. I wonder if love isn't the laziest excuse in the world for being weak? And the handiest. It was unworthy behaviour by any standard. I cannot shake off the grubby taint of dishonour.

I now know there was no alternative code of loyalty in this special place of ours. I have been faithful to Dan but he has not been to me. He couldn't have been, I know, and it was unfair and stupid of me to expect that he would be. I chose to ignore the inconvenient truth. It was easy for me to be for him alone because I *am* alone. He did not have that luxury, if luxury is the proper way of putting it. And, to be fair, he never promised to love me alone. In fact, he never promised me anything at all.

Donna is right to hate me. I hate myself for what I have done. I've been such a hypocrite, too, with my years of naïvely contemplating the way our friendship changed. I made that happen. I stole away her man and helped create a parallel life that made a mockery of their marriage. It's no wonder she cannot abide me.

I look at the allotments with new eyes, shaken to think this sacred place might become impossible for me to be in from now on. No, I can't let that happen. This is my haven, no matter what. It stands for more than Dan and me in my life. I could not bear to be without it. We all live with the sadness a loved place can bring, the memories it evokes and the disappointment felt there. I will have to adapt to this plot's new, leaner purpose, that's all. I hurry away, unable to deal with any further shifts of perspective. If I let regret take hold, it will devour me like a cancer.

Roly is hungry and vocal about it when I arrive at the office.

'Oh, hush,' I tell him.

He leaps on to the desk and head-butts me a couple of times. There are mucky paw prints all over my jotter when he descends to demolish his breakfast. I wipe down the mess without a murmur. Clearly I relish abuse.

Simon went over the items on his desk then checked them twice more. When he was fully satisfied that he was ready for all questions and eventualities concerning the boat, he called Kitty. He found the hand that was holding the phone trembled as he spoke to her. He was no better than a teenager with a crush.

'Why don't you come to the house after work?' she suggested. 'I'll heat up a lasagne and we can take it from there. I have to be on duty for Mum anyhow so I'm confined to barracks.'

He was delighted with the notion but tried to conceal that by his tone of voice because he felt he had made enough of a tit of himself as it was.

'You should bring Mona Fletcher too, you know. She's the

leading light of the local Historical Society and I'm sure she'd love to be involved.'

Simon's heart crunched into a tight ball as his hope of a sneaky date was blown out of the water.

'Of course,' he managed. 'Good thinking.'

He hung up, swearing at his own stupidity and Kitty's gracious inclusiveness.

'A person can be too nice,' he said aloud. 'And I don't mean that in a good way.'

He knew if he hesitated he wouldn't ask Mona along and would then have to lie to Kitty so he left his office immediately and located Mona in the gardening section, having a snooze. She was happy to accept their kind invitation. Was there a meaningful glint in her eye?

'Aren't you the sly one,' was all she said.

The newspaper tells me that celery is the new superfood to safeguard mental health. The thought of eating it in winter, particularly raw, actually makes me feel hungry and cold. There is a tortured pun about a worker looking for Celery Benefits, which actually makes me groan aloud. Hooray for celery, though, as it joins camomile and green peppers which contain similar helpful chemicals. This celery theory is based on experiments involving mice that have been genetically modified to develop Alzheimer's. I am in a quandary about that. I really don't believe in experimenting on animals, yet I want us to find a cure. I don't want other families to have to go through the hell we are. And the government wants to avoid further big bills: that should mean something gets done. Economics are a potent carrot, a vegetable that is probably another cure waiting to happen. It currently costs about seventeen billion pounds a year to care for dementia sufferers.

I have to remove Roly forcibly from the tartan blanket when its owner arrives. The man regards the cat hair, sniffs the cloth and looks sour. I half hope his head doubles in size from an allergic reaction, he's being so mean about my boy, however silently he's doing it. I decide to retaliate by printing off a form I keep on the computer for people I don't like to fill in and sign. I sweetly hand the man a pen and tell him, effectively, to get with the programme. Roly curls up on my empty warm chair while this is happening. He keeps his eyes on the action as he loves to see me waste nasty people's time.

Dan appears, long faced again, and it grates on my nerves. He may be sad we've parted but he is having a baby with the woman he loves and chose to marry, and both of his parents are still alive. By my reckoning that's a good innings. If he is adopting the sad expression for my benefit, he's wasting his time. The longing I felt for him at the allotment has mysteriously evaporated. The thought of him touching me now actively sends a shiver through me. I didn't know I had it in me to turn against Dan like this. I'm being unfair, I tell myself. I am venting everything on him because he is the person closest to me.

'What's up?' I ask, trying to sound casual.

'I miss you.'

'There's not a lot we can do about that.'

'I wish I could help you more. I should be here for you now.'

'Beware of sounding like a pop song,' I warn. It's unkind and I feel I should let him off the hook. This man is clearly suffering too. 'You have a lot to deal with yourself,' I concede.

'How did it go with the lawyer yesterday?'

'Fine. Dad left me the business.'

Dan looks utterly deflated to hear this.

'Would it be possible for me to take two weeks' compassionate leave, to have a think and sort a few things out?' I ask.

'Of course.'

I feel I am already halfway out the door.

Dan wondered how his voice could sound so steady? He marvelled that he'd got those two words 'of course' out without roaring them above the sounds of his whole world shattering into even smaller pieces. Careful with the pop song sentiments again, he told himself. Kitty was right: he was trite. He knew immediately that she would take up this escape route she had been offered. She would be a fool not to, and her father had counted on her common sense winning out. Dan wouldn't stand in her way. She deserved this chance.

But that wasn't the worst of it. This time she was leaving

him behind too and his sense of loss was so profound that Dan began to cry. Kitty did not move to comfort him. He had ensured that she could not when he had told her his news and ruined everything between them. You ruined it a long time before that, a voice inside him said. He wanted to throw himself under the next through train but knew by now he didn't have the courage for such decisive action.

In the past I'd often asked Mum, 'Why Pennick?' to which she would answer, 'Why not?' if she didn't want to talk about it, or else give a sigh before launching into yet another explanation. As it happened, it was a bit of an accident.

'Darling, your father and I love one another dearly but we cannot live together. We did try but it was a disaster.'

This was usually how the explanation began, the reassurance that all was fundamentally well in the world but human beings, flawed as we are, sometimes have to make do. Nothing much to worry about.

'I began to look for somewhere to rent and I don't know why but I didn't want to live in Norwich, as beautiful as it is. I wanted a bit of countryside round me, I suppose, with the benefits of a small town thrown in. On a drive one Sunday we stopped in Pennick and I thought it was quaint, the way people do until they get to know it properly.'

She never meant this in a cruel way. Pennick is so laid-back about itself it's hard to imagine any concerted plan to make it attractive to strangers coming together. It is what it is, and that seemed to have appealed to my mother.

'I rented a place for us both here and liked the way everybody accepted us without making a big deal of it. At the time that also seemed important to me. You loved it. We seemed to fit in here without too many problems. I could work from home, refrain from murdering your dad yet still nip into Norwich if I needed to. Stephen was only a train hop or a drive away for visiting you. We never left.'

I think the bland, humdrum nature of life in Pennick came as something of a relief to her. As a young girl, she couldn't wait to leave her home in Ireland. She loved her mother and sister but felt suffocated living at close quarters with them.

'There was an elemental misery in our household. We seemed to live permanently under a shadow, with my father taking off and the boys dying. I thought it would drag me under too so I had to get out. I miss it, in the way we all do the notion of home and heritage, but it would have killed me to stay. It would have sucked me dry.'

I had met my maternal grandmother and knew that she was a woman who would always pull you down. I don't know if she realised that she was crushing the life out of others, but it's more than likely she did. She disapproved of my mother bettering herself, 'having notions' she called it, which was rich given that she herself had insisted on having a job when she was a young mother. She stifled any striving for success in others, especially her own family, and, from what I can gather, mocked aspiration as a means to ending it. There was a sort of jealousy at work within her that couldn't bear to see others do well or have any luck.

After Ellen died, I think any good Mum saw in Ireland faded completely. Of course, then there was no one else but her mother to visit and she went back only on short, duty holidays to see her. She would often swear she didn't miss the place at all, but her eyes would sometimes tear up to see travel programmes about it or to hear sad news on a bulletin. Now, with the disease, she will probably never visit Ireland again. It has been taken from her twice.

I used to wonder if we were a household of single women because of my grandfather running off. It seemed harsh, though, to heap blame on him, he being all but a stranger to me, and it's not as if I grew up without a dad. Perhaps there's simply a trait running through us Fulton women that makes us pick unsuitable men. Or unavailable ones at any rate.

'Sly one,' May repeated after Mona.

Simon felt horribly uncomfortable.

'Never told me what he was working on,' the ex-librarian continued.

'It was theoretical until now,' he protested.

Kitty laughed. 'Don't let her get to you. We are all just overexcited to have a real, live man to ourselves the whole evening, to torture as we please. Isn't that right, Mona?'

'Oh, yes. We haven't had this much fun since we set fire to the Mayoral robes two years ago.'

'She made that up,' Kitty told Simon. 'I think.'

They cleared the table and he laid out his findings. This is my heart stripped bare before her he thought, then struggled after that line of Yeats about treading on his dreams . . . and told himself not to be a soppy idiot.

'History is an affecting subject,' Mona assured him. 'It's okay to be soppy about it as long as your research is scholarly and substantiated.'

Good grief, he was speaking his thoughts aloud now too. Simon cleared his throat and began his presentation.

'As I have mentioned to Kitty before, Pennick was used, briefly, as a Parole Town for captured French soldiers during the Napoleonic Wars in the early nineteenth century. The town was host to officers, for the main part, as they were deemed the most naturally honourable and it was assumed they could be relied on to observe the curfews imposed. These men were popular with the higher levels of Pennick society as they were educated, cultured, and could usually speak some English. In fact, many were treated more as guests than prisoners. Throughout the country, for instance, captured doctors and surgeons were allowed set up practice and a few were repatriated for their good deeds while on British soil. Inevitably, some soldiers fell for local ladies and even married into the area. When Pennick was decommissioned as a Parole Town, after one too many escapes, the prisoners were moved on. Some eventually made it home to France, some died here, and some returned to the war and were killed.

'One of the sidelines they had, to make some extra cash, was to fashion small *objets* for sale, using bone or sometimes fabric. These were also made as mementoes for sweethearts.' He dared look straight at Kitty then. 'The pieces are quite rare and much prized now. Plymouth City Museum has some very fine, very intricate examples made of bone, and there is a truly remarkable working model of a Spinning Jenny in a French museum, measuring just four and a half inches. I took the liberty of making some photocopies of those for you.'

He handed these to his rapt audience and gulped down a mouthful of ice-cold Pinot Grigio. He picked the ship up and held it out for the three ladies to see.

'I think that is what we have here. I am certain this boat is made of bone and believe it was crafted by a French prisoner on parole in Pennick. It is so rare I cannot find mention of another piece like it anywhere in the archives, and I'm sure it is very valuable.'

'Basis?' Mona barked, ever rigorous.

She was correct to question this bold statement of his, but Simon was ready for her.

'When Kitty and I cleaned the boat,' he said, delighted with the way that sounded and the closeness it hinted at, 'we discovered some initials on it. I have been investigating those further. They were FVAC, as far as we could make out.' He looked over to Kitty who nodded, enthralled. 'I now believe they are in fact two sets of initials rather than one: FV and AC. Extant records of the French officers held here are rare, as far as I can tell so far. Some turn up in legal documents because they spent time in the town jail for various minor offences. Incidentally, I visited the cell in the basement of the Town Hall and I am happy to report that there is some splendid graffiti still visible on the walls. One barely legible piece is in French. I hope to be able to have that restored, if the powers that be permit. It has been whitewashed over a number of times but not obliterated.'

'How exciting,' Kitty told him.

'Yes. It is . . . very. I'm glad you agree. I'm not suggesting it has any connection with your find, that would be too much of a coincidence, but it could be from the same time.'

'Or not,' Mona warned.

'Or not, of course,' he agreed hastily. 'It doesn't pertain totally or directly to our quest, at any rate.' He gulped some more wine. 'I have checked various rosters kept at some of the local big houses where work details of the French were employed. And the Constabulary kept lists of men who had to report to them each day while they were stationed here so I have put in a request to see those. A few of the merchant families also kept records which I have just drawn up from the archives. I may need help trawling those or this will all take much longer than I can stand because I really want to know as much about these people as I can find out. I know the work of a historian is painstakingly slow but I haven't been this revved up in years.'

'Do you have any clues about FV and AC yet?' Kitty asked.

Mona looked incredibly stern now so Simon tried to keep his voice as non-committal as he could. 'Well, I think I may know who FV is . . .' He paused, enjoying the thrall in which he held his small audience. He relished the moment. He had worked hard for it. 'In 1805 a François Villeneuve was sent to Pennick. His name is the only one matching one set of the initials.'

'So far,' Mona interjected. 'So far. It is a big assumption that those are the French initials. Perhaps AC was the French personage. Or perhaps they were both French.'

Mona was right. He had been so intent on impressing Kitty that he had let enthusiasm run away with him. It was hardly scholarly.

'That's true,' he admitted.

Mona was relentless. 'You *want* this piece to turn out to be a romantic gift, it seems to me. Well, you have a lot more work to put in before you can claim that.'

Simon took his ticking off meekly. He deserved it.

I really enjoy the evening. Simon and Mona are great to be with. She gives him a hard time, but only to keep him up to the mark. I think he was a bit embarrassed by her criticism but I feel sure it will spur him on. It has been a welcome escape to lose myself in good company and such fascinating discoveries. Mum too is diverted, if confused, by the history lesson. I send her to bed hoping she will have pleasant and romantic dreams based on what she heard tonight, and not of soldiers shooting at one another or Napoleon terrorising her. I don't want her to be 'frykened', as she puts it.

I tidy up and discover that Mum has been busy earlier. She has run the dishwasher full of woollens. Most are fine. However, one sweater has hated the experience and will only fit a nine year old from now on. When it is dry, I'll leave it into the charity shop and hope they don't display it in the window. I can picture Mum raging in and demanding her jumper back. She'll probably remember it better than she does me by now, such is the cruel nature of her condition.

My own comfort-cardi is among the damp items but it has escaped harm. It has been through so much I think it may be invincible. I'll need it tomorrow for my last day at the station. I drape it over a radiator and snuggle up in bed, listening to the wind build into a gale around the house. We have made it through another day.

THIRTEEN

Mum is blocking up the taps and plughole in the bathroom when I try to get in for a wee. She is crouched down below the cabinet over the sink in case her reflection sees her. She doesn't recognise herself up here either.

'We have to keep them out,' she tells me in a low voice.

There is no way of convincing her that these people are us, or that they don't exist, when she can see them every day in here and over the fireplace. The mirrors will have to go.

'I'll talk to them,' I say and buy some time.

She scurries into her room to dress. From the landing I see her hand mirror is face down on the floor under the bed. The proper place for a personal bogeyman. I take it with me, telling her it's broken, but she doesn't care about it or even realise what I have done as she's busy teaming an orange blouse with a red pullover. Those top designers who encouraged us to wear clashing colours recently should have her as their muse. I call Mum when breakfast is ready and watch as she comes down the stairs sideways, one step at a time, both feet meeting on the same tread before she moves on. She looks like a much older person. I cannot tell whether she is being careful or has forgotten how to do this small everyday journey the conventional way.

Hannah will watch Mum until it's time for her to go swimming with the support group. Our neighbour helps me lift the big mirror off the wall downstairs and we put it away in the garden shed. Next to be moved is the bathroom cabinet. Afterwards I take Mum to see the blank spaces.

'I asked them to leave,' I tell her. 'They've gone now.'

She seems content with that. She touches the wall above the fireplace and then checks the alcoves to both sides, to be sure the strangers are not hiding there. We watch her go upstairs to look over the bathroom again.

'I miss May,' Hannah says.

'Me too.'

'It's the other lass in her place now. Even though she looks and sounds just like May, she's different, isn't she? It's odd to see my old friend and hear her voice but not recognise what she's saying or the ideas she's having.' Hannah sighs. 'What's to become of us all?' she asks of no one in particular.

'We couldn't manage without you.'

'You'd do the same for me.'

Would I, though? Am I that generous? Maybe we don't know ourselves well enough to say until we are called upon. And we probably shouldn't wait till then, if we're any good at all.

'Today is my last at the station,' I tell her. It sounds ominous when I put it like that. 'For a while, at least,' I add, to take some of the edge off it. I pull my special cardigan tight about me. It smells clean and comforting.

Mum comes back and says, 'Napoleon was here last night.'

I see Hannah's perplexed expression but I don't have time to explain.

'He had a boat,' Mum goes on.

I am amazed. 'Long story,' I say to Hannah as she suppresses a smile. Unfairly, I'm leaving Mum looking as though she's off on one. 'He sort of was here, actually, with a boat.'

Hannah holds her hands up to ward off any more unlikely information. 'You can fill me in later.' She clearly thinks we're both unhinged.

'He was a lot taller than I expected,' Mum is telling her as I leave the house.

Simon had a new sense of purpose in his step. He all but skipped through the marble entrance of the Town Hall and had to stop himself from whistling. He saluted some lawyers he recognised and took the stairs two at a time. He greeted the library staff with extra cheer and could feel their scrutiny on his back as he tripped along the corridor to his office.

'Lovely day,' he declared to anyone who cared to listen. It was not. Wind and rain were mauling Pennick like a bear with a grudge.

He snagged a quick instant coffee and set about his acquisitions forms, determined to clear his desk of the dross he had allowed to gather and setting lunchtime as his cut-off point. He found it difficult to concentrate, wanting to delve more deeply into his private research yet not neglect his job. He would have loved some downtime to devote himself to the boat project but was new here and couldn't just bunk off because it suited him, even if he was the boss.

He had a hot date with a parish register later, and over lunch would look at some printouts pertaining to the nineteenth-century parole prisoners.

'Pennick's Parole Prisoners,' he said aloud, then repeated it quickly a number of times in the manner of a tongue-twister. He added some extra words and finally had 'Problems Pertaining to Pennick's Parole Prisoners' to contend with. Juicy and a challenge. 'And the tongue-twister's not bad either,' he said aloud to make himself laugh. He was an idiot, he decided, no two ways about it.

Life was good. Life was exciting. Kitty Fulton was in the world. As the song went, 'Who could ask for anything more?'

He sent off a request for information to the National Archives and emailed Mona to ask her to look up the local Genealogical Society's records. He wasn't sure if they were on-line yet. There were military records at Kew, too, which might cover the time they were interested in. 'Kew, too,' he repeated, and made himself chuckle again.

It wasn't much by way of a last day, if it was to be truly that at all. Passengers came and went. Kitty helped the oldsters who hated using the ticket machine. She warned off a few teenagers who were likely up to no good. They called back that she was a slag. No argument there. She fed Roly and patted his head when he demanded it. He was hard to shift from her lap. She took in a bag of shopping left by the coffee dispenser; no perishables so it was plonked straight on a shelf. Dan brought her a bar of chocolate. She wanted to cry. All in all, a regular day's work at Pennick railway station. She needed to keep it that way. If this was a momentous occasion she wanted to realise it purely in retrospect. Otherwise she might not get through it.

The wind rattled the windows and the rain was so heavy she could hear it bounce off the ground. It was a symphonic accompaniment to this new phase of her life. The concourse was littered with umbrellas blown inside out and abandoned, their spindly, broken struts set at painful, strange angles. She found herself being remarkably gentle as she picked them up and binned them. Dan walked the platforms advising people to stand well back in case they slipped in front of an incoming train. He terrified all but the most foolish.

At 15, The Cottages, Hannah passed the baton to Val when the swimming trip was over. He telephoned Kitty to say that May was complaining about sharing the pool with 'spastics' and he couldn't guarantee she'd stop using the word. She'd also put her dry clothes on over her wet swimsuit and no one had noticed. She was now in a new outfit and didn't see what the fuss was about. He confirmed there'd be a visit by a Healthcare Visitor next week to assess their request for more full-time care.

'If she's anything like this during the inspection, you are going to get all they can give,' he promised. 'Oh, by the way, she asked me if her father was dead. I said yes, and she was upset and wanted to know why it had been kept from her. She fell asleep crying, though it was forgotten about by the time she woke up.'

Before he rang off Kitty heard May in the background saying, *'Gracias'*. Val explained she was picking up a bit of Spanish from *Dora the Explorer*, one of her favourite television programmes.

'Great,' Kitty said. 'She can't remember me most of the time but she's learning a new language.'

Val chuckled. 'The mind is a different country, as someone ought to have said.'

I have a vision of a holiday we took once. I don't know exactly where it was but Mum, Dad and I were on a boat in the middle of a lake. Mum trailed her hand in the water and soaked up the sun with a lazy smile on her face, like in a movie. I remember her looking at Dad with what

I now know to be desire and love. It gave me a warm feeling. She stood up and dived into the water, making the boat rock and splashing water over us. When she surfaced many yards away she was laughing. Almost without reason, I thought at the time. I know now it was the sound of pure joy because of the place and the day and because we were all there together. She swam back through the glistering water, her strokes making regular and beautiful patterns on the surface. She reached the boat looking ecstatic. 'Look at me,' she'd said. 'I am so lucky.' She might as well have said, I love you.

The memory pierces me, hard and to the quick. The wonder is that I do not fall to the ground and cry out. I am so disappointed that I don't. Being constantly worn out lacks passion or rage. I feel I am betraying her with my apparent calm, as if I have given in to the unacceptable. I must seem like such a cold fish.

The shakes start again. Who am I kidding? I can't take on running a business I know nothing about, or any business for that matter. What am I but a glorified receptionist who knows her way around a wages spreadsheet? I calculate simple sums and present them plausibly with the aid of a computer program. I can issue a few tickets to people with simple demands. I have a ridiculously intricate knowledge of minor rail routes in a forgotten backwater of Norfolk, a specialised subject if ever there was one. This is my comfort zone. I've got this one sussed. Here, I can triumph. I cannot attempt to bring new works, pieces of art for heaven's sake, to a wider public.

I have to put my pen down before it stabs something as my hand continues to shake. I hear my father's calming voice. He says he wouldn't have asked me to do this if he didn't think I had something to give to it. That's not 'offer', he stresses, it's 'give'. You will bring a fresh eye and enthusiasm to the company. I rest my hands flat on the desk to still them. How will I do it without Dad? I will be there every step of the way, he says. I remember his letter said there were projects and publications underway. That will give me breathing space. I will try my best. It is all I can promise him. That will do, he says. I wonder if he will always be here to calm and support me. To be strictly accurate about it, I am hearing voices in my head. Which is not great. But I'll take it.

This will be an adventure, like the stuff of my bedtime stories. Another reason why Donna hates me, I'd say. I was read to every night of pirates and fairies, of derring-do and caves full of treasure, of magical lands and the creatures that inhabited them. All she could look forward to was a fight about her lowly status. As a younger member of her family, she was no one. In my house I was everyone. And when she did finally get anything of her own, I was on hand to destroy it or take it away. Dan's bar of chocolate does not taste so sweet now, more like a sour forbidden apple.

When the time comes to clock off I try to be as casual

about it as possible. I may be back to do it again and again for years, I reason, it's no big deal. I know secretly that this is disingenuous but it helps me along. I am terrified that Dan will appear and suggest a parting glass in the Railway Inn. The leavetakings are piling up. I cannot face the end of so many eras. Dad is dead, Mum is fading away. When I go out of that door, if I am finishing my time serving the travellers of Pennick, I am also truly ending my journey with Dan. I have no reason to see him any more once I leave this job. I need to ignore these thoughts as I am winding myself up into a useless hysteria. I have been through other tough times because of my love for this man and I have survived. I will get through this too. The longing for him is again visceral and crippling but I will have to endure it. I remind myself that this isn't formally the end, as I have not packed the traditional cardboard box of belongings that I see in all the television shows. That should get me out the door with some sort of dignity.

I look at my Lost and Found section and wonder what its future will be without me. I know why I do it. For separate, compelling reasons I cannot have my parents back, but I can at least help a few lost things get home.

Mona had been busy and had a little something she knew Simon would be interested in, or so went the telephone call. She arrived in his office nearly as soon as he put the receiver down.

'I may have found our AC,' she said.

Simon braced himself for another lash of the fact that presumption was poor scholarship.

'Sock it to me,' he said, without enthusiasm.

'Oh, stop that,' she told him. 'Kitty need never know.' She smiled and consulted her notes. 'One of the richer merchant families in the area had a mansion a few miles out of town. Very ugly building, it has to be said, and typical of the nouveau riche sensibility. Each generation added "improvements" in the style of their era. I have some photographs.'

She was correct: it was a hideous structure without any architectural coherence. Simon felt sure Mona was going to back up everything she said at this session with document- ation, to drive home the need for scrupulous accuracy in matters historical. The photos were just a start. They both shuddered at the images of the overblown house.

'Clearly more money than taste,' Simon said.

'Or sense,' Mona added. 'The family intermarried a lot, thinking themselves above the very community they had grown out of, and they died off without anyone mourning them too much. The house was razed after the Second World War to make way for an equally ugly housing estate. The family records came to the Historical Society for safekeeping and have languished in unopened boxes for years.' She looked up and let him off the hook. 'You couldn't have known about them. Most members have forgotten about their existence, if they ever knew at all.'

'I'm assuming you found a parole prisoner?'

'Yes, I did. I found Antoine Chaubert. He might be our AC.'

Simon must have looked crestfallen: he certainly felt it. The light at the end of the tunnel was fading away as more tunnel was added to the search.

'We need to look for a local with the initials FV in case that is an English half of the couple,' Mona continued. 'It could still comprise two French citizens, or one Brit and one Frenchie, of whatever initials. We have many permutations to consider and explore.' She caught Simon's expression. 'This is all to the good,' she said. 'Now we have real possibilities. We're not stuck with just one scenario.'

He grunted, knowing she was right.

'Further opportunity to impress,' Mona added, without looking up from her notes. 'Further opportunity to get extra help on board. Shall we call Kitty and ask if she'd like to go through some of the papers you mentioned you had?'

I am about to bin the latest edition of the *Pennick Post* when I see a story I had avoided reading first time out. It is the report of a car crash in which a mother and baby daughter were killed. The photograph is of the infant on the day she was christened, swaddled in her white robe with nothing to fear and everything to look forward to, so much to learn and do. Two generations wiped out, one before she even had the chance to know much at all. I think of the decades I have had with Mum, and my gratitude for that and sadness for the baby girl set me to crying again, great hopeless sobs that can never purge the cruel ecstasy of life and all it brings with it. I have been so fortunate. I have loved, been loved, and will continue to be, somehow, in the future. I have to believe that or I will never move another inch. I know why I skirted over the story initially: I have realised there is only so much tragedy I can take in a day. I am grieving for so much.

I sell a ticket to Richard Marlin, a chap I have known for years. He doesn't look surprised to see mascara streaked across my cheeks.

'Oh, Kitty,' he says, 'it will get better, I promise.'

I blub agreement; don't know why, because right now I know it will never get better. My heart has simply given up on that idea.

'Would you like a hug?' he asks through the window hatch.

'Your train is arriving at platform three,' I sob. 'Run.'

He starts into a lolloping canter, turns and yells, 'The ticket machine is bust.'

'So am I,' I shout, though I have no way of knowing if he has heard me. Is anyone listening any more? I wonder.

I put the newspaper in the bin, feeling like a betrayer of the woman and daughter who have died, as if I have thrust them out of sight and therefore out of mind. Dan used to call the paper the *Pennick Pravda*, giving it an ironic majesty and us a sneaky laugh. Everything about me is so bound up with him, I wonder if I have ever had a truly independent thought of my own in the years we have known and loved one another. In many ways I don't care if I have not. It has almost been worth it. Almost.

Kitty followed May through the supermarket allowing her to pile the trolley high, returning the superfluous items as they did their second sweep. They stopped at the refrigerated section and talked about cheese and yogurts, sausages and bacon.

'This one's hickory flavoured,' Kitty said. 'How about that?'

May looked doubtful. 'As in dickory-dock?'

'I suppose.'

'No. I won't eat a mouse.'

'I don't think it's made of mouse.'

'It might be, with a name like that. I won't take the chance. No, thank you.'

Kitty made a play of reading the label and confirming, 'It's not mouse.'

Her mother was adamant but not upset. 'I don't want it.'

Kitty was about to declare it was made of pig but thought better of it. If it was a day when pigs were high on May's love list they could be in for a scene. For some obscure reason, she remembered an advert from ages ago about a 'juice loose aboot this hoose' and couldn't shake the demented jingle from her mind.

As they got in their front door, with 'ooh' sounds still ringing in her head, Kitty said, 'I'm pooped.' It made May laugh and she repeated the word 'poop' many times over, shaking her head at the hilarity of it. If I could have made Dan laugh like that would he have been mine entirely, Kitty wondered. She had been a morose teenager, she reckoned, and looking back, Donna seemed always to be smiling then and, therefore, doubly beautiful.

Simon Hill arrived, apologising for another intrusion. Kitty was glad to be taken out of herself and told him so. She thought she saw his chest puff out at that.

'You may not thank me after you've waded through this lot.' Simon dropped reams of photocopied documents on the table in front of her. It shook under their weight.

'It's like being a detective,' she said.

He agreed. 'Just like that and, as far as I know, as utterly dull as surveillance is, but when you unearth a nugget of information the thrill makes up for all the long hours of mind-numbing boredom.'

'Sounds kind of pervy,' Kitty said.

Simon Hill laughed. 'And that too.'

This man enjoys what I say, she thought, I make him smile. The idea seemed startling and almost forbidden.

'I like the cut of his jib,' May announced.

He reddened and Kitty, without allowing herself to think about it, stretched out and touched his hand.

Mum goes to bed and Simon asks, 'How are you?'

I don't want to point out it is not quite twenty-four hours since he last saw me, in case this is rude or hurtful. I like the cut of his jib too, I realise, and that's something I may have to deal with. My heart gives itself up to a weird flutter that is not unpleasant. I guess I'm a sucker for even the tiniest display of concern now.

'I'm fine. A bit drained. It's been a rough time.'

'If you ever need to talk . . .' He lets the offer trail away. 'I mean, I know we've only, really, just met and all, but I might be a good sounding board for you? I don't come with any baggage.'

What is he trying to tell me here? Does he know more than I would like him to? Must I always assume Dan is at the back of everything that is said?

'I am heartbroken,' I tell him, and that covers it all. It feels good to say it out loud.

He nods. This simple, straightforward gesture is somehow encouraging and I know he won't be bored if I go on, or regret that he allowed me to.

'This base note of sadness in me won't go away, and I don't expect it to for a long time. If ever. It's like a cold I cannot shake off. It seems to have a chemical makeup like poison. It unbalances me. But I've made it myself, just as surely as Mum's mind has manufactured her Alzheimer's with its inappropriate proteins.' I sigh. 'Though there the similarities end. It's unlikely I will die of my broken heart.'

'Not on my watch,' he says, and smiles so, so kindly.

For the first time in ages I feel safe.

❈   ❈   ❈

Is this what it's like to have a friend? Simon wondered, because now he did feel that he had one. True, he would like it to become more than that but for once he seemed to be going about the process in the right way. Until now it had been bed 'em and shed 'em, sometimes that quickly, sometimes a lingering that suited no one ultimately. He supposed he'd never got to know any of the women well. He had been bad at the talking end of things, especially about himself. He didn't enjoy analysing his personality and behaviour to show how sensitive he could be. He didn't like it when a woman did it for him either, despite earnest assurances that it would help him be a better person. For his part, he didn't feel he knew enough about people, in general, to offer advice if someone needed it or, in particular, if they hadn't asked for it. He was not comfortable with those scenarios, or with being relied on by anyone but his parents, and their needs had been increasingly simple: they were old and needed practical help more than anything, as time went on.

Now he had someone to talk to and share with. He had someone to care for. This was a delicate situation. He had before him a vulnerable other, a woman he would not risk hurting. It was a long time since he'd made anyone a promise but he was on the brink of one now. He would take care of Kitty Fulton. He didn't want to go any further than that just then. He didn't want to break the moment.

She was pointing out she might be slow getting round to

the paperwork. He told her there was no rush. He neglected to mention that as long as they were communicating daily he was happy, couldn't give a fig about the research. At the door he leaned down to kiss her cheek, as was now their habit, and walked out on to the street feeling dangerously happy.

Kitty put the guard before the fire and cleared away the evening's dishes. She sighed as she realised it had not after all been the worst of days. She had a new friend, a new job, new prospects.

May appeared at the top of the stairs and said, 'Ellen's wet the bed again.'

FOURTEEN

'I am not a baby,' Mum shouts. 'I won't wear a nappy!'

'It's not a nappy,' I tell her, trying desperately to think of another way to describe the item so as to make it acceptable to her. 'It's a pad,' I say. 'A just-in-case pad. Everyone wears them.'

The day is going from bad to belligerent. Mum cannot be placated. I'm ratty and snappish. More than once I've had to turn away to keep myself from roaring, or worse. Mum's face is pinched with crankiness. I suspect mine is too. As usual, small things have escalated to unexpected crises. We went to a favourite restaurant as a Sunday treat and Mum wanted to know why the window was full of fish. Did no one realise the fish were all going to die if they were kept here? The tank was large but three-dimensional. I led her around it, hoping this would show it wasn't actually a window. By then, Mum had moved on to the idea that the whole world and everyone in it was dying. Her voice went up a key.

'I'm dying too, aren't I, Kitty?'

I had been 'Miss' or 'dear' until then, and to be called by my name might have made me happier were it not the fact that it was tagged on to this subject. I was so weary of being reasonable, actually fed up with it.

'Mum, we are having your favourite Chinese meal. We're happy,' I said, reining in my annoyance.

'Ellen is dead, so is Daddy.' An eruption of tears could be expected any moment now. I had a sudden hysterical urge to remind Mum that her mother also had passed away. The woman rarely got a mention in despatches at all so why not have her out there with the rest? My head felt oddly light and my throat parched.

The blessed distraction of a waiter bearing food saved us from a further outburst. Sunday, and God be praised. I was beyond worrying that it was frivolous or wrong to cherry-pick our religious moments. If it got us through the day smoothly, I was all for it. I'd pay my dues another time. I felt so grotty, I half hoped if there were a God, I'd be first to be called to heavenly bliss. Mum scoffed her chicken with cashew nuts and fried rice without another murmur, and entirely forgot about death and all who had been taken by it. She brightened up even further when her favourite dessert arrived: banana fritters and ice cream.

As we were leaving she pointed at the tank. 'Look at all the lovely fish,' she squealed. She cast her narrowed eyes around the restaurant, sizing up the clientele, and said, 'They're not going to eat them, are they?'

'No, those fish are far too pretty for that.'

She stalled at the door and I could not get her over the threshold.

'We haven't got our takeaway yet,' she pointed out.

Mum's voice was quite loud now and several diners gave us sly glances, as if they knew what was going on. It made me bridle. As much as I'm allowed to be fed up with Mum, none of these strangers had any right to sit in judgement. We are not a freak show to make you all feel better about yourselves, I wanted to tell them, but the effort wasn't worth it. My head was aching with stress and the stirrings of a classic winter cold. It is always the case that if I don't feel good, our whole day is in jeopardy. Our system is balanced so precariously there is no margin for error or being less than one hundred and ten percent committed to whatever a situation might require. I'd bombarded myself with paracetamol and the hottest thing on the menu to unblock my bunged-up head but neither had worked. I hadn't even tasted my food. Now I wanted to lie in bed and be cared for, brought hot drinks and nibbles, to sleep at will and sweat out this lurgy. Fat chance of that. Today is a series of arguments with every last subject up for debate, and reason a casualty each time. I want to dissolve in a heap but that is a luxury we cannot afford.

Mum says, 'You're very pale, young lady, maybe you

should get some vitamins. My daughter could tell you which ones.'

I cannot resist saying, 'She's great, your daughter, isn't she?'

'Yes,' Mum says, proudly. 'You'll like her. Everyone does.'

At least the notional Kitty is wonderful.

I put soiled sheets into the wash and replace the linen on Mum's bed. I'm glad now I let Val convince me to get a rubber cover for the mattress during the funeral week, when the bed-wetting started. Like an idiot, I had supposed it was a one-off incident.

'Just be thankful we're not at solids yet,' he'd said, to make me laugh a little even though it was in horror at the notion.

Mum is stuck into a Lassie movie and thrilled with it. I praise all responsible for television as it is my little helper. She told me politely earlier that she's having a lovely day. She is having trouble concentrating on reading so I might get some audio books from the library for her. I jot that on a pad so I won't forget. My head is like marshmallow and can't be relied on. Everything seems to be on an even keel now so I make myself a hot toddy and curl up opposite Mum, in front of the fire with the Sunday papers. I need to smack this cold right in the kisser if I am to start at my dad's firm tomorrow. My business now, I remind myself, and am filled with the strangest, nicest mixture of terror, excitement and whisky.

I doze off because the next thing I know I hear shouts

of 'Snap' and wake to find Simon playing cards with my mother. I have lost track of time and it terrifies me. I spring up and look at the clock, realising I have been out for two hours. Two whole hours. Anything could have happened. The house might have burned down. Mum might have hurt herself. I fell asleep on duty and am appalled at myself. I find I cannot stay upright. I am dizzy and in a lather of sweat. It's a nasty sensation. Then I am floating. Simon rushes over and catches me as I begin to fall.

The next bites of consciousness are woozy and bent out of shape. Simon is carrying me upstairs and placing me in my bed. I think he helps me undress but I am raving now and incapable of figuring out what should or must happen. The sheets feel nice, then hot and wet. Simon returns from the bathroom with a cooling flannel and strokes my back and neck with it and tells me I will be fine. I love him just then. I ask him if Mum is safe. He tells me not to worry, that he has everything in hand. I will have to trust him on that as I am incapable of doing anything for anyone, even myself. The pattern on my wallpaper is moving about and making me uneasy. I shut my eyes tight but then my head spins. I am so tired. The cold flannel is so good. I feel safe but terrible. I drift off.

I burst awake, shouting 'Dan', though I don't remember dreaming about him. I am freezing, my teeth chattering and my body shaking. I cannot speak properly, only in bursts of nonsense. I don't recognise the words and I don't seem to be making sentences although I desperately want to say something coherent. Simon tells me I'm burning up but puts an extra duvet over me even so. I chatter some more then warm up again. My body feels heavy. I drift away.

It is 4.15 in the morning before I am able to think straight but not in any conventional way. I feel so ashamed that I lost control. I have let everyone down. Simon is asleep in a chair by my bed, his hand resting by my pillow. It looks so tender. I try to shift out of the sodden bed without waking him but cannot. He is suddenly alert.

'Kitty,' he mutters in an odd tone I cannot quite identify. 'How are you feeling?'

'Ravenous.' My voice is hoarse from a dried-out throat.

I am floppy and weak so he helps me out of bed. I am wearing a truly gross nightgown, a pink flannelette confection that I meant to throw out ages ago. It does nothing for me. Not only that, it is probable that Simon was the one who put me in it. I shouldn't fear for my modesty now, I know, as I may have none left in this man's eyes. I smell dreadful, too, all grease and perspiration.

'Let's get you fed,' he says. 'Would Madam like to be carried to the kitchen?'

I laugh weakly and say, 'why not?' because things are going that way and I don't think I have the strength to walk that far. I cringe at the state of myself. We muddle down the stairs, my clammy arms and breath on his neck, my feet hitting the walls on the narrow stairwell.

'Hardly *Gone with the Wind*,' he remarks.

'Though it is another day,' I manage.

I hear the laughter in his chest.

It strikes me that Dan never did this with me. There was never a moment like that. But then, there never could have been, either.

Simon can cook. He explains it is one of the necessities when you've been a bachelor as long as he has. This doesn't quite cover it, I decide, but he is so lovely about it all I decide to be gentle, by which I suppose I mean I get coy. I am also, still, tremulous and weak.

'Nice seduction technique, too,' I offer.

I am sure he blushes. He doesn't deny the charge. I know I am digging, wanting information and sneaky with it, using the situation.

I try not to gulp down the carbonara he makes too greedily as that would make me ill as well as looking even more like a pig. A pig in a pink flannelette nightmare. Something about the way he slices bread and puts it in front of me makes me dissolve and suddenly I am a weeping heap and embarrassed with it. Simon puts his arms around me and says, 'Sweetheart, don't. Don't do this to yourself. It's all under control now.'

Strangely, it feels like it is but my tears are redoubled. And what did he just call me? I finally get a grip and say, 'Was it just lucky you came by or what?'

This sounds like both a statement and a question and, really, I would love it if it were left hanging without a reply. That way I can convince myself later that no harm at all was done. But I have to know how he came to be our saviour. I want it to be an innocuous reason but I keep expecting catastrophe, or near avoidance of disaster, because that is my territory, the place where we live. I am not wrong.

'I met May on the street,' he says.

I am devastated. This is the worst news but he is right to tell me. She should not have been out, not without me. She cannot be alone any more. I have failed the most vulnerable person I know.

'Kitty, you're not well,' Simon says.

Simon says. Isn't that a game? I feel sleepy again but must try to keep going here. I focus on his earnest face but it's hard when the handsome prisms keep shifting. I bet I look drunk, eyes drooping.

'You can't do it by yourself. Not all of the time. May hadn't gone far. She was looking for Hannah because she had an "intimate problem" and she didn't want to bother you because you were sleeping. She said you deserved it.'

'Mum said that?'

'Yes. And she called you Kitty.'

He holds me in his gaze and I notice that his eyes are a devastating grey-green-turquoise combination. A person could lose herself, if it weren't for Dan. He says, 'The only one being unfair to someone round here is you to yourself. You take on too much and leave yourself open to the failure you expect. Give yourself a break. Some of us think you're great, even without the heroics.'

It's nice of him to say so. I am grateful. He's wrong, though. I messed up today, no way round that fact. It won't happen again. I want to change the subject and, without thinking, I ask the first thing that comes into my scrambled head: 'Why are you single?' 'At your age' is a given, as in 'at mine too'. He is not looking at me as he answers, those wonderful eyes choosing another point to address. His turned-away neck looks wonderfully vulnerable. I'd like to bite it. I must be raving still.

'I never met the right person. Or no one I recognised as being the one. Does that make me a cliché? I dunno. You?'

I won't blame my fever or say I am disorientated. The fact is this; I want to tell someone. For the first time ever I admit, 'Mine's a married man.' I try an ironic shrug but it hurts my weary bones.

'Dan,' he says.

It seems we are both up to speed and I don't know how we got here. Now I want to tell him everything. No, that's not it, I have to. I have to tell him the entire story. It spews out of me in an unstoppable flow. The phrase to 'spill the beans' hops into my mind then and I know that there is probably a very ordinary story to explain the phrase and I think then how odd that this occurs to me at such a crucial moment. But the mind is a strange place, as Mum and I have discovered.

'I have done a very bad thing,' I say, and then I cannot stop. I bare my soul. My mouth takes over and I tell this man, whom I have only just met, about my life and how it has come to an impasse and now I feel I cannot go on but I must, because to stop is not an option. It is incoherent and heartfelt and although I fear I will regret this, I cannot stop now. I am so depleted, physically and mentally, that the easiest course is to tell all and deal with the fallout later. When I am done I am sweating and shaking again. I yawn and find it difficult to keep my eyes open. I am dizzy with the euphoria of it all.

Simon tells me I should have a bath while he changes the bedclothes. I haven't the energy to argue. At least there is no longer a mirror in the bathroom to show me how wretched I look. I might feel I was seeing strangers, too, if I could see this person I am tonight, all pale and broken. When I am washed and changed, into a slightly less hideous nightgown, I crawl into the clean nest of duvet and fresh cotton sheets and Simon lies on top on the other side and we both sleep.

'Thank you,' I say, as I drift away.

'Any time,' he whispers, and I know he means that. 'By the way,' he adds, 'you can forget going to Norwich later. You need rest.'

I am glad to let him take over even if it's only for a short while. We'll worry about the big things then too. For now there is nothing to do but to sleep.

✧　✧　✧

Simon listened to Kitty's story. Although it cut him to hear about Dan he felt he now knew this woman better than he did any other person on earth: a strange new situation for him. An added responsibility. He was both gladdened and appalled by this. He now knew her history and who 'the other man' was. Well, he had worked that out quickly enough in the hours when she'd called out the name 'Dan' repeatedly as she raved in her sleep and he waited for her fever to break.

He did not judge her in the light of her aberration. He was not a man who was quick to point the finger in these matters. He thought no less of her for it. What he saw was a beautiful and haunted woman who was capable of love and courage and fidelity.

May appeared at the bedroom door.

'Has Ellen had her baby?' she asked. 'It's very quiet.'

He went to her. 'Go back to bed, May, there's nothing to worry about.' He had no idea who Ellen was, but perhaps neither did May. Keep it calm, he thought, and say nothing definitive.

He watched her climb into bed and settle herself, fretting, murmuring to herself.

'Ellen's baby died,' she told him. 'And then Ellen was dead too.' She sighed. 'At least, I think that's what happened.' She shook her head sadly. 'Sometimes it's hard to remember.'

'Go to sleep now.'

'Yes. Thank you.'

279

He was unused to this sort of gratitude. Usually he didn't deserve it, he thought. People thanked him superficially every day, for advice, a business transaction, a tip on a book or a courtesy, but he was observing no more than old-fashioned manners, essentially. Alexis Montford once thanked him 'for the shag'. Mind you, she'd meant it. Often the women in his life used their thanks as a heavy irony, which he was well able to ignore. For people to be genuinely grateful to him for a kindness, a good deed, was a new sensation. He was well beyond his comfort zone here, he knew, and probably should be scared. Too late. He was in this to his neck and beyond. Was that good? He wasn't sure. It shook him, that much was certain.

He watched Kitty sleep and wondered where her thoughts were now. He would have liked to have been in her head, to share some more of her, or wrapped around her like a lock, to protect her, keep her safe. The thought of touching her brought with it a reminder of other needs and passions.

He hadn't had sex since arriving in Pennick. With anyone but himself, he qualified. It didn't feel like a hardship, though, as he'd have regarded it elsewhere. He seemed to be keeping himself for a woman in love with a man she could never have, a woman who might never shake off the ghost of her first and only affair of the heart. And he didn't care. He was prepared to offer himself and take the chance that she might love him, eventually. There, he'd admitted it: love, the worst of all afflictions. The surrendering of the self into the hands of another in the hope that they would not reject or simply be careless with your gift. He wanted to know this woman's greatest hopes and worst fears, as surely as his mouth and tongue wanted to taste her physically. He wanted to become necessary to her.

It's like I have a Mum Monitor in her head: when she stirs so do I. And so does Simon. In the morning he looks tired, stubbly but kind. He gestures quickly for me to stop what I'm attempting.

'No, Kitty, you are to stay where you are. Hannah said to call her when May got up. You are not to move an inch.'

'I really do feel a lot better,' I insist, and I do.

'I'm not interested. You are staying put.'

I quite like this bossy edge to him. 'Can I at least use the telephone to tell Miss Marshall that I won't be in?'

'I'll think about it.' He smiles. 'Tea and toast first.'

That does sound divine. I lie back against the pillows and try to relax. Mum is jabbering away downstairs and I wonder if she is talking to someone else or to herself. Simon appears with breakfast and asks if it would be all right for him to shower. That makes me laugh out loud.

'I think it's the least you deserve after last night's shining armour routine,' I say.

He runs his hand through his hair and shifts from foot to foot. If he has more to say he thinks better of it and soon I hear the noises of a man washing in our little bathroom. They are happy sounds.

'There's a new toothbrush under the sink,' I call to him.

'Are you the least vain family in the world, or else vampires?' he asks on his return.

'Worse,' I tell him. My voice falters for a moment but I rally. 'Mum was seeing strangers in the mirrors so we got rid of them. I have a little hand one if you're worried about how you look.'

'I'll settle for you telling me I'm fine.'

'You are.' Better than fine, I could have added, but that would be impertinent and I don't want to embarrass him in any way.

I find I don't want him to leave and I get the impression that he doesn't want to go either but he must and he does. Hannah yoo-hoos as she comes through the front door and I hear her chattering with Mum. I can doze again. I'm hoping my dreams won't bring Dan as close this time, or at all. I must move on. I must make something of life without him. The last face to drift through my mind as I slip away is Simon Hill's. I lie with eyes closed, trying his name for size. 'Si' makes my face stretch into a smile then 'mon' forms a pucker, like the prelude to a kiss. Such silliness makes me grin, eyes still shut. I have a new friend.

The next time I wake, my head pounds as if I'm hungover. The house is quiet. I look around the room and the walls seem far too close to the bed. It's a sensation I recognise.

When I was a child this skewed perspective always heralded a nightmare. I force myself up and out to thwart it. I shrug into a fresh outfit, promising my body a shower as soon as it is fed.

A note on the table says Mum and Hannah have gone for a walk. Mum has signed it and her handwriting looks as if a spider has crossed the page dipped in ink. I am alone and that should be bliss but the silence agitates me. It seems unfriendly. I am used to bustle at work, mayhem here at home. I turn on the radio and refuse to let melancholy make me cry. Simon has left a sheaf of papers to be checked for any mention of French parole prisoners. I spread them out and begin to read.

I finally get into the swing of the day. It's so different from other weekdays, it takes time for me to shake off my vague anxiety that I should be doing something else. Margo has taken over in the station in my absence so that assuages some of the guilt. I find myself wondering if the 15.10 to Norwich will be on time and whether Dan will have to calm anyone down if it's late. There are times when that particular service is like the last train out of Dodge, with passengers desperate to be on it, and we have never figured out why. Dan loves to quote the local saying that Norfolk is cut off on three sides by the sea and on the fourth by the railway.

Mum returns and stands with her hand on her hips, singing 'el nombre' along with a caped cartoon mouse on the television. I wonder if it's just a coincidence that so many programmes seem to be teaching Spanish or perhaps I have not been around long enough to see the other stuff she likes to watch. I know she is not learning the language, as I joked she was with Val. Mum is not able to make new memories so she's mimicking the pleasant, catchy sounds and maybe here and there is a word that is steeped in her head from long ago and can be rooted out now to suit the moment.

We had another kind of moment earlier when I found her wandering about naked from the waist down. She had 'done her business', as she put it, and had left all of the clothes taken off in the process on the bathroom floor. She still hates the incontinence pads but fights them less each time. I am glad to see a flashpoint losing its significance. I am less thrilled to be seeing my mother's privates on display, as accustomed as I am becoming to them.

I have asked Simon and Mona over to review our findings. I did wonder whether I just wanted to see Simon again, plain and simple, but I think it's clear enough we're likely to be friends rather than anything else. My mind is too full of Dan to be going anywhere new. Also, I don't feel I could have the presumption to ask anyone to take on a woman like myself, so much on the rebound, so full of grief for a lost dad, complete with a glorious but batty mum. It is what it is and we'll leave it so. My heart warms with gratitude to think of him, though, and what he has already done for us. He didn't have to but he stepped in when needed. He is a good man.

I have become engrossed in my study of the French prisoners throughout the day. I think we should begin our own record of each of the individuals we encounter. I have fallen under the spell of local history. And there I was, thinking that Pennick had none.

Out of nowhere I remember Alice North's attempt at making money from Pennick's past. She bought a rickshaw one summer and could be hired to conduct an historical tour of the town. It never took more than thirty minutes. The main problem was that she wasn't fit enough to be cycling anywhere, let alone pedalling for three. There also wasn't that much to see. She had to give the venture up before it killed her. She uses the rickshaw now to do her shopping at Tesco but has to put up with a lot of teasing along the way.

Kitty had made a discovery and Simon wanted to praise her fulsomely but it was another nail driven through his own initial academic arrogance. He had so wanted to impress her in those early stages he had forgotten the basic tenets of his craft and presented too early and neat a solution to the mystery of the initials. They now had a second FV. Kitty had found mention of a Fenella Vickers in the annals of the house occupied by Dr Monroe of Cross Street in the early 1800s. Fenella was known as Nelly in the records, for the most part, but one pertinent mention in the good doctor's diary had led Kitty to make the connection.

'She was the household maid. There's talk of *soirées*

involving the captured soldiers so perhaps she knew one of them?' Kitty stumbled charmingly on the word *'soirées'* and Simon felt a heel as he cautioned her then.

'Let's not jump to conclusions,' he warned, just ahead of Mona doing so, he guessed. 'Much as we'd like to,' he added, softening the blow.

'I understand,' she said, and he knew she did.

Kitty had joined them now. They were three historians.

Mona was working her way through sundry official documents of the time and Simon had commandeered parish records as his field.

'Rather you than me,' Mona had said. 'Norfolk does not lack for churches, that's for certain, and Pennick is no exception. Dr Monroe's house is still standing in Cross Street, by the way. A family called Richards lives there. Lovely garden out back.' She shuffled her papers into order and prepared to take her leave.

May called, 'Good night, Jessie,' as she made for the door.

Kitty apologised but Mona would have none of it.

'She's spot on,' Mona said. 'That's my nickname, after Jessica Fletcher the television sleuth. I would love to think it's also because I look like Angela Lansbury, but I fear not. I spend my life nosing about, sniffing through local history, so I have a bit of a reputation. Can't help it, I was born curious. Isn't that right, May?'

'What?' She looked from Mona to the others, a rabbit caught in the headlights. 'Do I know you?'

'Ah, well, it was nice while it lasted,' Mona said. 'I'll let you young things get on with it. Shall we fix our next meeting for the weekend? Should give us time to get on top of our assignments.'

Kitty and Simon agreed and were left feeling like awkward teenagers after she'd gone. May was giggling at the 'And finally' item on the news about a naughty squirrel that had teamed up with a thieving robin in a London park.

Simon began, 'I should have said this morning that Hannah helped you with changing and so on last night, as well as May, in case you thought there was any impropriety or anything you might have been embarrassed by.'

'Thanks for that,' Kitty said, remembering that Simon had pretty much undressed her when she was first put to bed, and stroked her naked back with a facecloth. It was nice that he tried to put her mind at rest, though.

'I do hope we'll find them,' he said, referring to the papers.

'Yes.'

May's laughter broke into the near silence of the room. A fire crackled in the grate.

I am wishing goodnight to Simon at the door when my mobile rings. It is Dan. Simon sees the caller's name, or guesses, and says he'll be off but I know he is reluctant to leave me to take this call. I answer and know immediately from the sounds on the other end that Dan is close by. Simon does his foot-to-foot routine, raises his hand in a half-wave and starts slowly down the street. I watch his back, not quite retreating, more stepping away so as not to interfere but available should he be needed.

'I heard you were unwell,' Dan says in a low voice.

Perhaps he doesn't want me to hear how close he is.

'It was just a twenty-four-hour thing,' I say.

I don't want to get into a conversation with him. I am trying, with every last shred of common sense I have, to extricate myself from him, and us.

'I could come round if you need me,' he goes on.

'No. Thank you, but no.'

I want to say I don't need him; that's what the 'no' means, but I can't get those words out.

'Kitty, I . . .' he falters, tries again. 'I . . . that is, we . . . no, me, me . . . I probably never . . .'

I don't want to hear whatever the never is. It's too late. I must refuse to go back.

'It's okay, Dan, I know. It's fine. I have to go now. Mum needs me. Thanks for calling.'

'I'll see you,' he says. That's one of those loaded questions couched as a casual statement. It exhausts me.

'Yes, you'll see me. Goodnight.'

We are done. Simon is at the corner and looks back. I wave with the phone hand so that he can see that I have finished with Dan. For some reason this is important to me and also, I think, to him. He waves back and blows a little air-kiss. I suppose Dan has seen this from his hiding place. As I turn to go it is Donna I think of and how she must feel now, sitting at home, assuming he has come to me.

Did I think of her down the years? Yes, occasionally, but not as much as I should have, that's the shameful truth. If I had, I wouldn't have let the charade go on for as long as it did. At least I hope that is true because the alternative is not something any decent person could live with. In the depths of my heart I know I will always make excuses and seek to explain my actions. That is the life sentence I will endure. I wish I had some way to atone for it all but, just at this minute, I have no comfort to offer her.

FIFTEEN

May was trying to pee in the kitchen sink when the Healthcare Visitor arrived, which was excellent timing, Kitty thought, if undignified. The woman took it in her stride. She looked as if she'd seen it all before and nothing startled her any more. She radiated pure indifference. Kitty sent May upstairs with clear instructions to use the proper loo, wash her hands and then come back to talk to the nice visitor. She made a pot of tea while trying to keep up conversation with the stranger who, for her part, spent the time making notes about the house. May arrived back on the scene in her incontinence pants but without her plaid trousers. Kitty told her to go back up to put them on. May snapped.

'Shut up! Shut up, you. It's all "don't do this" and "don't do that". Nothing I do is good enough. I'm sick of it, so shut up you!'

She stormed upstairs and banged a few doors for good measure while she was there.

'Is that regular?' the woman asked.

'Arguing, yes, though the temper display is unusual.'

A scribbled note.

'Do you work?'

'Until now I have but my dad died a fortnight ago and I'm on compassionate leave.'

She was granted a curt nod of acknowledgement while the writing continued

'Just you, is it?'

'Just me,' Kitty confirmed. She wondered if this woman ever broke double figures when choosing words for a sentence. 'I have great neighbours and there is a very active club locally that helps out with people like Mum.'

'She's a handful.'

'Yes, she's been called that before.'

'Have you thought about residential care?'

'Not really.'

'You should.'

'I'm hoping that's a way off yet.'

'It may not be. Consider it. Here's a list of places you can visit, put her name down for a vacancy. In the meantime, I'll recommend you get all we have to offer in the way of home help, such as it is.' The woman took a swift slurp of tea, for form's sake, then changed gear. 'This is now about what's best for both of you, not just her, although she needs her dignity maintained and good care, of course. You have to think of yourself too. You're no good to anyone, especially your mother, if you're worn to the bone. Don't overdo it or play the martyr: that way you'll both sink and you'll be doing no one any favours. I'll give you my lecture about not being fair to your mother by keeping her here too long without professional care on my next visit. You'll love it, it's a real corker.'

Seemed she went to double figures when it really mattered. Kitty had a bad feeling about that promised lecture. Time was shifting again: the sands were slipping away faster than she'd anticipated, and rapidly running out.

On Thursday, Benny arrives at the door, in bits.

'It's Roly,' he says. 'He won't stop crying and he's off his food.'

It looks to me like Roly is not the only one.

'Kitty, you have to do something.'

I am terrified Benny will burst into tears in front of me and wreck the delicate balance he has achieved between his own extreme oddness and the ability to interact socially with other people. I agree to come to the station but point out we'll have to bring Mum along too. We muffle ourselves up against the cold while Benny has a quick cup of instant coffee then venture forth, a motley association of oddballs and misfits.

I wave to Jed at the allotments. Benny is appalled to see such an elderly man pushing a wheelbarrow. He goes over to help and the two strike up a conversation. Benny appears to have no problem understanding Jed's archaic drant. Someone should be recording this. The two are conversing in a musical score, inaccessible to anyone but the players. Soon they are laughing. I realise I know little enough about the night watchman. He might be steeped in deepest Norfolk tradition like Jed. I think he's from Gately, just out of town, but I'm not sure. I really should ask.

I take time to check my plot and Mum wanders about chattering. I notice she is carrying a framed photo of Dad and me.

'I'm bringing these people for a walk, dear,' she explains, then mutters, 'not that it's any of your business.'

I am a pest and a nosey-parker. Donna used to call me that when we were kids. I am again touched with regret for our lost friendship, in the very spot where most of my crimes against it took place. Dan's plot is neat and tended. He has been here recently but I am glad he's not here now. He'll probably be at the station when we get there. However, I am travelling in an entourage and unlikely to find myself alone with him. There should be no visible awkwardness.

When we resume our journey Benny is full of chat about Jed and how he is going back to help him with a leak in his shed roof later. All the lonely people, I think.

In the few days I have been gone, Margo has clearly barred Roly from the office. He is on the concourse, curled up in a ball under a bench. As a rule, he wouldn't get so close to the passengers, though he is not above begging if they are feasting on something nice. I call his name and he looks intensely suspicious of me. He circles slowly to make sure he knows me then lets out a wail that would cut glass. His coat is matted and he looks thin. I reach down to stroke him and he leaps into my arms, overbalancing me. There's a bit of weight to him yet. I rub his head and he puts his paws on my shoulders and presses his furry face to mine. He's still crying out about being abandoned while searching my face for answers. I see I am doomed. I catch Benny's eye and find he is holding a cat carrier, ready for me to take Roly home with me. I have been ambushed. There is nothing for it but to give in.

Passengers congregate and the familiar ones tell me about offering him tidbits that he was not interested in. 'That's not like him at all,' Vivie Stephens says, and she's right. Roly lives for his grub.

Vivie is delighted to see Mum, as are a few of the others who know her. She is polite to them although she doesn't recognise anyone. She holds out the photograph and introduces people to her husband and daughter. It is the first time I have heard her refer to Dad in that way. I wonder why they never told me they were married. It's something I will probably never know the answer to. Dad has taken his reason to the grave with him and Mum has had hers stolen by Alzheimer's. 'A lovely man,' is the consensus. I decide we'd better hurry away before grief undoes me again. The lovely man is no more and he will be missed forever.

We load Roly up and leave without encountering Dan. I don't know whether I am grateful or sad about that. Margo will report this theft of the station cat to him later, if she can be bothered. I will text to explain. I wonder how he is and if he too looks thin and matted. Does he cry for me?

Benny carries Roly back to our little terraced house. The neighbours hear the cat calling from a distance, still complaining about his lot, and appear at their doors to welcome him. You'd swear we were coming home from hospital with a new baby, the fuss they all make. Roly Fulton arrived today, they'll say, sitting around the dinner table later. A big lad, a healthy six-pounder, great set of lungs.

By the time we get home, the people in Mum's photograph are Ellen and her dad. They have enjoyed the walk greatly, apparently. Inside, I open the door of the cage and Roly emerges cautiously. He takes a moment to stretch and look about him then, with an elegant leap, joins Mum on the sofa in front of the fire.

'Pegasus,' she says to me, and I understand this is her word for 'cat' now.

'I'll make us a nice chicken risotto,' I say.

Roly gives a yawn and looks as though he was always destined for that couch and this house and our lives. He's home at last.

Miss Marshall assured Kitty she did not need to come to the office for the time being.

'Are you absolutely sure you don't mind?' Kitty asked. 'Please tell me if you do. I don't want it to look like I don't care or I'm taking advantage of you. I would just like to get sorted here before I start.'

This was the closest she had come to admitting that she had forsaken her job at the station. As the hours went by she knew she could not go back. There was only forward now, the past would have to look after itself.

'There's nothing you can't do from home, for the moment,' Miss Marshall assured her.

Kitty had a moment of sheer panic then, thinking of what might happen if Marie Marshall decided to retire. There was no reason for the woman to feel any huge loyalty to the business now that Stephen was gone. That was a conversation to be had face to face, and soon, another pitfall identified, underlining the fragility of all Kitty's arrangements.

'I'll send you some manuscripts that need looking at,' Miss Marshall continued. 'We all look forward to you joining us.'

'I'm looking forward to being there,' Kitty told her. As well as feeling terrified, she might have added.

The poetry was a revelation. Kitty had assumed she wouldn't be up to expressing any views on the work, but her father and mother had always insisted she was more than capable of simply enjoying a poem for itself and declared that that counted as much as any other consideration. So, she let the words play out before her and, while sometimes she got lost, found she could identify the basic themes underlying the poets' intentions and still appreciate those when all else failed her. She would have to take specialised advice on the academic side of the business, of course, and could only hope she would be as good at weeding out the worthwhile from the nonsense when it came to choosing projects for that area in the future. 'When in doubt, ask,' her father had always said. 'There's no shame in admitting you don't know it all.'

Kitty was surrounded by books and manuscripts at home. She had both her firm's work in progress and the historical research to get through. Hours would fly by as she immersed herself in one or other, the only punctuations May 'moments' or Roly demanding attention. Both had to be watched carefully. The cat could not understand why the door was not left open all the time for him to come and go.

'Listen, mate,' Kitty said, 'talk to Benny if you've got issues. You cooked up this scheme between you and now you've got to stay in here till you get used to your new home.'

'He's not listening to you,' her mother told her. 'He's a . . . hairy thing.'

May had seen the cat use his litter tray a few times and decided it would be good to adopt the same practice. A plastic domed roof was quickly added to Roly's loo and May escorted to the human one whenever it was clear she needed it. A lot of the time it was immaterial and the incontinence pad had to do its bit. Then it was up to Kitty to spot this as her mother didn't always remember to tell her. Kitty had become adept at reading the signs. There is not a lot we cannot cope with between us, she reasoned. Each new detail and difficulty could be worked through, added to their routine and dealt with accordingly.

Sophie was the first of the new home helps to arrive. May was fascinated by the woman's black skin: she touched it, then checked her fingertips to see if they'd changed colour. Sophie laughed off Kitty's embarrassment at her mother's behaviour.

'If that's the worst that happens me, I'll be doing well,' she insisted.

'That makes me even more nervous,' Kitty said. 'Like disaster is just waiting to pounce.'

'Nah, it's not *about* to get you, you're living it. That's why I'm here to help.'

It felt good to have that acknowledged.

'I don't recognise May's accent,' Sophie commented.

'Mum's Irish. Grew up in a small town north of Dublin. But she's lived here for longer than she ever spent there.'

Kitty felt uncomfortable talking about her mother as if she was not in the room, though May wasn't paying much attention. She had other things exercising her, which she decided to offload.

'You're black and you're fat,' she told the care worker.

Sophie laughed heartily. 'That's true. Now we're cooking.'

'I'm so sorry. She goes through phases of brutal honesty.'

'I prefer that. I don't have enough time left in my life for people to waste it with lies or platitudes.'

Kitty found the way she elongated 'plaateetyoods' wonderful. It gave it the extra 'oomph' a word like that deserved.

'Can we have some of Granny Larkin's cake?' May wanted to know.

Having Sophie here feels like luxury. I can take my eye off the ball occasionally without worrying that there'll be a disaster, or even a minor incident for which I must blame myself. I notice the magnitude of it more now than if I was out at work all day, and that makes me appreciate how generous friends and neighbours have been to us throughout the course of this disease. I have paid Hannah and Val for their time and work in the past, but not enough and I know that. Now, I am the owner of a business and have the money Dad left for Mum's care, so I will give them a pay rise. The opportunity to do this feels so good. It's such a shame Dad can't be here to share it.

Mum is taking a nap and I try one too. I can't lie on the bed with her as I would like to. When I am Ellen she clings to me or follows me around asking questions. It really is like having a pesky little sister. When I am Kitty she smiles a lot and hugs me. But mostly I am no one special. Then, she sees me as friendly but I can tell she isn't entirely sure of me, so sharing an afternoon snooze with her is out of the question. I lie on my own bed conscious that I have rarely shared it with anyone for very long. That's about to change.

Roly has set his sights on it and, specifically, me in it. He lies on top of the duvet covering me, the length of him stretching from my chin to my legs. I am pinned to the bed with very little wriggle room. I can feel his purring vibrate through him and the sound is all around us in the room, below it the bass drum of his heart beating against his ribs in counterpoint to mine. The only other heartbeat I have felt this strong and this close is Dan's.

'I don't suppose it's of any interest to you,' I wheeze, 'but I cannot breathe properly.'

Roly blinks at me, not a lot more. He's got inscrutable down to a tee.

'How about a deal? You sleep on one side of the bed, me the other.'

No go.

I close my eyes and enjoy his heart beat fluttering with mine, grateful of the affection, wondering if I'll make it to waking up, what with the oxygen deprivation and really not caring if I don't. This is as close to perfect happiness as I've been in a long while. I am flying on the wings of a cat named Roly Pegasus, a magical creature who brings great joy for the price of a chicken risotto. There's not a lot to argue with there.

The trick with the Parish Records was not to get side-tracked by other interesting stories. There were so many, Simon found. Open a bound tome at random and there were a hundred fascinating details of town life, often written in a beautiful hand. He would look at the roster of priests and deans and match them to their handwriting, forming whimsical images of them in his mind based on the slant of their letters and their idiosyncratic flourishes. He would read between the lines of the births, christenings, marriages, funerals. That wasn't very scholarly of him, strictly speaking, but some things could be inferred: many events were perennial; others carried the weight of history and had a pattern. He particularly loved stories about those married before or during a war, always a sucker for wanting to know what became of the lovers.

He had expected some French parole prisoners might have married into the community, and here at St Cuthbert's there was the record of a marriage between Armand De Louis and one Margaret Gibson of Bishop's Lane. A scant three months later their son was born and baptised Jean, but sadly died within a few weeks. Kitty had suggested they log all of the information they encountered about the parole prisoners and he thought that a good idea. It was more work, sure, but it was a fascinating and much-neglected part of the town's history and their researches would not be wasted. It occurred to him that to trace the graves of those people they identified would also be an idea.

He found no one with the initials FV or AC, and decided they needed to check whatever census results were logged for the early 1800s as well as the church records. The United

Kingdom census proper was started in 1801, championed by an English statistician called John Rickman who was responsible for the first four, until 1831. What excited Simon most about that fact was that the census, although little more than a head count at the time, was set up in part to ascertain the number of men available to fight in the Napoleonic Wars, exactly the period they were investigating. He loved an omen, and this seemed a good one.

Yawning, he glanced at the wall clock. The evening had galloped by. It was 10.30, probably time to call it a night. He still had St Melchior's and St Peter's to visit as well as a full-time job to keep. Perhaps Mona could concentrate some of her undisputed energies on census results. After all, she was the one supposed to have time on her hands now.

Simon's neck cricked as he stretched it. He was glad the Dean had left him to his work in the church sacristy and had not invited him into the parish house next door. Being inside church homes meant tea and explanations, polite chitchat, when all he wanted was to get stuck into the records. He took off the cotton gloves he wore when handling delicate books and records. He gathered his papers, collating loosely as he went, and put them in the battered satchel his parents had given him when he left for college. The buckle always made a satisfying clunk as he pressed it home. Sometimes he did it twice to hear the sound again.

It was too late to go calling on anyone now. Or rather, not just anyone, Kitty. He would text to say that he was doing well and looking forward to swapping notes with her. He couldn't help wondering if they would ever progress beyond this project and on to another level, as a couple, but a complication like romance was the last thing Kitty needed right now. He would cultivate her friendship, in the traditional way, and hope that the future would deliver something more. Just as well he had the dual patience of a librarian and historian. Mentally, that is. Physically, he was crying out for attention. It was not a situation he had regularly found himself in and he was unsure how to handle it. Pennick was a small town and to go about the business of a dalliance, just for base relief, was fraught with the potential of discovery. He didn't want anything to put Kitty Fulton off. No one was removed more than a few degrees from anyone else in this place. On top of that, he found he wasn't interested in becoming involved with anyone just for the sake of sex, a new feeling that surprised and slightly unsettled him. He would hold fire, for the time being; perhaps join a gym to expend excess energy.

He yawned again and watched the vapour of his breath disperse towards the high ceiling. It was time to search out the Dean, to thank him and ask if there was a map or list of the graves surrounding the church. He passed the wall plaques commemorating those fallen in the wars. He loved these places, silent monuments acknowledging great sacrifice. His footfalls echoed against the stone, a small tribute from the living to honour the dead.

*　　*　　*

I try to explain to Mum that we'll have new people helping us from now on. She is worried about her friends although she finds it hard to name them. I tell her they will still be here too. She gets into a lather about where everyone will fit. She is clearly fretting and I know it's because she is frightened at so much apparent change and struggling to come to grips with the idea of new personnel. She has probably forgotten that I go to work most days, too. She wants to trust me but she can't, as benign as I look and sound. I start to make a list and try to go through it with her.

'I don't want Ursula again,' she says. 'She slaps me.'

I don't know who she means by Ursula. Is she getting someone's name wrong? Is it possible someone is hitting Mum or treating her badly when I am not around? That cuts me to the quick. I trust all of the people I let mind her. I have to hope she's confused and not referring to one of our carers. I will have to be extra vigilant.

She is moving around the room, touching photographs and things she's known for years, using them as talismans to ground her. She is trying to rebuild her shrinking universe, hoping that a touch or glance will unlock new meaning. Each item, and its present worth, is probably lost to her the moment she moves on. Still, it seems to bring some sort of comfort.

'Who exactly are you again, dear?' she asks me. 'Remind me. My memory is not what it used to be.'

'I'm Kitty.'

'Kitty?' She frowns. 'That's the same name as my daughter. Are you sure you're not trying to make a fool of me?'

'I am your daughter Kitty.'

'No, you're not,' she says with conviction.

'I am, you know.' Stupid to say 'you know' when clearly she does not know any such thing.

'No,' she reiterates.

'I'm Kitty,' I insist, as calmly as possible.

This is getting us nowhere and she doesn't believe me at any rate. I don't know what to do to prove my case. I might cry but I must not. It will upset Mum. It will upset me.

'You are not my daughter. You couldn't be. You're English.'

Wow. The sheer logic of the statement stuns me. I didn't see that one coming. Never would have, I don't think. It has not been an issue before. I'm not sure we have ever spoken meaningfully about her being Irish and me English. It's just something that we are. She has never particularly worn her Irishness as a badge and I have never really explored it as part of my heritage. We put on a bit of green on St Patrick's Day but that's for fun, not for any great nationalistic reason. This, now, has left me lost for words. And if it is important to her that she is an Irishwoman amongst so many English, she must feel very alone.

Why has it become an issue? I wonder. It's probably random. This creeping disease has no system for selecting the parts of her brain to shut down. It started in her hippocampus and simply followed the trails of its own destructive path. Today, it might just as easily have stopped her gag reflex. Instead, it is still chiselling away at her life's experiences, taking them from her one by one and leaving her with a set of ideas she cannot join up in any effective or cogent way. Her being Irish is something she grew up with. Experiences in childhood are deeply entrenched, more than those of later years, having been mulled over so often in a lifetime. This aspect of her identity has far more chance of being remembered by dint of being there from the start. I was not, and therefore my details are more easily jettisoned. It is another withering blow.

But I am glad that she has something of herself to hold on to. She is Irish. Bully for Mum, genuinely. It's a shame her brain won't allow for an English daughter but I cannot blame her for that. I have to remind myself sternly that this is the Alzheimer's talking, not May Fulton, not my entire mum, because she is unavailable to us any more. In the meantime, I am not her daughter and therefore, in part, she is not my mother. This is so unfair and sad I want to give up.

Mum has never needed to make a big thing of being Irish. Her accent has mellowed slightly through the years but still readily proclaims her, and apart from that she's never wanted anything more of it or what it stands for. Singsong Norfolk it is for me: as you were, Kitty Fulton.

I think of the few times Mum took me to Ireland. I could always tell she was reluctant to go, bent as she was on making it exciting for me. On the first occasion we visited, I was very small and I remember she said, 'We'd better give your grandmother a go of you.' I was sick on the boat and wan and vague-looking by the time we got there. The gnarled old witch held my chin in a vice-like grip to check out my face. I can still feel the cold imprint of her bony fingers digging into my flesh. I didn't recognise any trace of myself in her but children probably don't see such things. I got malice all right: it would have been hard not to pick up on that.

'She's the living image of your father,' she told Mum, and I was sure that wasn't a compliment.

'Would you listen to the little English accent on her,' was another comment repeated to all who came to check out the returned prodigal and her foreign offspring. Again, I didn't get the impression she was pointing out anything that pleased her.

Still, she pressed money into my hand as we left, even if it wasn't sterling, and I got to go home and boast that I had a grandmother.

Subsequent visits revealed that cold hands were good for making pastry, not that Gran ever wanted to, and religion was a curse and all who practised it to be avoided. There must have been something familial in that notion because Mum agonised about sending me to be schooled by the Benedictines. I couldn't have cared less. I wanted to be with Donna, and hang the rest of it. Dad said they gave a great

education and these days they weren't allowed to look sideways at you without dire consequences. He wasn't much of
a one for organised religion either. He had his own indi-
vidual morality which he discreetly passed on. Come to think
of it, I don't think I'm even baptised. They were rebels after
all, my parents.

I try one more run through the list of carers with Mum
but she seems to have given up on me, and the day, and wants
to go to sleep. That has become her favourite activity of late.
I allow myself to be a pushover, yet again. Seems to me I
have spent a lot of my life not rocking the boat. And if that
is so, then I deserve all I've got, or not, to date. I never pushed
Dan for anything, and got nothing. I never pushed myself till
now. The care worker is right: I am no good to anyone else
until I am good for me. I will try very hard to make things
acceptable for Mum at home and a tribute to Dad at work.
And, yes, I will factor me into all of that, too. I wish Simon
were here so that I could discuss this with him. He'd have an
intelligent outsider's perspective, I know. I make a note to ask
for pictures of everyone new to stick on a wall so Mum can
see and check them. I put Simon's name on the list, along
with Mona's.

Pennick station was Kitty's first stop on her way to work as
a commuter. Margo was not yet in so she had an opportunity to peek into her old office without provoking comment.
It looked small and mean from her new vantage point. Still,

she had a huge battle with herself not to go in and open up, then had to hide behind a pillar as she saw Dan pass along the opposite platform. Her breath caught painfully under her ribs and she felt sure he would sense the panic coming off her in waves. She had dressed well and taken especial care with her makeup but, at this last moment, she knew she couldn't face him. The self suspicion that her efforts were probably in case she met Dan, rather more than her first day at Duke Publishing, made her even more agitated. She started as his voice came over the Tannoy, announcing two delays and a platform change, then groaned aloud like any other traveller. Buying her ticket was a useful distraction and she was pleased to find the machine had been fixed. She was first to board her train when it finally arrived.

Kitty rustled through sundry relevant papers on the journey, hoping to arrive in the mindset of a publisher, but was more taken with the faces around her and distracted by the smell of damp, over-perfumed humans. Her stomach was knotted with apprehension. She tried various ways to promote inner peace. She listened to the hum of the engine and clicketty rhythm of the tracks carrying the train along. Facts were a balm so she gave herself over to a few of those. Norridge, as Jed would have it, got its first rail link in 1845. Until then, it was said to be quicker to travel from Norwich to Amsterdam by sea than Norwich to London by land. Her mind was packed with trivia, she decided, though it was a comfort to be distracted by it.

At the other end of the journey she was carried off the train in a swell of early-morning commuters, as anonymous as the next person. She changed into her smart shoes too early, only to go over on her ankles repeatedly and feel the leather pinch as she walked from the station to her city-centre office. Kitty had always loved the cobbled streets leading to her father's business. Now they were to be her own route to work and she was too jittery with nerves to enjoy the walk. Hadn't Noël Coward once remarked, 'Very flat, Norfolk' in a play? But Norridge had undulations, hills even where buildings could rise above others. It seemed odd by comparison with Pennick's flatness. I am in a flat Panic, Kitty thought, placing one foot in front of the other very deliberately, to resist stopping altogether from terror.

The office was on Lily Lane, so-called in the days when the city was renowned for, and awash with, flowers. More incidental tidbits to clutter the mind of this hick from a hick town she thought. And all the more galling as Norwich itself was often regarded as a backwater. London was a metropolis, Manchester too, whereas Norwich was regularly dismissed at national level as a country town rather than a proper city. Yet here she was, frightened by it and what it now stood for. Sod it, thought Kitty and stopped in a doorway to change back into her sheepskin boots. Better, much better. She felt more like herself and a bit more up to continuing on her way.

The streets were full of quirky art galleries and antique

shops. She wanted to dawdle by their windows, be tempted by things she didn't need. But she had to get to work and there was no more putting off her date with the future. She was reeled in, street by street, resisting the funky shops and cafés, until she stood before the brass plate bearing the words 'Duke Publishing'. Kitty walked through the office door like a condemned woman approaching a scaffold.

Miss Marshall looked genuinely delighted to see her. She had brewed coffee and there were Danish pastries to eat before tackling the post and, perhaps, the rest of Kitty's working life. They chatted easily, which was a tribute to the older woman who gave her new boss the equivalent of a verbal massage. Kitty relaxed a little and was brought up to date with the business. Basically, orders were steady and correspondence unusually high, as notes of condolence continued to arrive each day.

'Some are wonderful celebrations of your father and stories that you may not have heard before. I only opened those that were generally addressed,' Miss Marshall added quickly, keen to avoid appearing intrusive. 'Anything for immediate family is on the Desk for you to deal with.'

The Desk was now hers. Kitty foostered about the office, unwilling to sit at her father's place yet. She felt like a fraud. At least her toes were warm enough again to risk her court shoes. Miss Marshall had rescued the few plants her father had in his house, and the finest, a large rubber plant he'd called the Triffid, was now settling in to its new spot by the window. Kitty knew it liked the cold end of a pot of tea, no milk or sugar. 'Good morning,' she finally said to the room in general and sat down.

Her father's desk diary read like a work in progress, with dates to meet people and see films and plays, but also quotes he'd especially liked and jotted down. This was not the schedule of a man who was expecting to die any time soon. Today, she noticed, he would have lunched with an author at a wine bar two streets away. An attached note read, 'Remind that manuscript due end of month.' Miss Marshall confirmed that the work was due in and Kitty decided she would chase it up. I am living my father's life now, she thought, but I will have to do it my way.

His handwriting was measured and handsome, a lot like him. It touched her to sit and read about his world in his words. Kitty went to the beginning of the book to see what he'd put for the start of the year. It was a quote from 'Ars Poetica' by Archibald McLeish:

A poem should not mean
But be.

Stephen had written beside it, 'A poem need not mean, but should be?' Between those two was where he would pitch his year, one he would not live to see out.

Miss Marshall knocked on the open door and said, 'I wonder if I might have a word.' She looked troubled and

Kitty thought, This is it, she's leaving. She girded herself for the worst and hoped she wouldn't cry when it happened.

'I realise this is a very difficult time for you and I don't wish to add to that in any way.'

Kitty's jaw began to tremble as she clenched her teeth, awaiting the killer blow.

'I want you to know that I have had many good years with the firm . . .'

Yes, here it comes.

'. . . but I will understand completely if you want to start afresh with a new team of your own.'

Kitty waited for more then realised that Miss Marshall had expected to be let go and not the other way around. 'No,' she said, too loudly. 'Oh, no, not at all. I was worried that you would leave me,' she explained. 'I was afraid that you wouldn't want to work for me.'

Miss Marshall looked as though she didn't understand that concept and might say, Don't be silly. Kitty wanted to go to the other side of the desk and hug her for that. However, it didn't seem very businesslike, even under the circumstances.

'Thank you so much for wanting to stay with me,' she said instead. 'I am so glad that you do.'

There were two other members of the small team: Victor Long and Cameron Field. They worked part-time but had arranged to be in for Kitty's first day. When they arrived they greeted her as if she belonged. They ignored her nervousness and filled the office with pleasing chatter and industry, which she realised was partly from good manners but also because that's how they liked it too. There was no fustiness, but intelligent banter and fun. Kitty discovered how brilliantly rude Victor Long was about competitors he felt ranked beneath Duke Publishing. He was wearing a worn sweatshirt with an illustration of a sock, a rat and some golf tees on the front. He told her he'd designed it himself and had lots more in the pipeline.

'Don't doubt it,' Miss Marshall said. 'He's working on his Byron at the moment because he's determined to rehabilitate not just philosophers but poets too. So far, it's a picture of someone waving at Ron Atkinson.'

'Good, if you recognise Big Ron,' Cameron Field said.

Victor, head of academic publications, led the fun. He was giddy, gay and mid-forties. Cameron Field liked to hold fire before delivering his own bombshells, with deadly accuracy and wit. 'Timing is all,' the poetry editor would say when they laughed. Miss Marshall steadied the ship, delicately poised for action and intervention. She was a naturally precise woman without being prissy with it. She also knew how to dress the part. Kitty marvelled at her stunning but understated ensembles of classic pieces, all made of the finest cotton, silk or cashmere. Kitty knew her yarns from her mother's heyday as a knitter. She would take bets that Miss Marshall looked after her clothes very well and that her vintage pieces were originals she had bought at the time and carefully held on to. Kitty realised she needed to work on her new look as a publisher. And perhaps when she was comfortable in her new role she could progress to calling Marie simply by that name.

She was consulted about a jacket for a book of poems on the theme of water. Kitty had read the material the week before and been struck by the robust images of water's strength and power over us, our dependence on it. She put the decision to a ballot and a painting by a local artist came out tops. This was fitting as her father had always fostered such work, and the small assembly agreed the most appropriate and deserving image had won.

'It's so good to have some of Stephen back here,' Victor said.

Kitty took a moment to twig. 'You mean, me?'

'Of course. You are the person most like him left in the world.'

SIXTEEN

The audio books are not the success I'd hoped for. They have made Mum paranoid. She thinks she is hearing voices in her head. The narrators have done too good a job and she is totally immersed in the world they have created using the author's words. I should have foreseen this but I was distracted by Norwich and heedless of the main thrust of our life, which is my mother's welfare. My mind was elsewhere and now poor Mum's is in a mess. She was fine when we had the books on the speakers in the room, but a move to head-phones scuppered her. We chose a well-reviewed novel and just one thriller, meant for young teenagers, as I thought these would be easier for her to follow. We even got some poetry, but it is the thriller that has done the harm. She's convinced someone is trying to kill her. I really should have known better and am ashamed of myself. Even answering the telephone is a problem as it's more disembodied voices for her to deal with. I bin the headphones for starters.

Pauline McLynn

I try to explain how the telephone works and find that I don't actually understand it all that well myself. It is one of those things we take for granted. Who remembers how they set up their email account, even, let alone an invention that has been around as long as the phone? I might as well try to explain electricity, again something I am hazy on and inclined to file away under magic, though not the kind that drives me around the bend. Electricity is good magic, for the most part, it's magic with an edge and a purpose, not trickery like sleight of hand is.

I get to thinking that poetry is sleight of hand in its way. It weaves a deliberate magic, moulding words for a purpose, to delight and astound but also to bedevil and entrance. Again, I can't accurately explain how that's done. I seem to understand little enough about life's embellishments. Yet I am a woman who decides to unleash such trickery as poetry on the nation. A smile has crept on to my face. I may be as maddening as any other hoaxer now. Somewhere a reader may be cursing me. But it's a benign magic, I hope, and one that will help. I am certainly under its spell.

When Mum was first diagnosed we had a conversation with Mr Bishop about anti-psychotic drugs. We didn't want to go down that road. I am happy to say Mr Bishop agreed, yet another reason to be a little in love with him. What we have always clung to is that Mum is not delusional, she is simply unable to reason out something new or remember it long enough to understand and assimilate it. The voices in the telephone need to be explained in language and terms she can recognise. I find this is best achieved by comparing it to something from long ago. I tell her our telephone is like the one in the callbox outside her mother's house in Ireland but we have a small version here and that the people calling are doing so to tell us good things, good news.

'I don't have to talk to them if I don't want to,' she checks.

'No, you don't.'

'But I might, sometimes.'

'Yes, you might. That's good too.'

'They're not in the telephone, though, sure they're not?'

'No, it's like a tube that's carrying their messages to us in our house along this wire from where they are.'

'They're not in the house, so, hiding on us?'

'No.'

'Good.'

She is calm again. It's all about the even keel, making her feel safe and able to cope.

'We put money in the big, black phone in the box outside Mam's and you press button A when you get through and button B when you want the money back. Me and Ellen always go in and press B when we're passing 'cos sometimes there's money still in there.'

The telephone wins a reprieve as Mum searches for the A and B buttons and wonders why it's so small.

I love my time at the Norwich office although I cannot go in for the full nine to five each day because of Mum.

In particular when she is upset, like she's been about the voices, it's wrong to leave her for others to deal with, as wonderful as they all are. I can easily work from here when I need to, though all of my papers have to be cleared away in a box under my bed when I am done so there is no danger of Mum making something from them, usually after a craft demonstration on daytime television. I saved a manuscript from becoming a Christmas garland yesterday. It still bears two fine scissor slashes across the title page: blunt though the instrument was, it made its mark. There is a lot of Make and Do in the house at present as Roly has decided to take up knitting, or at least the unwinding of balls of wool that they might be ready for use by a human companion. Mum finds this most entertaining and will throw balls around for him for as long as he wants her to. I have lucked out there because he never goes more than fifteen minutes before needing to eat and sleep a few hours.

At the height of her powers Mum looked like she was in a hypnotic trance when she knitted. It was fascinating to watch. She found it a great way to tune out or to meditate. Slowly, as her faculties waned, it looked more like she was in combat with the needles and yarn. Now, she is chucking wool around for a cat to chase.

Roly is allowed to use his cat flap to go forth and terrorise the neighbourhood with general prowling and the chasing of wind-strewn cartons and cans. We have dispensed with the cat litter so Mum isn't tempted by it any more. She is resigned to her incontinence pants and constantly checks she has supplies of both the day and, larger, night-time varieties, each of which has its own brightly coloured box in her room. She chose cerise and lime green there, and I must admit they look pretty stacked together. Aside from the strangers in her head, all is well.

The visit to the library was fine but odd. Mum loved being surrounded by the masses of books and went from section to section running her fingers along the spines. Sometimes she touched those she may have half-recognised or perhaps it was the covers that pleased her. She opened one or two but immediately lost interest. It reminded me of when I was a child and played librarian at home. It was the act of opening and stamping the books that pleased me at the time, not reading the classics. I checked out *Lorna Doone* and *The Count of Monte Cristo* innumerable times to imaginary friends without ever reading a word of them.

Simon proudly walked us around his kingdom. It was lovely to have a friend along. I have lots of new ones now, though I worry that it has been at the expense of my father in an unfair cosmic trade off. Some are as a result of his death, you see, but I would far rather have him alive, given a choice. It chokes me to think of him and then my heart beats and aches so hard I think it may explode. It never does, of course, that's the stuff of proper, dark fairytales.

We stopped at the poetry section and I noticed some with Duke's imprint. It was hard to see Mum as having anything to do with them although she edited many of the works on display. I watched as she cocked her head to the side, trying to figure out the familiar emblem on the book spines, then giving it up as a bad deal and skipping off to dawdle and sing quietly among other shelves and genres.

Everything is changed, a lot of it for the better, but the important things are still so wrong. The magnitude of the change frightens me and I say as much to Simon. He says I will cope, and I hope he is correct. He seems to have great faith in me, or hope on my behalf.

I miss the stamping of our books when we are ready to go. I did love the little card bearing the details that was stored at the library while a book was out, and the random way some of the date stamps were slanted or added to a rogue new column on the card-holding insert inside the cover. Still, a book is a book and that much hasn't changed, yet. It will, I am assured. It is changing even as we speak but we will be of a generation able to ignore that if we choose. I hope the public will always opt for handling an actual print and paper book. I publish those now, after all. I love the feel and look and smell of books at all stages of their existence. Anyone who doesn't experience that is missing out, I think.

Another change from my childhood is that library etiquette does not dictate absolute quiet any more. It doesn't mean anyone is shouting, of course, except Mum as she waves goodbye. A few readers actually wave back.

It makes me think of Dan and the trains and then I am floundering all over again.

Simon had watched a new drama on television where archae-ologists solved an ancient mystery within the allotted viewing hour. The series was hokum but fiercely entertaining for all that, and a bit of encouragement for him. He might have liked to be a digger, once upon a time, but ancient records, searching through fusty books, suited him better; the mind game of the quest. He thought that historians had so much more at their disposal to flesh out a story with, not just the artefacts from a dig, chipped from prior use and buried in the dirt of centuries. Historians were allowed to take leaps that were not tied to a few specific items in a circumscribed patch of earth. An historian had the whole world from which to cull reason and fact, the greatest possible wealth of detail, and therefore was potentially a better storyteller. The best historians, he felt, were those who accurately conveyed their story while making the necessary mindshift to bring it alive with contemporary relevance and interest. A local historian, of course, bore witness to the smaller lives spent in the bigger picture. That was what Simon hoped to do.

St Melchior's was a parish on the outskirts of town which not been totally outstripped by urban renewal. It had a fine view of the surrounding countryside on two sides and a very pretty seat from which to enjoy it, or so said the Vicar. As it was presently dark, Simon took the man's word for it.

The church was neat and well tended and also attended, according to the Vicar, who was a round man with a shiny pate and pleasant demeanour. He looked a lot like the church felt, Simon decided. The Vicar offered him tea, which Simon politely refused, plugged in the two-bar electric heater and left him to it.

Simon liked to start some years before his target date to get a feeling for the time and the names involved, allowing his brain to click gradually into detective mode. It meant that tonight he was looking for the ancestors of those initialled FV and AC, should they be present in the register. He patiently let his gloved finger run down the cast of the town's characters laid before him, keeping a keen eye out for initials that might be of interest. He'd been sitting at his task half an hour when his spine began to tingle. He found the first mentions of the family Kitty had unearthed, the Vickers. Here was the marriage of Louise Martin to Albert Vickers in 1765. Simon calmly made his notes and continued until he hit pay-dirt with the baptism of Fenella in 1766. He had found Kitty's Nell. He steadied the page and resisted the urge to whizz through the names and dates, instead transcribing those facts that were pertinent and hoping for more. He found the death of Louise recorded in 1778 and her husband Albert followed her two years later. There was no mention of Fenella's demise in the register, even if she'd lived to be a hundred. Along the way he also encountered one Anne Clarke, initials AC, but removed her from the list of possibles as she had died an infant.

Simon was not above getting his hands dirty which was exactly what he found himself doing the following morning before work. The graveyard attached to St Melchior's dated back to the seventeenth century and, like the church, was pleasant and well kept. He saw that the Vicar had not lied about the view. The outer reaches of the small plot were those holding the most ancient remains. Subsidence had left its mark over the years so stones and markers were askew in the sunken earth. He began with the graves most easily accessible in order to inspect names and dates, but couldn't find the Vickerses' plot. Acid rain and the elements had sloughed the lettering from most of the ancient markers. He had to resort to rubbings of the stones to read some of those most worn, each charcoaled stroke adding to the tale of a citizen long gone, remembered now only by a stranger looking for someone else. Here were the basic details of life and death, the rest of their story consigned to oblivion. He read of Caleb Hough who departed this life 12 June 1807, aged 15. He met relicts and the stillborn, and Zarius Lovelace who went to God aged 19 hours. Simon knew his statistics: in 1800, two out of every five children born alive died before they reached the age of five. Sabina Willbond, who 'died in year 20 of her age', had a headstone with a couplet warning:

Be humble mortals, learn your doom;
To this cold bed, you all must come.

Simon's hands and face were frozen by the time he located Louise and Albert and two of their sons, Uriah and Jacob, but there was no sign or mention of Nell. It was unlikely she had a grave here all to herself but he checked the rest of the stones before giving up and making for work. He was an hour late and frigid with the cold. Still, he had found some useful information and was eager to tell the others.

The light is on in Dan's allotment shed as I trudge to the station on my way to work in Norwich. The morning is dull and grey and the light shines jauntily through the little windows. The shed looks so friendly and inviting, I stand to consider my options even though I know I should walk on. I decide to creep closer, I don't exactly know why; every shred of reason is screaming at me not to. He is inside, puttering about. I can hear his shuffles and the odd, small cough against the cold morning. In the old days I would have joined him, in the days when that was normal for us. I am not sure what normal is any more and am not the person to ask about it, I daresay. Normal for me is a strange place that most other people will never know, with a ghost mother and a house full of Post-it instructions. I have no instructions for the here and now. For one insane moment I think about turning the handle and going in. Instead, I go around the corner and press myself flat against the back wall, to be as close to Dan as I can allow myself now.

This is probably just as insane a move as the alternative I quashed. I try to imagine what he feels like. It isn't that difficult because I know his body as well as my own. I hear him drop something and swear, and just as I am smiling I hear a woman's laugh. It is Donna. I start back, stung. He has brought her here, to this place that used to be ours. My mind sharply dismisses the perceived hurt. Of course he has brought her here: it proves to her that she belongs with him. It proves that to us all. And, irrationally, I also wonder why he is not at work. I have removed myself from that part of our life, too, so I don't know the answers to even the simplest things now. This is as it should be but it hurts all the same.

I am shocked by my own foolishness. I really thought I was past such idiocy. I stumble away, desperately careful to remain silent. I am a grubby spy and detest myself for it. I am light headed with the notion of my narrow escape from disaster. What if they had seen me? How would that have seemed? I will not allow myself to come so close to ruining things, ever again. I am done with that life. I have to be. Still it is difficult for me to breathe and I don't want to look anyone else in the eye for the rest of my journey.

Duke's is my refuge. It is a new world where I am almost reinvented. I am amazed by the stimulation I find here, every day. It is so different from my job in the station at Pennick. Here there are creative decisions to be made that are more than what colour the walls should be painted and if we can afford new shelves.

I find it is easiest to call myself Kitty Fulton Duke, as hard as I resisted it once, as this announces me to my new business colleagues without too much explanation. It's very posh-sounding and I have to resist giggling at the pretension of it, the ridiculous double-barrelled sound. I am not prepared to lose any part of it, however, as that would mean denying either Mum or Dad which is not on, as far I am concerned.

I speak on the telephone to an American who calls me 'Miss Dook'. He is the first American I have spoken to over the phone, though I must surely have helped some with timetable information in my day. It is such a simple 'first' to happen to me at my age that I am slightly shocked by it. I have to get over that sharpish as he wants to talk about work we are to co-publish. He uses words like 'implacability' and 'per se' and I'm not totally sure I understand them. He's in love with the phrase 'the human condition' and also 'Beckettian sensibilities', which I take to mean minimalism and despair.

When I check that with Miss Marshall afterwards she smiles happily and says, 'Yes, exactly.' To be honest, I don't want to have to read all of Beckett to find out, I really do prefer a good thriller. I like the sound of 'sensibilities', though, and think I must cultivate some if I don't have them already. I murmur general light assent down the line to the American and try to make that sound both quiet and enigmatic. It's treacherous, actually. I don't want to overstretch myself and use a term or phrase wrongly, thereby blowing my cover. I find the call terrifying. The truth is, he knows the material in question a lot better than I do, but he also loves it and that's good. I hold on to that and get out the other end with plausibility intact, I hope.

It's great to be able to talk to the others here about Mum. They know her, of course, from when she was fully May Fulton. She's not here with us today so I feel no guilt about discussing her, whereas sometimes, at home, it's as if I am discussing someone who isn't in the room even when the new version of her is, and it's all very strange. This distance is affording me an overview of her condition. It's frightening because, if the disease follows regular patterns, Mum's time is running out. She will never live to be old. The cruelty of that fact is almost overwhelming and I go out walking to pound off the depression that threatens to overtake me. I am also putting off the conversation with Miss Marshall about when we will clear Dad's house and what is to be done with it in the long run. I feel as if I don't have any 'long run' any more, just borrowed and unreliable time.

Norwich is lighting up for Christmas. The shops have colourful window displays to lure in customers. Glitter twinkles and even the rain seems less intrusive as a result. Normally, I love to browse. Normally, I adore the festive lights of a town. I'd like to see coloured baubles in the trees and windows all year round. But today I cannot settle my mind.

I worry that elderly travellers at the station may not be cared for by anything more than a cranky ticket machine. Chances are Margo is not a lot better, mind you, but still, they need the chat and the help. I can't bear to think that they'll be dismissed by her and then distressed if they miss a connection. This leads me to think of Dad's distress as he suffered his fatal heart attack. I can only hope he thought it was indigestion as many people do. A doctor explained to me it's usually very unlike the chest-clutching attack of television medical dramas or the movies.

As upset as I am about all of these different things, I know they are a deflection of sorts, though the station is at the centre of my problem. I still see it and use it most days. I cannot continue to skulk through like a criminal. I need to talk to Dan about my official resignation and it is not something that can be undertaken simply by letter. I will have to face him and that is what I most dread. I need to make that clean break, that act of closure, so we can both walk away with dignity. From here, it looks like the hardest thing ever to tackle but it must be dealt with. Otherwise I will never truly move on and neither will Donna and Dan.

Kitty drafted a letter, worrying over it for the whole afternoon. She picked up the phone and dialled Pennick station.

Dan was not available, Margo said, but she could leave a message. Ask him to call – could Margo make doubly sure he got that? The sigh from the other end of the line was all the response Kitty got and the call ended with what sounded like Margo hanging up. Kitty decided to text Dan with the message, too, having little faith in her replacement by now. She asked if they might meet later that day, when she was on her way home from Norwich. His answer was prompt and by text also, naming a time. Kitty felt sick with apprehension about the meeting, thinking even the message about it looked sinister on the screen of her mobile. The minutes ticked ominously by. Miss Marshall sensed her mood.

'This is about more than leaving the old job, isn't it?'

Kitty nodded miserably. 'I'm cutting the ties of a lifetime, really. And the worst of it, for me, is that I want to cut them but that makes me feel like I'm betraying all involved. I'm very mixed up about it.'

If Marie Marshall was puzzled she didn't show it. 'You must move on. It will be the best thing in the long run.'

The long run, the thing Kitty felt she didn't have but apparently did. There was a whole future out there for her to discover. To ignore that would be an unconscionable waste. She knew all of this but it didn't make it any less daunting.

'It's almost out of your hands, if you want to think of it that way,' Miss Marshall continued. 'Your father's death has given you a new course to pursue, should you choose to.

I think you should, even if it's not my place to say that. Make him proud.'

None of this lifted Kitty's mood of dread and the afternoon trailed miserably by. The train journey home was equally interminable but she relished the delays. She opted to stand in case sitting allowed her to curl up and deliberately miss her stop. She knew Dan would guess which train she would arrive on. It gave him the advantage, she decided. Not that this was a competition. How would he play things? Would he see the train coming down the tracks and go to the office to wait or meet her on the platform. She hoped for the office; anything else cast her too much as Celia Johnson in *Brief Encounter*, and she didn't want to get sentimental or sloppy. There had been enough of that to fill a few lifetimes.

Dan was on the platform and waved to her as she arrived. Kitty was saved from greeting him with more than a hand waggle by a passenger on crutches, needing assistance. As Dan helped the man, Kitty stood by the door to the office and was glad to see Margo still on duty inside. Each precious second spent acclimatising was helping her to keep calm. Kitty looked at her father's watch and saw that Margo would soon be knocking off. She willed Dan to come over now so that she might get through the business of leaving and go while they were still in company.

'How is Norwich?' he asked, as he ushered her into the overheated office. It smelled of stale coffee and hard-boiled egg.

'Fine. Odd. A challenge.'

Margo barely acknowledged her, preferring to bang some stationery around the desk before grabbing her bag and leaving. She barely said goodbye to either of them. It made Kitty feel guilty for something she hadn't done and she resented the girl for it. Dan shrugged as if to say, Issues, ignore her.

'I presume you're here to hand in your letter of resignation?'

'Well, yes.'

'I've been expecting as much. We'll all be sorry to lose you, Kitty, myself most of all.'

She was afraid then of breaking down and fudging her exit. She buried herself in her handbag to find the letter she'd written earlier. Why did she have so much junk in there? She swept aside loose items of makeup and a hairbrush. There was a diary, pens, some bills, her umbrella, a purse, perfume, the evening paper, and several half-empty packets of gum. Her keys rattled, underscoring the chaos. Finally she located the envelope and put it on the desk. She couldn't risk any physical contact that might occur if she handed it to Dan, she felt too precariously balanced. He did, too, she guessed, standing with his arms tightly folded for protection.

'I don't know how much time you'd like me to work out,' she said.

'Don't worry, that won't be necessary.'

She was grateful for his understanding and restraint but

wary of showing any emotion. It wasn't him she was most worried about here but herself. If she allowed her resolve to melt she would be the one to ruin this perfect leavetaking. The simplicity of it was unexpected and threatened to wrong-foot her.

'We'll all miss you,' Dan said, 'especially me.' He looked down at his working boots, encrusted with the dirt of his day. 'Thank you, Kitty. For everything.'

'Thank you, Dan. Really. It has been a wonderful time but we need to move on.'

'We do.'

'Goodbye.'

There would be no handshake. They had never in their lives done that, not even at her father's funeral. Then, he had lightly touched her forearm in sympathy as she longed for him to envelop her and make her safe and able again. Donna had nodded and scowled her condolences. This stilted little scene had gone unnoticed by all but the three of them in the confusion of mourners. As huddled together as they might have seemed, they could not have been further apart. The Three Amigos had come unstuck.

There was nothing more to say and nothing further to hold her at the station. Kitty practically ran through the door and out into the cold Pennick evening. And what she felt then was not the sorrow she'd expected, but relief. She was free.

◦   ◦   ◦

Exhilaration rushes through me like a drug in my blood-stream. I am high on the adrenaline of my straightforward exit and slightly worried that I seem to want to sing from the mountaintops in the manner of Maria in *The Sound of Music*. Pennick's flatness would save me from part of that scenario and I know I am spectacle enough without bursting into tuneless song. The trouble is, I am so grateful to Dan for his unfussy handling of my leavetaking that I am in danger of falling in love with him all over again. I haven't yet fallen out of love with him, I suppose, but I must ignore that and hope that time will dim it as it has so many other things. I step gaily along the pathway by the allotments, heedless of the drizzle and cold. My mind throws up the odd warning about pride and a fall but I don't care. I fret that I have no one to tell about this. Then . . . Simon, I think, he'll understand. I'll call him when I get home.

There is no need to phone Simon because he is sitting at our table drinking tea with Benny, who has Roly on his knee and looks as happy as I feel. Mum is playing perfect hostess. There is water in the milk jug and crackers on a plate instead of biscuits but she has done well.

'Ah, here's that nice girl who helps around the place,' she tells them, then turns to me. 'I'll let you do the introductions yourself, dear.'

I'm just thrilled she's properly dressed and not sharing the mysteries of her incontinence pants with two relative strangers who might not be ready just yet for that sort of frankness in their lives. She busies herself in the kitchen again and returns with a decanted tin of cat food, which she smears generously on to the crackers. Roly now looks very interested in the snack.

'Mum, you'll spoil your appetite for dinner if you eat anything now.' I wrestle the plate from her. 'Would anyone like a glass of wine, or is it too early?'

'Wine,' Mum says. 'I think I like that. Do I?'

'I'll join you,' Simon says, but Benny looks uncomfortable.

'I'm teetotal,' he explains. 'Never even wanted to try it, to tell you the truth. Too many alcoholics in my family. Best avoided, I always thought.' He's stricken that he might have given offence and quickly adds, 'For me. Best avoided for me, you understand.'

I pour the drinks but it is Benny, on his third cup of tea, who gets talkative. 'I've been over the allotments,' he reports. 'Helping Jed out. Enjoying it, too. He's got good stories, you know.'

I am not the only one forging new relationships. This thought and the wine give me a further warm glow. I am in love with life. I'll even let old Alzheimer's off the hook for the evening, as long as it doesn't upset my mother or cause her to look foolish. I have enough foolishness for us both now, grinning as I still am and giggling silently about the sheer range of possibilities open to me at last. I wonder, idly, if I have been unhappy much longer than I ever knew?

Simon smiles at my good humour. 'You are elated,' he says.

'I am unleashed,' I tell him.

'Should I be afraid?'

'Oh, yes, I think so.'

'Good.'

We both think that worth drinking to. The laws of gravity dictate we all end up in the dirt, so the bottom line is this euphoria can't last. But, while it does, I will enjoy it fully.

'I miss the two of you,' Benny tells Roly and me. He's like a kid whose parents have separated. When he gets up to go to work, I make him promise he'll visit again. He says he will and I believe him.

Simon offers to cook and it looks like there'll be a second bottle of wine opened tonight. The Town Librarian is becoming quite the regular at 15, The Cottages.

'I like having a man about the place,' Mum says. 'Will you be coming every day?'

'I will if you'd like that,' Simon replies.

She's content, which is the main thing, even if she thinks he's one of the new carers. I see no harm in that. He's done his share of caring for us, in fairness.

I like to see him work the kitchen. He has a lovely slicing action with the big knife I rescue from a locked cutlery drawer for him.

'Can I offer you an apron?' I ask.

'I'll wear one if it'll give you a thrill, Kitty,' he says, without missing a beat in his dicing.

I feel weird about that, in a really good way. I laugh. I suspect he's flirting with me but I could be mistaken. It's not something that ever happens to me so I'm probably misreading the situation.

I describe my week and adventures, without dwelling on my final exit from the station. I think Simon knows its larger significance without being told. He says he can feel my joy and I'm happy about that. It's nice to be able to spread it around. Mum is smiling too and I really don't care why, just as long as she's enjoying herself. The aim of my life is to make her comfortable, safe and happy. It's my turn to care for her as she has for me for so long. This is the indentured service owed to family and I am determined to give it my all and acquit myself well. Besides, she is also my best friend.

Out of nowhere, I begin to cry. I have hit the earth quicker than anticipated. I blub on and tell them both it's because I am so happy. And I am. I am so damned happy. Roly climbs on to my knee and I tell him I love him. I love the three of them. I tell them that, a number of times. I am so lucky. I am so happy. I am so drunk.

SEVENTEEN

It's hard to describe the suffering. I can barely open my eyes, though it is still dark when I wake, as these winter mornings always are, so it is not the light that hurts but a more profound pain trapped inside me. It takes a long time to summon the ability to raise my head from the pillow then follow it with my body and finally get out of the bed. Just standing upright is a challenge. I begin to move slowly. Every step generates a seismic and nauseating shudder. I cannot breathe without wanting to retch, and at times I do. Happily, if that's the word to use, these are dryish and don't make too much mess. I have to sit on a step halfway down the stairs to allow the nausea to recede.

I very, very gently knock back fizzy painkillers and fully expect them to come back up again so I sit very, very still in the armchair till that danger is past. Roly is intrigued but not enough to interfere with me and for this I am thankful. My hand is able to rub his head without involving the rest of me. There is one unexpected bonus to the ghastliness: I am so hungover I don't feel low; this pain is too great to allow for the subtlety of depression.

Eventually the agony is numbed enough for me to deal with Mum's ablutions and breakfast before I hand her over to Hannah. My neighbour laughs when she sees me. Mum joins her and says, 'Isn't she a terrible sight altogether?' She's right, I am. 'The demon drink,' Mum says, shaking her head and laughing some more. She doesn't remember last night so it must be so obvious what's wrong with me even the addled can tell. I am tremulous from the poison still racing around my beleaguered body and move like a newborn foal.

I don't know how I manage it but I get to work without any disaster of note. There are several incidents of misjudging the depth and width of puddles and some bumping into parked cars and rubbish bins. I may still be somewhat drunk. I get to the door of Duke's and it is Marie's turn to laugh, which she does. 'I take it your mission yesterday went well,' she remarks, and I admit that it did. Too well. 'I was feeling as free as Adam and Eve in the Garden of Eden,' I tell her, 'and made as poor a call.' She brews me a milky, decaffeinated coffee from freshly ground beans and adds a little sugar. It is delicious and I feel compelled to say, 'I love you, Ms M.'

I decide to use my numbed condition to push through the other big thing I have been avoiding. I arrange to clear my father's house. The pain in my head is so searing that any grief associated with this step is overshadowed. It is the perfect moment to tackle the unpalatable. I remember some government underling getting fired for suggesting a disaster day is a good one to leak and lose other bad news, and then making good on that theory. With everything around me looking vague and out of focus, even my reflection in the mirror, I ask Marie to accompany me this coming weekend and arrange for Simon and Benny to be on call too should any big items need to be moved. Between the retching and the headache, the day I have long postponed is chosen, noted and will have to be dealt with. Too many people now know about it and would have to be cancelled and lied to if I chickened out. One other thing has come of this: I have begun to call Marie by her first name.

We have brought out a book of Christmas poems for the seasonal market and the local radio station wants to do an interview with me. Today. I try to wriggle off the hook.

'Does it have to be today?' I wheedle. 'Tomorrow would be so much better.'

No, they cannot do it tomorrow, yes, it has to be today.

'To be honest with you, Marie Marshall here at the firm is the expert on this book. She's the one you really want.' The telephone receiver is digging painfully into the side of my pounding head.

No, Miss Marshall won't do. They want the new young face of the firm. I'd like to point out that it's radio and my face won't be on show, but I haven't got the strength. This is great publicity and I cannot turn it down.

I am not shy of strangers, thanks to working in a train station, but I am quaking to think the general public will listen in and expect me to be interesting. I have nothing to say, probably never had. I feel as if I am floating in a surreal dream where colours are too bright and sounds too loud and tastes too magnified. But, as terrified as I am about speaking to a faceless public, even that cannot hurt as much as this hangover. I'm actually lucky it's radio and no one can see the wreck that once was Kitty Fulton. The listeners are about to be introduced to Ms Katherine Fulton Duke of the distinguished Norwich publishing firm. May the Lord have mercy on her pickled soul.

It all passes in a blur of introductions to the studio staff, the refusal of a cup of tea, the grateful acceptance of ice-cold water, and entry into the muggy booth. The atmosphere and odour in the padded cell are a lot like the station office on a day when the heating is on full blast and Roly's food is on the turn. I clutch the hardback book and remember Marie said to mention the name as much as possible. 'Yule be glad you did,' she joked.

I am asked to read out a poem and choose a short comic one about our famous Norfolk turkeys. I am certain I read it badly but the interviewer is smiling and begins to read out texts and emails people send in praising the book. One is from someone with the initials MM and I suspect that has come from our office. I say nothing to alert the good folk of the county and can see how easily big corporations could fall into similar phone fixing. It makes me chuckle but I have a dangerous moment of bile-churn and remain as still as possible thereafter. We chat about other titles on our list and, when asked about our future plans, I mutter about some academic texts, the next Harry Higgins collection, and then announce that I am working with some local historians on a study of the Napoleonic Wars and their effect on Pennick, my hometown. As Mum might say, 'Sweet holy Mary, mother of the divine Jesus.'

What's possessed me?

There is a flood of messages wondering when that book will be out and I have to backtrack and stress that it's merely on-going work at present. Suddenly I am out of there and on to the freezing street, clutching a piece of paper with the presenter's mobile number on it. He wants me to call him so we can go for a drink sometime. How did all that happen?

Back at the office the company of three have gathered to congratulate me on my turn. We find we are all very curious about the Pennick book. 'I guess I'll have to make good on it now,' I say.

'Best to,' says Marie. 'The advance word of mouth is very good.'

I crack open a bottle of Chablis because I need a cure

and we appear to have much to celebrate. The strangest thing is that I now feel attuned here. This is my job, this is my place, these are my people. I wonder if the Triffid enjoys a glass of vino at all? The phone begins to ring and Marie starts to take orders for the Christmas poetry collection and to field enquiries about the upcoming historical study of Pennick in the early-nineteenth century.

Simon sat with Mona Fletcher listening to Kitty on the radio. He felt a bit heated by the presenter's obvious flirting. If the man called her attractive or beautiful once more, in those cloyingly honeyed tones of his, Simon was going to have to ring in to interrupt the conversation. He hoped the man's voice didn't match his appearance and that he was ugly as sin. When the surprising announcement of the local history book came, he and Mona both gasped at the same time and quickly looked to check if the other had already known of the plan. Clearly not.

'It seems we have a lot of work to do,' Simon said.

'And contracts to sign. Marvellous. I've always fancied seeing my name on the spine of a good book, so we'd better make it one. Meeting, tonight, Kitty's house. I don't think she can argue about that after dropping a bombshell.'

Kitty answered her mobile, saying, 'I have become a lush so forgive any slurring. I am drinking again, but only to dull the pain of my hangover. Do I need to apologise for anything I may have said or done last night?'

'Sadly, no. Well done on the radio interview. Was it just me or was that host a bit smarmy?'

'Oh, I thought he was a lovely man. Actually, he gave me his number so I imagine he has a book in a drawer somewhere that he wants me to consider. It all comes with the territory now.'

Simon eased up when he realised how unaware Kitty had remained of the presenter's intentions. 'It certainly made me want to read the book,' he said. 'Or should that be books?' He was laughing now.

Kitty joined him. 'I don't know what came over me. Why in the world did I announce it? I had no right to do that without consulting you and Mona but it just came out of my mouth. My brain has been slightly on hold all day. I was rash, I know, but I do think it's a good idea. Shall we?'

'Oh, yes. Besides, I don't think there's any choice in the matter now. I listened with Mona and she's fired up to the point of being scary – eleven on a scale of one to ten, I'd say. I don't think you could back out even if you wanted to.'

'Which I do not.'

'Just as well, because she has called a meeting of the Council of Three tonight at your house to discuss it.'

'I'd best switch to coffee immediately.'

And I need to find Nelly Vickers, Simon thought as he hung up.

I look at my local train station with new eyes. It's a ramshackle lean-to of a place, but I've always known that. It hasn't seen much in the way of architectural upgrade since it was built in the late-nineteenth century when it would have been bijou but worthy. There are modern painted signs and some that light up, none of which do much to flatter the building. It could do with a little café-cum-shop. I do worry that automatic beverage machine will poison a diabetic some day because there's no warning about just how sweet the brew it spits out is. And it does spit. Al Faber runs a newspaper stand in the morning for a few hours but he's threatening to retire and there is no heir apparent. Dan should really look at sprucing the place up. I won't be the one to tell him that, necessarily, but I am sure there are many ways of getting the message to him.

I probably look like I'm loitering, fondly remembering my time here, but I am not, or not in any meaningful way at least. I feel a presence hovering and when I look over my shoulder Donna is standing by an iron pillar watching me. I hope she doesn't think I'm waiting for Dan.

'You're out of here then,' she says.

'Yes. I'm seeing about running Dad's business.'

'Heard you on the radio.'

I wait. It's the best way with Donna.

'He was the only dad in the area didn't try to feel my tits.'

'Really?' I am shocked. It had never occurred to me that it might be on any parent's agenda. No one's father tried to grope me. I must have been one dull girl.

'Quite the gentleman. Wondered if he was gay for a while, be honest with you, but he had manners was all, and a bit of respect. I liked that.'

This is the most I've heard from her in a long, long time. It's a fairly one-sided conversation but it's communication and I won't care if she starts to swap recipes as long as she's talking to me. It's more than I deserve.

'How's your mum?'

'Escaping, bit by bit.'

This makes her smile, just the tiniest bit. 'Never thought she'd be the one to leave.'

I return the smile, but bigger. 'Yeah, who knew?'

Donna is unafraid to hold my gaze. She really knows how to put it up to a person.

'Congratulations on the news,' I say.

She holds her bump, tenderly, and says, 'Thanks. Dan and me are delighted. Made up.'

Made up: yes, they are. I can't put it off any longer.

'I'm sorry, Donna.' There's not a lot more I can say to cover what needs to be acknowledged between us.

'Yeah.' She doesn't grant forgiveness and I don't expect her to. The best I can hope is that, in time, she'll mellow. She can never forget.

'The local Historical Society teamed up with the Women's Institute about ten years ago to make a record of the really ancient gravestones in the area,' Mona told Kitty.

'We had a hunt through what they have but we can't find Nelly,' Simon added.

Kitty sighed, disappointed.

'However,' he continued, 'part of St Melchior's graveyard was decommissioned to become part of the neighbouring housing estate.'

'Mock-Tudor, ghastly,' Mona interjected.

'The poor souls resting in the decommissioned area were moved to what's now the municipal cemetery.'

'That graveyard has been in use from the eighteen hundreds as a secular burying place so our lass might be there anyhow, even if she's not one of the ones who got replanted.' Mona caught sight of their expressions. 'Well, whatever they call transferring human remains.'

'Reburial?' Kitty said.

'They have been reinterred,' Simon tried.

'All right, all right, point taken.'

'I don't suppose the WI made a study of that graveyard?' Kitty asked.

'Wouldn't you know it, no,' Mona said. 'I suppose we all thought it wasn't as interesting or old as the church ones, but it is.'

'We're also going to check the records of the Monroe family's burials as Fenella worked for them,' Simon offered.

Kitty thought about it. 'But what if Nelly left Pennick? What if she's not buried here?'

'That's another possibility,' Simon agreed. 'And then, there is no guarantee we'll ever find her.'

'I hate to bring us back to basics,' Mona said, 'but can we also bear in mind that the ship may not be anything to do with Nelly and may have two sets of *French* initials on it.'

They all sighed at that.

'I have been in contact with the French Military,' Mona continued. 'They've put me on to a very nice chap who's interested in this, one of their historians. Between us, we might get together a definitive list of who was stationed here and what happened to them . . . or as far as it can ever be definitive at this late stage. I told him we are particularly interested in Antoine Chaubert and François Villeneuve. We want to know about them all, what with this book we're doing, but it would be nice to have a singular story to hang it round.'

Mona was wearing a flowing scarf tonight, which Simon suspected was a writerly affectation. She'd have him in a cravat next if he wasn't careful.

'I'd hate to think we might not find them,' Kitty said.

'Unfortunately, it's a very real possibility,' Simon admitted.

The little boat sat on the table before them as it always did at their meetings.

'Who are your people?' Kitty asked it.

I've always enjoyed a walk through a graveyard. I find cemeteries calm places to be, unless you're attending a funeral with all of the raw sorrow that brings. I like the regular lines

349

of the layout and visiting the people I have known. My father is now in Pennick Municipal Cemetery so any visit, from here on out, is always going to be horribly personal. I take Mum along, though we are not just here to visit Dad. We are going to look for Nelly too.

We're wrapped up well against the cold, which is bitter according to Mum. It's funny to think of the weather as having moods or vendettas that require it to be 'bitter' or 'soft'. There are other people scattered about today, heads dipping as they pause to greet an old friend or relative. We have not been here since the funeral and I feel guilty about that. I really haven't been ready to visit and Mum is oblivious to the situation again, which is partly a blessing.

It's too early to put up a headstone for him so Dad's name and dates are still on a small wooden cross. It will be six months before we can erect anything more substantial. The cemetery staff told me we must wait for subsidence. I know all too clearly that my father's remains are decomposing under that soil and nature must be given a fair chance to do what's natural in this first half-year. It's unsavoury to dwell on it. I have to tell myself it's just his mortal shell, he is long gone. I cannot imagine a time when six months of this grief will have passed, but they will, as sure as night follows day.

I clear the spent flowers and tell him what we've been up to. I keep a hawk eye on Mum who is busy wandering hither and yon without too much focus on the graveyard or its inhabitants. I worry she'll take flowers or items she fancies from some of the more ornate arrangements people have left to commemorate departed loved ones. Simon is locating the areas we need to concentrate on for our Nelly Vickers search. I think Dad would have been fascinated by it all. I tell him I miss him and the words sound puny compared with the rending in my chest. I let myself cry when the tears come, devastated all over again to be without my father, my dad, Daddy.

Mum comes back and asks where we're going next. She's bored. I have a contingency plan and ring Val to come and get her. He'll take her on his weekly super-market shop. She still loves a bit of retail therapy and her happiness on a trip is easily ensured by a Mars bar. This may be dodgy practice but it's true so I let myself off too much wasted self-recrimination.

Simon joins me at the grave. 'It's hard when they go,' he says.

I agree with him. We stand and look at my dad's final resting place and the silence between us is comfortable. There is a lot that I can share with this man, I find.

'Did you ever want brothers and sisters?' I finally ask him.

'From time to time I did, but not in any pitiful way. I didn't long for a family. We moved around so much, I would have liked someone my own age to moan with about that. I wanted straightforward whingeing and complaining about my sorry lot. Mum and Dad could only justify the upheavals rationally. I think they secretly felt guilty, so they wouldn't indulge me because it made them feel bad too.'

'I have moments when I wish I had family back-up. All out whingeing sounds good to me too.'

'You've got me for that now,' he says, simply, and I feel I do.

I hook my arm through his and we go to get Mum for the handover to Val. It goes so smoothly she doesn't even look back as she leaves and I feel slightly hurt. Rich, I tell myself, as I am the one offloading her for a few hours. At the gate, Val turns back to wave. My face must have a sorrowful expression on it because he makes Mum turn around too and I can see that she's now arguing with him about that. He raises his hands to heaven for me to see. I know he doesn't really mind; it's all part of the May merry-go-round.

'How long has that man been in love with you?' Simon asks.

He doesn't miss much, I'll give him that.

'Forever, according to him. I love Val, too, just not the way he'd like.'

I can't tell what Simon makes of that because he suddenly gets all businesslike and steers us to our first target area, for the hunt to begin in earnest. The modern section where Dad lies gives way to more and more ornate backwaters. The Victorians, in particular, loved their mausoleums and monuments. There are a lot of huge crosses and weeping angels. As we progress towards our first search area, the stones grow plainer and the pathways less trodden.

We chat about the French prisoners. Simon tells me they had a curfew of 5 p.m. in the winter months and 8 p.m. in summer. If they wandered past their allotted mile from the outer reaches of town, there was a reward of ten shillings paid to whoever apprehended them. If they stepped out of line, they were banged up in gaol. They received a subsistence allowance from the British Government, to pay for their food and lodgings. That really surprises me. Senior officers were awarded one shilling and sixpence a week, initially, with the junior officers on one shilling and threepence. They complained that it wasn't enough to meet the high cost of living in England and got the French Admiralty to write letters on their behalf and did actually win an increase.

I tell Simon I can hardly believe these men lived in Pennick, however briefly.

'Not only that, I have a theory that the house on the corner of Cross Street and High Street was decorated by French soldiers.'

That stops me in my tracks.

'Have you ever noticed the plasterwork on the front of the building? It's like a swirling vine. That's quite typical of their work. There's some like it in North Tawton in Devon, another Parole Town.'

This is Pennick we're talking about here. My nowhere of a home town, a place no one but its inhabitants knows or cares about, which is meant to have nothing of interest about it. I say as much to Simon who looks at me with a mixture of pity and disbelief.

'Kitty, Pennick is lovely. It's pretty, situated in a wonderful part of the county and it's teeming with history. What's not to love about it?'

This man is opening my eyes. I chance a fresh look around but realise I'll be changing my opinion only a little at a time.

The first delight for Simon was to be alone with Kitty, even if they were in a graveyard. He had her all to himself. It was astoundingly satisfying to watch her hoover up information and see how it transformed her face. She had a poor outlook on her hometown, though. He'd never lived anywhere long enough to have one so he didn't quite understand that. To have your roots in one place seemed very desirable to him, and to have a shared story with others in a community. He wondered if that's why history called to him as it did. Was he trying to root himself more strongly in the past, so as to know the feeling of homecoming? Was Pennick the town where he belonged?

They began to study the stones in their allotted area. An hour later Kitty let out a small yelp and summoned him. She had found a marker with a French inscription. They stood for a moment to calm themselves then they began to read and translate the wording on the stone. Simon took a photograph of it for their records.

> *Ici Repose Le Corps de*
> *Vincent Le Stum*
> *Natif de Lorient*
> *Lieut. Au 16 Regt de Ligne*
> *Age de 33 ans*
> *Décède le 10 Avril 1807*
> *Requiescat in Pace*

'A Breton,' Simon said. 'A lieutenant who died aged thirty-three. Rest in peace.'

Kitty had put her hand in his and he gave it a squeeze. He always found the strangest mixture of ease and difficulty in breathing when he was around her. At that moment, he would not have traded places with any other person, alive or dead. They had found a Frenchman and Simon was holding Kitty Fulton's hand.

'We'll press on,' he said, reluctant to let go but wanting to make the most of the light while they had it.

About twenty minutes later he came back to her side, breathless, and asked her to look up.

'What do you see?' he asked.

'Graves, fields beyond, trees, grey sky. A woman wearing what looks like a one-piece skiing outfit in an unforgiving purple.'

'Go back to the trees. What kind are they?'

'Some yew, an oak and a willow, I'd say from here.'

Simon began to walk quickly in the direction of the willow she was pointing at. 'I think we've found another one,' he said.

I have to run to keep up. Simon is burbling about a theory he has, how it may be nothing, and I am getting very excited about what we might find. The stone is partly submerged and it may be that the roots of the tree are responsible for that. It is also old, or course, and the earth is subsiding as it likes to do. Why has he targeted this grave above all the others?

'Napoleon is buried on St Helena and his tomb is close to the spring where his drinking water was taken from when he was alive. This spring was surrounded by willow trees. Hundreds of British and French army officers attended his funeral. After the ceremony everyone took sprigs of those willows with them, sometimes whole branches, as mementoes. Later still, when British forces withdrew from the island, a sergeant who had married a local woman was left behind and appointed guardian of the tomb. He was a bit of an entrepreneur and set up a small business cultivating willow shoots to sell to visitors. He rooted them in old wine bottles, filled with spring water and sealed. Several are known to have made their way back to England and there is one in Ashburton in Devon growing beside a French soldier's grave.

I'm hoping that this is planted here to mark something or someone special, related to a parole prisoner.'

It is. We clear away the weeds that have grown about the stone and try to read the inscription. It is badly worn so we do a rubbing, and that is when we find her. This is the final resting place of Fenella Vickers who died in childbirth in 1807, aged 19 years. We don't know how to celebrate. It doesn't seem right to whoop and holler triumphantly by a grave. It is a sombre moment, difficult to process fully. In my mind I had given up any hope of locating her.

'I know it's circumstantial,' Simon says, 'but I think Nelly was involved with a Frenchman and I think he planted this willow to watch over her, as its cousins did the Emperor.'

'The stone doesn't mention her baby,' I say. 'The child may have lived.' I know the search for her offspring will be high on our list from now. I cannot wait to tell Mona. We have a sad and wonderful story to hang our book on.

'She died in childbirth, unmarried and possibly in disgrace, which might explain why she is not buried with her family.'

'Poor Nelly.'

It is getting dark now so we quickly record our findings and start to make our way home. The ground is bumpy and more treacherous in the waning light and we both stumble about. We are just outside the gate, about to hit concrete pathways again, when I miss a step up and fall over. I am unhurt, just shaken. Simon helps me to my feet and waits while I brush dirt off my coat. I look up when I am done and we gaze into each other's eyes. I cannot look away and I am sure he cannot either. I don't want to.

Something has changed, displaced the air around us. He reaches for me and I am willingly drawn into his arms. He kisses me and I am breathless with how good it feels. It is so gentle at first, and then passion mounts and it is as if we have waited all our lives for this. When we break the embrace we move together at speed to my house and, without words, climb the stairs and fall into my room. I don't remember clothes being removed, just Simon's hands and mouth on me and mine on him and the ecstasy of it. I look into his face and his lovely smile, which is all for me, and I feel whole and so lucky that he found me. He kisses my lips, lightly this time, and says, 'I love you, Kitty.'

EIGHTEEN

The man beside me is a miracle and I cannot sleep for looking at him. He spends the night here often and instead of becoming used to that we are still devouring one another. I never thought I could give myself up so completely again. There is a subtle sense of treachery in this invidious comparison that I try not to dwell on. This is so much better because Simon is all mine. I have not betrayed Dan, any more than he did me. At the beginning there were times when Simon's breath on my skin, or even his voice in my ear, were foreign enough for me to start at the notion that I was cheating on Dan, but that was ridiculous and I soon gave up thinking that way.

What a wonderful thing it is. I feel as if I have blossomed. There is a skip in my step and a confidence about me which are astonishing and a relief. I was so worried all of the time; now I have moments when I think I might just about get by, that nothing too awful is happening every day beyond the substantive issue of Mum's disease. I am more relaxed and happy and I think Mum picks up on that. She has taken our new situation in her stride and is perfectly content to have Simon in the house. Roly is a bit put out that his place on the bed is taken by a much larger male but he's dealing with it in his way and is still lord of the sofa so one status quo is maintained.

I don't discuss Mum with Simon. He knows that is a situation he will have to roll with and that she is uppermost in my priorities. What I feel for him is so different. If it lasts, as I hope, it will have utter loyalty underpinning it also. I suppose this is love, as I cannot think what else to call it, how else to describe it. I pinch myself sometimes to check that I haven't sunk into a delusion. Simon says he has never felt this way, has never been so sure of the rightness of something. It is such a gift when he tells me these things. He wants to yell from the rooftops that we are together. He is delighted with me. I feel so healthy, fit for my new challenges. He is proud of me.

I don't want the household upset in any way. We are trucking along as best we can. But I keep coming across the social worker's list of residential homes in my bag and I feel I must deal, at least in part, with all that it stands for. I make an appointment to see Mr Bishop at the hospital but I go alone to meet him. He is giving me ten minutes from his lunch break and I am extremely grateful. There is mayhem in Accident and Emergency and I see staff running and calling out to one another. A bystander knowingly says, 'Work van incoming.' I can hear sirens in the distance, dashing the broken to be mended. I wonder if the man who commented is the equivalent of the train spotters at the station. Pregnant teenagers smoke outside, oblivious to the cold and the poison they're inhaling for two. They're sure they will live forever and they are reproducing to prove it. Proud parents come through the doors swinging tiny newborns in baskets and car seats. A man attached to a drip sits in a wheelchair, whistling the 'Toreador's Song' from *Carmen*. I make my way indoors, along the familiar corridors, and take the turning for the Department of the Mad and Bewildered.

Mr Bishop is eating a sandwich at his desk and consulting vast folders of notes. He has another, sweating in its plastic wrap, in case I want to join him but warns me it will taste as disgusting as his own. 'Hospital food.' He shrugs. 'It's a wonder any of us makes it out the door at the end of the day.'

He tells me I look well and I know I do. I am glowing. I don't explain why but the consultant is a savvy man and I don't doubt he can guess a thing or two. He looks at the list I have brought. It is not extensive, as few places want to take someone like Mum.

'There are two here that are over-fond of medicating the problem, in my opinion,' Mr Bishop says. 'I know you don't want to take that route unless absolutely necessary, and I agree with you and applaud the decision. I wish I had more relatives like you.' There is a moment then when I see his utter exhaustion and I fully expect him to slide off his chair into a deep sleep. He shakes it off. 'How about I mark them as if I were choosing one for myself?'

'Thank you, Mr Bishop, that would be a great help. I won't tell or show it to anyone, I promise.'

'You'd better not,' he says, and though he is laughing I know he means it. 'And I do wish you'd call me Desmond.'

'Desmond,' I try for size. It feels strange, but it suits him. 'Mum's fine with me right now and I hope it doesn't come to this at all, but I'm guessing it's like trying to get a kid into a decent school: you have to have their name down from conception.'

'Not unlike that,' Mr Bishop agrees. His eyes are a muddy, humane brown. They make me believe there is nothing we cannot achieve if we put our minds to it. 'With any luck you will never have to face the situation,' he adds delicately.

We are not talking of a cure here, simply that Mum might pass away before the worst ravages descend. I do not want her to be humiliated by them, even if she remains unaware. Was I wrong to call her back in from the sea that day in Egypt? I did not let her go, on her own terms, as she'd wanted me to. No, I would do the same again today. I am still not ready to give her up.

'How will I know if it's time?' I ask, trying not to cry. This is what I wanted to ask him all along. I don't want to miss a sign and do her harm.

'Do you mean, to let her go into residential care?' he says. 'Or beyond?'

'Both.'

'Kitty, you will know,' he reassures me. 'You are the person who most loves and cares for May and you are the one who knows her best of all. You will not make any mistakes. Trust yourself. She is extremely fortunate to have had you thus far, and I was a lucky doctor the day you walked in that door with my new patient. You have made my job easier by far.'

He doesn't have to say any of this and I cannot thank him enough for doing so. I know he isn't allowed gifts but I leave him a copy of the Christmas poems book, which both Mum and I have signed. It seems so little to acknowledge what he does for us, but it's all I have.

Simon didn't dare measure how happy he was. He had finally found his life partner and they matched perfectly. It was as if all of the living he had done to date had simply been to prepare him for this moment when he could be with Kitty. She didn't think him shy or odd as some had. She didn't ask about his previous lovers. His life before wasn't an issue. He was accepted into the little world of 15, The Cottages and felt he had a family again.

Kitty talked him through the photographs labelled for May's benefit, naming her ancestors as she went, laughing at pictures of herself as a girl. May followed along, touching the pictures, looking at the strangers who had once meant something to her, when the world and everything in it was hers to play for. Kitty showed Simon her vegetable plot, a sacred place but one she now wanted to share with someone else. One day, he went with her to the station to collect the items she had left behind there. She was making her clean break. A sullen Margo ignored the ringing phone and told them Dan had advertised the post and she would not be applying for it. As they left Kitty signed something out of the Lost and Found book and took it to her allotment where Simon helped her dig a hole on the very edge of the area. She buried the padded envelope without ever telling him what was in it. 'It's something I should have dealt with a long time ago,' was all she said. He didn't pry.

'If you had come to Pennick even a year ago, I don't think we would be together now,' I tell Simon. I have been thinking a lot about this. 'I wouldn't have been at a point where I needed change as much as I have done in these last months. In spite of what was happening to Mum, I had a system going and I thought I was doing okay. I know now the system was dysfunctional, probably did then too, but it was all I knew and I had no ambition beyond that.'

'Strange for me as I never would have said timing was my greatest strength,' Simon admits.

'You should talk to Cameron at the office about that, it's his hobby horse.'

We are going to Norwich to make a start on clearing Dad's

house. I regard it as a visit to him and try not to think of the parting it really represents. Mum is looking out of the carriage window at the rain sleeting down.

'The sea will be cold today,' she says.

'We're not going for a swim.' I tell her, again. 'We are going to tidy up Stephen's house and collect some things for you.'

I do think she'll want some of Dad's things, even if their significance is lost on her. She still appreciates something pretty to look at and any other unconscious attraction she has to it is a bonus and doesn't bother her unduly. The disease gives her a freedom that is sometimes almost enviable.

'Says here blackcurrants can help the prevention of Alzheimer's,' Simon reports from his newspaper.

'Prevent is a big word,' I observe. 'Too late for us. The saddest thing I ever read was about a study done in a convent. One of the nuns had Alzheimer's and her greatest worry was that she'd forget God.'

'God won't forget her,' Mum says, and goes back to drawing faces in the condensation on the window.

It's impossible to say if she means this as a good or bad thing, this God who forgets nothing and no one. I think of Donna. I am no longer so confident. I dread seeing Dad's house, a reminder of the past and how I must deal with it in order to move on. Mum has no such worries.

We stand in Dad's main living area wondering where to start. Simon advises that I see this as a reconnaissance

mission and I think he's right. There is no hurry to obliterate my father's presence from this place. In fact, it may be
nice to become reacquainted with some of his things. Mum
told me that when she first met my father: 'He had a lounge
and a linen cupboard, so I knew he was a Protestant. That
fact alone made me love him from the off, because I knew
it would drive your grandmother mental. She was never a
religious type, but in her narrow mind Protestant meant
Brit and that was a pejorative term.'

Mum took no prisoners with me when it came to words,
and if I didn't understand something she sent me to the
dictionary to look it up. I think that's why my vocabulary is
as good as it is, and not a whole lot to do with my formal
education at school.

'I don't think she ever thought through why that might
or might not be a bad thing. I cannot abide pat acceptance
of old myths or lazy thinking. It engenders prejudice, and
nothing that comes of that can be a good thing.' Mum again,
in the good old days. Today she is merrily ringing a bell she's
found on a sideboard. Inside that older woman is a young
girl I have met only recently. I'm hoping she wants to be
my friend.

I keep stopping to read notes that Dad's left and poke
through drawers full of correspondence. I know it will take
me an age to get through everything here, and that's a
comfort. I would hate to think his life's possessions could be
swiftly disposed of. There is an album of photographs that

is too tempting to leave unopened so Simon makes tea and we sit down to view the contents. There is a series I haven't seen before but they match a framed photo of me that is hanging on a wall. I don't remember it being taken. I am three or four years old, standing on some stone steps in a pretty, frilled dress. The story is that I burst into tears when I first saw the photograph and wanted to know where everyone else was. I didn't want to be alone. I thought I had been abandoned in that unremembered time.

Now I see it comes from a whole set taken on that same day. My mother and father pose on the steps too, in their best clothes, eyes squinted against the sun. Sometimes it's just Mum and Dad, sometimes I am between them. I look at the back of one and see that Dad has marked it 'Register Office'. This then was their wedding day and I was there. Mum is not the only one with a dodgy memory. I stare at the picture hard for a long time, willing it to speak to me, and still it unlocks nothing. It was obviously not an important day in my life, though it was in theirs.

I show one of them to Mum and wait for a reaction. 'Pink dress,' she says, and that is all.

Mona came to the meeting bearing many treasures. She was clearly chuffed with herself. Her flowing scarf was of a becoming amber hue and Simon couldn't help but comment on it. He got a 'This old thing' and the suspicion of a blush.

'I have found a Monroe,' she announced. 'Her name is

Audrey and she is a direct descendant of the Dr Monroe we are interested in. Not only that, she has primary source material. I spoke to her over the phone and, although she sounds frail, her mind is alert. She says she has very old diaries that she's certain go back to the eighteen hundreds. They're in storage in a bank vault somewhere and she'll call them up for us. It seems Nelly's Dr Monroe was an inveterate record keeper, bless his woollen socks. Audrey is very ancient and in a private nursing home outside Bishop's Cross. I think a visit may be in order.'

Kitty immediately volunteered to accompany her, as she also wanted to see how an institution of that sort might look and be run.

'That's not all.' Mona brandished a letter. 'The French have been in touch with news of Antoine Chaubert. He was killed in battle in 1815. They have no further data at the moment but my new best friend over there, lovely man named Jean Marc de Beauvier, is on the trail. He's as hooked as we are.' She was fanning herself with the letter now and both Simon and Kitty fancied it was to do with the living man behind the correspondence rather than the dead soldier.

Audrey Monroe's retirement home had once been a grand mansion in the Palladian style. It still had the proportions and façade to announce that, and any additions had been tastefully tucked away behind, at the business end of the beautiful building. The staff was smartly uniformed and the house smelled fresh.

'I bet it costs a bomb to stay here,' Mona commented as they were led to Miss Monroe's suite. Kitty thought it bore more resemblance to a hotel than any of the public nursing homes she'd encountered to date.

The lady who greeted them admitted to being ninety-seven years of age. 'Hoping to hit the ton, as the young folk now put it,' she said. She seemed hale enough to do so, in her rickety way. She was a fragile arrangement of spindly limbs and wrinkles, with darting active eyes and an air of curiosity. 'And you brought me a lovely man. How kind.'

Simon preened. Audrey Monroe knew how to work a room.

Kitty poured the tea their hostess had laid on and they set out to explain their research, saying they were interested in learning more about a servant called Fenella Vickers who had once worked for the Monroe family.

'Obviously I don't know much about that time, old as I am. The good doctor would have been about five generations before me. I have racked my brains for anything that might have descended through the family as gossip, but nothing has cropped up as yet. The noggin is not what it once was. So I have put out a call to my younger brother Antoine. He's the baby of the family, a mere whippersnapper of eighty-two.' She took in their astonished faces. 'Have I said something wrong?' she asked.

'Antoine?' Kitty repeated.

'Yes, it's an old family name. Traditionally, the youngest son is called that, though it's sometimes hard to guess which boy will be the last, don't you think?' She laughed at the eccentric family trait.

I have had the turkey on since eight and it's doing nicely. Mum, Simon, Roly and I had a breakfast of scrambled eggs and smoked salmon, with Buck's Fizz for the humans and some special cat milk for Roly. The fire is blazing and Mum is playing her favourite Christmas jingles on the stereo. She is bursting to open the gifts under the tree but knows she has to wait until the others arrive. It is my first Christmas catering for more than three and I am a bag of nerves about the food. Simon is helping, when I let him, and will serve the meal when we are ready to sit down. He stands behind me as I prepare Brussels sprouts I grew at the allotment. My own potatoes, carrots and parsnips from the plot are already in the oven. Simon puts his hands on my waist and leans in to whisper, 'I know what I'd like for lunch.' He kisses the side of my neck and presses against me. It's wonderful to be so desired.

'Step away from the cook,' I order. 'I can't concentrate when you do that.'

Our guests will arrive within the hour and he insists that I have enough done and must sit down for another glass of champagne. The air is filled with the aromas of spicy mince pies, roasting turkey and plum pudding. If only Dad were here the day would have a chance of perfection. I make a little toast to him.

We have decided to have a gentle, indulgent end to this year. We will stay at home and treat ourselves to the best of everything we fancy. It may be the last such celebration of its kind. Mum is deteriorating fast now. She has trouble with darkness behind a window when it renders it a mirror and she imagines there are people spying on her. They mock her, she says, waving and threatening. She heard someone playing the piano in the house yesterday and was upset by that. We don't have a piano so I assume it was a piece of music on the radio. She still enjoys herself, however, and her frustrations and fear pass quickly, but she is less and less able to reason and hardly speaks much any more. Physically she is becoming a slighter woman and that's heartbreak to behold. And yet, I have so much hope for us. My biggest is that Mum's brain will simply shut down some night and she just won't wake up. She will simply forget to breathe, in her sleep, and slip away without realising. That would be such a peaceful end. Why not? It could happen. I'm allowed to hope, to dream.

Benny and Jed arrive together, all scrubbed and excited. Jed has made a holly wreath for the front door. Its red berries and glossy green leaves are in happy contrast to the dark wood. He has a talent for display and could go into business selling these wares. The planter he made for Dad's funeral is still utterly lovely. I have added some festive decorations to it and it shines outside the back door of the house. Mona arrives and we raise a toast to absent friends. Mum threatens to burst if we don't open some presents.

We have imposed a £10 upper limit and the only person I have broken that for is Mum. She gets pink wellingtons because that's her favourite colour. She tramps about in them proudly. Roly looks less certain about the studded collar with his name on a disc hanging from the front. It may or may not last the season. Benny and Jed look happy in the new hats and scarves I have bought them. Jed is thrilled with the earmuffs I found and says they're the business 'fer that 'lott-ment. Cold's suffin savage thair'. Mona loves her pen and pencil case. It has sequins that sparkle happily like the flashing lights on the Christmas tree. 'This will go into my parole prisoner bag,' she informs me. She keeps her notes and papers in a special briefcase for that subject alone.

We still await Dr Monroe's diaries, and in the meantime our favourite theory is that Nelly's baby was adopted by the family and named Antoine after his soldier dad. It's a possibility and some day we may know the truth of it.

Mum's gift to me is some beautiful yarn. Simon helped her choose it. I will use it to finish the bedspread she started but can never finish. I see in its pattern the lines and drills of my allotment, Simon the order and colours of his book-shelves at the library. Who knows what it means to Mum now, if anything at all.

Simon and I do not exchange gifts. Instead we have made something together. We unveil it for the company. It is a ship made of lollipop sticks in honour of the boat that brought us together. On the underside are the initials KFSH. And that might be a good story for another generation long after we have gone.

It is the story of ordinary people, who lived and loved in a small town in the middle of nowhere. I think it's worth telling.